HALF MOON AQUA

HALF MOON
Aqua

HALF MOON AQUA

Half Moon Bay Book 7

ERIN BROCKUS

Chapter One

DECEMBER...

Sara Collins crossed her arms as she stood on the beach, staring at her dream. Correction—her dream in progress. She drew her brows together, indicating the mixture of anticipation and dread roiling her stomach. The long rectangular building stretched out in front of her, even whiter than the sandy beach of Half Moon Bay Resort in St. Croix. The far-left portion of the enormous structure was complete, and its dark, smoked-glass exterior mocked her, its success evident. The art gallery—Ember—had opened recently with few delays or complications.

The same could not be said of her project, Aqua, which encompassed three quarters of the building. Designed to be one of the premier spas on the island, Aqua's lack of progress had been a trial for Sara since construction began.

That would change today.

With a determined sigh, Sara strode toward the spa's double entry doors, contained within a smoked-glass wall. The entry complemented Ember next door, giving the building a harmonious look. Behind her, the late-afternoon sun cast the white walls on either side of the dark glass into blinding brightness.

"I'm calling it Aqua for a reason," she muttered. "And this time I'd better hear water when I enter."

The glass was only tinted on the exterior, and after opening the door, a modern, bright lobby greeted Sara. The air conditioning wasn't operational yet, making her grateful for the breezy, rose-colored sundress she wore. After gathering her long brown hair and arranging it over one shoulder, she swiped a hand over the back of her neck, wiping away the sweat.

On the far side of the room, a floor-to-ceiling reinforced wall ran nearly the width of the large lobby. The main entrance door from the parking lot, a smaller version of the glass doors she had just passed through, stood to the left of it. The towering wall would eventually become the undeniable focal point of the lobby.

If the stacked stone that was to cover it ever arrived.

Several burly men in construction vests clustered around a broad, two-feet-deep rectangular basin in front of the expansive wall, their hands parked on their hips. But the floor occupied Sara's attention. More specifically, she focused with laser intensity on a four-feet-wide channel meandering through the lobby.

An empty channel.

As her gaze followed the bare, white-painted concrete trench to its source, the rectangular basin at the base of the wall, her stomach twisted. The winding canal originated from the basin, then split in two directions. One offshoot channel wandered to the salon on her left. The other curved to her right toward the treatment and massage rooms.

The shallow pool at the base of the wall was filled with water, which set Sara's heart racing. But that was the only water in evidence. She approached the foreman, a tall, lanky man named George. Sara's professional eye noted his light-brown hair was overdue for a cut and curling at the neck. He carried a clipboard and had a walkie-talkie clipped to his belt.

She pasted a smile on her face and kept her voice pleasant. "I thought we'd have water in the canals today. What's up, George?"

The foreman turned around and gave her a tight smile. "Afternoon, Sara. We're just about to open the valves."

Hallelujah! About goddamn time. "Sounds like my timing is perfect. I can't wait."

George nodded to another man, who held his thumb over a button in a nearly hidden recessed panel next to the wall. All eyes focused on the base of the channel leading from the pool. When the worker pushed the button, a white panel slid open, and water poured into the two-feet-deep canal. It trickled by Sara before splitting to run in the two directions.

She broke into a broad smile and couldn't resist clapping. "There it goes! This is so exciting."

George grinned back. "Hopefully not too exciting. We'll fill it an inch deep and keep a close watch to see if the water holds."

Sara's smile disappeared. "Holds? What do you mean?"

George shrugged but eyed her evenly. "It's water. Flowing in a brand-new channel for the first time. Don't be surprised if there's a leak or two."

"Oh, don't tell me that!"

"Just being honest. I've got guys stationed throughout the building so we can shut off the water if anything dramatic happens."

Sara ambled toward the salon. Halfway across the room, the meandering river took a turn and a shallow bamboo bridge rose over it. She stopped on the bridge, delighting in the serene sound of the water trickling below. Eventually, the entire canal —floor and sides—would be covered in gray, flattened river rock.

But that would come after they were confident the channel would hold water.

Continuing, she stopped at the broad open entry of the salon. Eight hair stations would line up on one wall, with mani-pedi stations along the other. She was even considering a fish pedicure area. Her station, at the far end, was the only one in semi-operational order.

The water-filled channel continued its lazy path through the salon, two more bamboo bridges providing crossings. A large man with chocolate skin and heavy work boots paced back and forth at the far end of the salon, his thick brows drawn as he studied the small river. He raised a walkie-talkie to his mouth. "George, we gotta problem here. Turn off the water."

"Roger that, Harry. Turning off now."

The man hunkered down on his knees and bent over the channel. Sara rushed across the room, crossing two more bridges. This time, she was too worried to enjoy them as she hurried toward Harry. Opening her mouth to ask what the problem was, it became obvious when she neared. Water was draining at the seam where the channel ended at the far side of the room, the water level noticeably decreasing.

Harry vaulted to his feet and grabbed a nearby sandbag, throwing it into the channel. Then he followed with two more. The small dam held most of the water back, but the section near the end of the little river drained steadily. He looked up at the sound of Sara's rushing footsteps. "I'm sorry, Miss Sara. There's a leak here for sure."

His walkie-talkie squawked with a new voice. "We have a leak on the other end by the treatment rooms too. Maybe two of them."

"Dammit!" Sara said, panic clawing its way up her ribcage.

George and another man arrived and stopped next to Harry, staring at the channel. "Good thing we had the sandbags ready."

"What's underneath there?" Sara asked. "Is something under the floor getting flooded?"

"Yeah, no doubt." George said. "Plumbing, electrical, and all kinds of stuff run under the floor. We'll tear out the area around the leak and mop up the water." Sighing, he shook his head as he kneeled and ran a hand over the canal's wall. "Our usual sealant was on back order, so we used a new kind. Can't say I'm real impressed with it."

Sara snapped her head up. Panic turned to fury as she closed the distance to stand directly in front of the project manager. He towered over her, and she bent her neck back to glare at him. "A *new sealant?* You tried something completely untested on this project? We aren't paying a single extra penny for this, George!"

He held up a hand, taking a step back. "I'm not asking you to. This was the best solution we could come up with, but it obviously isn't going to work. Getting supplies to an island in the middle of the Caribbean is always a challenge. We all agreed on the bid amount, so any cost overruns are ours to eat, not yours."

"Damn right they are!" She swept her gaze around the room, wanting to explode but looking for a more productive outlet. "Maybe we can install the stations and get things running without the water feature. Could we open, then get the river inspected later?"

George's shoulders sagged as he shook his head. "There's no way they'd give you the final permits with something that major still unfinished. I know setbacks are frustrating, but hang in there. It will be worth it in the end. I promise."

"If the end ever gets here!" She sighed, stepping forward as she looked down at the water-filled channel on the far side of the sandbags. The water was almost gone, and her anger bubbled up again. "Why isn't the channel made of waterproof material?"

"We thought the sealant would work just as well. We could put in a complete liner, but that will increase the cost."

Sara whirled around. "What? You just said—"

Harry took a large step back. George stood his ground this time, though he held out a placating hand. "I said we agreed on a specified bid. Sara, a full waterproof liner isn't in the contract. Look, I know you're mad. I'm not real happy about this myself. Let me make some calls and see if I can find the sealant we usually use, and we'll go from there. Everything will work out, ok?"

All the energy drained out of Sara. Her shoulders could have weighed a thousand pounds. "Fine. I need to discuss this with Hope anyway."

Sara pushed through the back door and stepped onto the beach. She raised a hand to her forehead, shielding her eyes as the sun neared the horizon. The turquoise water of Half Moon Bay lapped softly on the beach, and she took a deep breath of salty air, making an effort to shake off her frustration.

She turned left, passing by seven wooden bungalows. Four were on the beach with direct ocean views, and three more sat behind, at the edge of the thick tropical vegetation. Next was the main resort complex, with a rectangular infinity pool and attached bar. The restaurant sat on the far side of the pool. The lobby was a separate building near the restaurant. Four more bungalows were on the south side of the complex and construction had begun on the three Rainforest bungalows which would sit behind them. But this late in the day, the sounds of hammering and sawing had quieted.

Voices coming from the long pier to the right drew her attention. Two men walked toward the resort, and her bad mood faded as a smile rose on her face. One man rose over six feet tall and was light-haired, while the other was of average height with neat, dark-brown hair. Sara's heart soared at the sight of the shorter man. Then she saw the bulbous-headed three-feet-long fish he carried.

Huh? A fish?

Jack Powell saw her and returned her broad smile as he scratched his trimmed, dark-brown beard. The other man, Alex Monroe, was married to her sister Hope. The Monroes owned Half Moon Bay Resort and lived in a house distantly visible at the south end of the beach. Alex and Jack were integral members of the resort dive team.

The men descended a short staircase onto the sand, and Jack reached out an arm, pulling Sara close for a hello kiss. She leaned into him, avoiding the fish but melting into the softness of his lips. "Thanks. I really needed that."

He backed away, wrinkling his brow. "Bad day?"

"Just another problem with Aqua. Again." She turned to Alex. "I was on my way to give Hope an update."

Alex pointed to the iridescent blue-green fish, and Jack held it up triumphantly.

"You can tell her later when we come over to your house," the tall man said. He was in his early forties, but you'd never know it from his muscular build. "We threw out a couple fishing lines coming back from the afternoon dive and landed this mahi-mahi."

"I invited Alex and Hope over for dinner," Jack said. "This fish is too big for just us. I'll fillet it up and grill it."

Sara's frustration slipped off her shoulders and disappeared into the sand, replaced by excitement. She turned to Alex. "Oh, that sounds perfect! Jack just built a fire pit, so we can officially christen it." And it had been too long since she and Hope had relaxed together.

Alex waved goodbye. "We'll be over in an hour or so."

Sara's gaze returned to the pier. Halfway down, a building stretched across it, creating a tunnel for people to walk through. Her current spa, Hibiscus, took up the entire second floor.

Looks like we'll be staying there for a bit longer...

As they walked along the sand, Sara gave Jack a quick update on the water fiasco at the new spa. Then she asked about the other major item on her mind, considering it was December 20th. "Is everything ready for our trip?"

Jack nodded, a smile lighting up his face. "I confirmed the hotel reservation in Galveston. Stop worrying, darlin'. My family will love you."

She put on a brave smile, knowing how important this visit was to him. "I hope so. This is a lot of pressure, you know. Meeting your parents and your ten thousand siblings for the first time. At Christmas, no less."

Chapter Two

SARA CLIMBED the steps onto the back porch and entered her and Jack's cozy cottage. The sound of Hope's laughter from the beach followed her inside. Her eye fell on a packing list sitting on the laminate countertop, reminding her of Jack's earlier reassurances. Ten thousand siblings might have been a bit of a stretch, but not much. Jack was one of six children, a far cry from how Sara had grown up. But Jack couldn't wait to introduce her to his family, and Christmas was a natural time for a visit. At least that's what she kept telling herself.

But I don't have to worry about that quite yet.

As Sara removed a bottle of white wine from the refrigerator, she glanced around at what she had named the Love Shack. They were renting a three bedroom and two bath, somewhat ramshackle, cottage. The kitchen opened to the living room, though the natural wooden walls and ceiling made the cottage somewhat dark. The older kitchen appliances were degrading from the constant salt air, but their home was rustically charming.

Jack's modern, dark-gray living room furniture was more out of place here than in his former apartment, but two brilliant watercolor paintings depicting nearby Frederiksted gave the room life. The cottage had one primary appeal, which became obvious as she returned to the porch and the sound of ocean waves enveloped her. The house sat at the end of a bumpy dirt road and boasted its own beach at the head of a small private cove.

More laughter drifted over as Sara made her way over the salt and pepper sand to the brick firepit Jack had built. The simple construction consisted of four layers of bricks arranged in a circle on the sand. An assortment of weather-resistant seating clustered around it. A homey fire sent up a crackle of sparks, highlighting Hope's lean, attractive face as she laughed at something Jack had said. She and Alex snuggled up on a couch, her legs across his lap and an arm draped over his shoulder. Her chestnut hair was pulled back in a ponytail and she had dispensed with work attire, dressed in a purple T-shirt and white shorts. Alex absently brushed one hand over her ponytail as he smiled at her. Sara enjoyed watching them together. Hope was thirty-eight and Alex four years older. Their obvious love for each other only enhanced the fact that they were a gorgeous couple.

"Who's ready for a refill?" Sara asked, holding up the wine bottle. She filled Hope's and Alex's glasses before splitting the rest between herself and Jack. She took a seat in a chair next to him.

"I was just remarking how well it worked out that you two moved in here right when I wanted to get new living room furniture for our house," Hope said. "I love our new set!"

"Well, you should," Sara said, laughing. "You picked it out. I just broke it in for you. Though I like the two paintings you bought me. I'm glad I kept those."

"More than your own?" Alex asked.

Painting watercolors was one of Sara's great passions. "Oh,

yes. His style is completely different. I don't have any desire to display mine."

The artist in question was a street vendor in Frederiksted. "I might ask him if he'd be interested in an exhibit at Ember," Hope said. "I'm trying to find more local artists to showcase."

"Judging from Robert's success with his exhibit, the man would be a fool to say no," Jack said, brushing his hand down a lock of Sara's long, brown hair. "Just remember, your sister's a local now too. You should feature her paintings."

"Oh, no!" Sara said. "I have way too much going on with Aqua right now, not to mention Christmas. The last thing I need is more work."

"He's right, though," Hope said, tilting her head to the side. "You're definitely on the list. But maybe we'll wait until the new spa is open."

Sara sighed and took a long drink. "I can't believe there's been another delay. This is so disappointing."

"It'll work out in the end," Alex said. "Working with water adds to an already complicated project. It will be spectacular when it's done."

Hope nodded. "Your design is something else, sis."

"As long as my spectacular design doesn't bankrupt the two of you."

The $100,000 gift Hope and Alex had given Sara still sat in her bank account, reserved as an emergency fund for unexpected expenses with the new spa. But the Monroes had provided the primary budget. As co-owner, Sara would receive half of the profits. Her money had come from a Spanish treasure Hope and Alex had found in a nearly hidden cave on resort property. They wanted to share their windfall with family, but Sara hadn't been comfortable accepting the generous gift. When Aqua became a reality, her answer was clear. She had wanted to add her money to the construction budget, but eventually she and Hope decided to keep it in reserve.

Hope shared a private smile with Alex before turning back to Sara. "Don't worry. Our second auction cleared even more than the first. Even after buying the north end of Half Moon Bay, there was still enough to finance Aqua and Ember, with money left over. We're considering other projects around the resort."

"Yeah," Alex said, pointing a finger at Sara. "Like your current spa. We're bursting at the seams on the pier. I want to move the dive shop upstairs to open more room for gear storage. So hurry up."

Sara laughed. "Oh, it's my fault now, huh? Blame George, not me."

"If the delays keep mounting up, I will." Alex examined the cove before them, the last vestiges of light casting a lavender sheen on the water. "Have you guys dived out there lately?"

Sara shook her head. "Not for a month or so."

"We'll dive it after we get back from Texas. The reef is great out there." Jack was the main divemaster at the resort. Alex was a scuba instructor—among other things. One of Jack's greatest hopes was to become an instructor as well. Despite Sara's prodding, he was hesitant to bring it up though, not wanting to encroach on Alex's territory.

"There's a coral head in shallow water that's full of baby fish!" Sara said, leaning forward in her seat. "They're so cute. I always make a point of visiting them when we dive."

Alex nodded. "The juveniles like the isolated bommies in shallow water. Less predators there."

Hope turned her attention to Jack. "Do you still hear from Dexter?"

"Yes. We've talked several times on the phone."

Dexter Ridgeway had been an integral part of their

purchasing the land Aqua and Ember now sat on—he had owned it. Dexter was over seventy years old, and after selling, he moved to South Carolina to live with his son's family.

"He sounded really happy," Jack said. "He misses the ocean, but he's teaching his grandson how to make birdhouses, which they place around their property."

"Good for him," Hope said. "And now we have enough land to expand however we want. Though we'll still keep the small, exclusive feel to the resort."

"Alex is right about the dive operation bursting at the seams, though." Jack said. "I finished the extra racks and hangers for the gear, so that gives us a little breathing room."

Hope looked at her husband. "Do you have any idea how lucky you are to have a divemaster who not only is as fastidious and organized as you, but has construction skills too?"

"I'm not complaining, believe me." Alex smiled and shook his head. "I hardly recognize the place anymore."

"I think that's a good thing," Hope said, entwining her hand in his. "That just means it's truly our resort now." They hadn't had an easy time since taking over the property after the previous owner retired, but now Half Moon Bay Resort bore little resemblance to its original incarnation. Hope smiled at Jack. "I might have to hire you to work in the kitchen. That mahi was amazing."

Jack laughed, almost choking on his wine. "Don't be too impressed. I know how to filet and grill a fish, but the seasoning was all Gerold." Gerold Harrigan was Half Moon Bay's executive chef, who was developing an island-wide reputation as the resort grew.

"You two fly out the day after tomorrow?" Hope asked.

Jack nodded. "We land in Houston in the early afternoon, and it's an hour and a half drive to Galveston."

Hope slid her eyes to Sara, and the two shared a sisterly

look. Hope was aware how nervous she was about meeting Jack's family. Sara breathed a sigh. "I really did think we agreed on a January trip, you know."

"What's got you so concerned?" Alex asked.

Sara hesitated as she stared back at him. His voice had been soft and warm, but the former SEAL was the embodiment of confidence. And she wasn't.

How could you understand? You've never faced a situation in your life you weren't completely confident about.

But Alex had experienced plenty of hardship and loss in his life. Sara glanced around the fire, surprised when three pairs of eyes were trained on her, awaiting her answer. A truthful answer would reveal her deepest insecurities, which she tried to keep hidden.

That she wasn't good enough, that Jack's family would only notice she was overweight.

Jack and Hope were the only ones who really saw the hidden side of Sara. She loved Alex like a brother, but that made their relationship a bit feisty at times. And she didn't feel like baring her soul at the moment, anyway. "It's just that it's a big deal, you know? Meeting your boyfriend's family for the first time?" Then she winced. "That word sounds ridiculous at our age, doesn't it?" She was thirty-four to Jack's thirty-three.

"We're very casual, Sara," Jack said softly.

"It's just so different from what we grew up with," she said to Hope.

"Isn't that a good thing?" Hope asked with a smile. "We didn't exactly have the greatest home life. Now you get the chance to be a part of a big, loving family."

"It's still a hell of a lot of pressure."

Jack reached out and ran his hand down her arm. "Not unless you make it that way. Relax, and everything will be fine."

. . .

Sara leaned into Jack's side as they waved goodbye. Alex helped Hope into his classic Land Cruiser, then they drove into the dark night. The air became silent once more except for the timeless wash of the ocean onto land. Jack turned Sara toward him and cupped her face in both hands. He softly kissed her, his lips warm and gentle, and she melted against him.

He wrapped her tightly in his arms, drawing her against him as he murmured in her ear, "You understand I'd never let anyone mistreat you, right? You don't need to be afraid of my family."

She stroked her fingers down his back, settling her face against his neck. "I know. My mom and dad just screamed at each other all the time. I always thought it was my fault—Hope was the only one I felt secure with. Maybe it's time to learn new ideas of what families can be."

She moved her lips to his, once again drawing comfort from him. At the same time, they both opened their mouths, deepening the kiss, and a tremor ran through her. Tracing a line of kisses to his ear, Sara whispered, "We can worry about your family later. Right now, there's only you and me."

Chapter Three

THE NEXT MORNING, Jack led his dive group through a broad channel covered in lavender pillar coral, reaching toward the sparkling sun far above. A large school of yellow-tailed snappers parted like a curtain around him. A glance at his dive computer informed him they were forty minutes into the dive. Stopping before a coral head, Jack hunted for a frog fish who liked to hide there when several strong tugs pulled his fin. Turning around, he was presented with an explosion of bubbles emanating from a diver's regulator.

Instead of delivering a steady stream of air activated by his inhalation, Dennis's regulator was free-flowing—the inner diaphragm of the mouthpiece was open and producing a froth of bubbles. Even through the curtain of air rising in front of Dennis's face, Jack had no problem interpreting his wide, panicked blue eyes behind his dive mask. A free flow wasn't an emergency. The diver received more than enough air, but water often entered the mouth along with the excess air. Not a good thing deep under the surface.

Jack surged forward, grabbing his yellow octopus second-air source. He purged it and pressed the regulator into Dennis's mouth while removing the malfunctioning one, sharing his own air supply. Dennis closed his eyes and took a deep breath as he breathed off Jack's tank, his long, dark-blond hair waving around his head. Jack pressed the purge button several times on the man's second stage, but the froth of bubbles continued. He turned off Dennis's tank valve, shutting off the air supply before opening it again to see if that would reset the regulator.

No dice. Bubbles tumbled out of the mouthpiece.

Ok, looks like Dennis is breathing off my octopus for the rest of the dive.

Jack turned off the diver's tank valve again. He dropped the now-dead regulator, where it hung at Dennis's side, dangling from its attachment at the tank valve. He signaled to Dennis that they would buddy up and got a relieved nod in return. Dennis's concerned dive partner hovered a short distance away, as did the other five divers. All watched raptly. Four were resort guests, and the other was Zach Turner, a part-time employee who had graduated from high school the previous June and was soaking up all the diving experience he could get. He stared at Jack, his eyes a vivid white against his dark skin.

Good, they're all getting a little extra education today, especially Zach.

Jack gave the entire group an ok signal, letting them know there was no emergency and patted Dennis's shoulder before linking elbows with him. But the incident completely changed his dive plan. Jack peeked at his computer—he still had half a tank of air left, which would be plenty to get Dennis back safely to the surface.

Within five minutes, they were under the boat, and Jack disengaged from Dennis and took out his dive slate. The other four divers were very experienced, and he'd dived with them for several days. So he had no qualms about leaving them to finish the last fifteen minutes of the dive without him. He wrote instructions on the slate for them to remain near the boat and got four nods in return, plus one high five from a diver who was pleased Dennis's regulator malfunction hadn't cut his dive short. Jack grinned back and signaled Dennis and his friend to ascend and begin their safety stop with him. He waved to Zach to come along too. The kid didn't have a designated buddy, so he went with Jack.

As soon as they surfaced, they inflated their buoyancy compensation devices, and Dennis handed Jack back his octopus. "That was a little more exciting than I bargained for. Thanks for the help."

Jack was pleased the diver wasn't too shook up. "Don't mention it. You handled it great."

Alex's group was already on board. He saw them and came to the stern platform, frowning. Jack and the two divers moved toward him. "Something wrong?"

"Dennis's reg has a free flow," Jack said. "We need to swap it out for a spare."

Dennis laughed. "What? I don't get to spend the second dive arm in arm with you?"

"Sorry to disappoint you, but I'm already involved with someone."

They laughed as they removed their fins, but Alex wasn't smiling. Boat captain Tommy Williams came back to help, and Alex maneuvered Dennis so the guest could sit down and get out of his scuba kit.

Jack shrugged out of his own BCD and joined them as Dennis reassured Alex he was fine. "Jack knew what to do and settled me right down."

Alex gave the diver a crooked smile. "Yeah, I'm sure he did. Free flowing doesn't happen very often, but I guess it was your unlucky day." He turned to Jack as he unscrewed the first stage of the faulty regulator from the tank. "You want to grab the spare?"

Nodding, Jack made his way to a storage cabinet at the front of the canopy and kneeled on the fiberglass deck. He pulled out a basket of spare equipment, quickly locating a regulator.

Alex appeared beside him and placed the broken reg in a different cabinet. "I'll have to look at that and see why it malfunctioned."

After performing a count to confirm everyone was on board, Tommy unmoored the boat and climbed the ladder to the wheelhouse above them. The engine roared to life, and they motored slowly toward their second dive site as Zach changed each diver's gear over to a fresh tank. The two men stood from the deck, and Alex nodded at Jack. "Good job handling that. You have a quiet, reassuring manner divers really respond to."

Jack knew he was good at what he did, but he still flushed at the compliment. "Thanks. This is definitely a job that keeps you on your toes."

"That's for sure." Alex sighed and ran a hand over his short, wet hair. "Not sure I can get to that reg anytime soon. Good thing we've got several spares. I'm teaching a Nitrox class this afternoon, and a couple in my group wants an advanced class the next few days." He paused, eyeing Jack evenly. "Have you ever thought about becoming an instructor?"

Excitement tickled down Jack's spine. *Only since I became a divemaster...* "Yeah, I have, for a long time."

"I could sure use some help teaching. Though if you become an instructor, we'll need another divemaster too. Hell, we already do."

Jack smiled. "There are worse problems to have."

"Yeah, I know. I've got some ideas about that, but they're more long term. I'll start looking into an Instructor Development Course for you."

Jack burst into laughter. "That just kills me. You trained Navy SEALS, yet you can't teach recreational instructors."

Alex smiled, but waved him off. "I just never went through the extra coursework. Didn't see the point. In the seven years I've been here, this is the first time instructor training has come up. Besides, I want to find you an IDC at a busy dive shop, so you get plenty of experience teaching. I'll find something."

"Thanks, Alex."

Jack could hardly keep the grin off his face as he returned to Dennis's tank to attach the new regulator.

AFTER THE AFTERNOON DIVE, Jack stood in the cramped gear storage/air compressor room. Even with the new shelving and storage he had built, there was barely enough room for all the scuba gear. The large air compressor and membrane system for producing enriched air took up half the room, which didn't help.

Alex is right—we really need the extra space that will be freed up once the spa moves into the new building.

He returned to the wooden dock, happy to escape the stifling room. As he closed the door behind him, Alex walked into the dive shop with his Nitrox student, not even close to being done for the day. But Jack was. He strolled up the pier, enjoying the warm sun on his back.

His phone rang and he pulled it out of his pocket, breaking into a smile at his little brother Will's face on his screen. Will was Jack's closest sibling. "Hey there. What's up?"

"I'm on a break and thought I'd give you a call."

Will worked at Galveston Island State Park as a ranger, something Jack had always envied. Until he became a divemaster. Now he figured he had Will beat on the job front. "On a break? I didn't think you ever worked."

"Like you should talk. You're the one who watches pretty fishies all day long."

Jack laughed. "It's not all fun and games. I had a near-emergency today, but the guy handled it fine."

"Yeah, yeah. What kind of emergency—did someone forget their sunscreen?" He laughed, and a smile rose to Jack's face as they bantered.

"If you think it's so easy, you try it sometime."

"Maybe I will. I've been diving more. I got my advanced certification, you know."

"What, a month ago? That course just exposes you to more advanced conditions in a safe setting. The only way to become an advanced diver is more dives, Will."

"Oh, stop lecturing me. You sound like Dad."

Jack laughed as he walked by the lobby on his way to the parking lot. "I'm your big brother. I'm allowed to give advice."

"Bite me. So, you still coming home tomorrow?"

"Yeah, we should be at the house by late afternoon. You're staying at Mama and Dad's for the holiday, right?"

"I am. Mama was disappointed to hear you're staying in a hotel."

"We'll spend plenty of time at the house. We just wanted to be able to get away from the chaos. Sara's a little nervous about this."

"Gee, I wonder why? You're kind of an asshole, Jack."

"Language! Priests aren't supposed to say words like that."

"I'm not a priest!" Will sighed. "Why do I always rise to the bait?"

Jack laughed again as he tossed his bag in the bed of his Ford Ranger. "Every time. I kind of expected you to have figured it out by now, but you're a slow one, Will."

Will had gone through Methodist seminary school and was an ordained minister, though he had never worked as a pastor.

He tended to flit around from one interest to another. Which their father was becoming less and less tolerant of as Will got closer to thirty years of age.

"For a guy who wants me to make sure his girlfriend has someone in her corner, you're not exactly killing me with kindness here."

Jack's smile fell as he climbed in and started the engine. "I really do need you in her corner. Sara's important to me, Will. I want this meeting to go well on both sides."

"Is she a shrinking violet or something?"

Laughter burst out of Jack's mouth. "Not in the slightest. I think you'll get along well with her. But she only has the one sister, so a big family is a new experience for her."

"All right. Just for you, I'll try to keep any family members from attacking your girlfriend."

"Thanks, Will. We'll see you tomorrow."

THE DIRT ROAD that led to their house was in terrible condition. Not for the first time, Jack was grateful they both had four-wheel-drive vehicles. When it was dry, the road was ok as long as the driver went slow. But it turned into a slippery quagmire during rains, making 4WD a necessity. "Yet another thing Calvin should do a better job keeping up with," Jack muttered. Calvin Emory was their landlord and counted on the property's incredible location to keep it rented, not its condition.

A fact Jack was less than thrilled about.

As he drove out of the jungle, he saw Sara's RAV4 parked in front of the slightly dilapidated one-story cottage. The house was the brownish gray of weathered wood, and the green shingle roof had a patchy carpet of moss growing on it. But how many places could you live on your own private beach?

He opened the front door and tossed his keys in a basket on a nearby end table. "I'm home, Sara!"

The furniture from his old apartment graced the living room —a dark gray couch and loveseat, plus Sara had purchased two armchairs to complement them. The open kitchen was on the far end. The three bedrooms and two baths were off to one side.

"I'm in here!" came the distant response from their bedroom, and Jack entered to find a suitcase open on the king-size bed. The bed had come from Sara's apartment, which Hope had equipped using the same linens and bedding the resort beds used. Sara's furnishings were a major upgrade compared to his homely purchases from Walmart, which were in the guest room and bath now.

Sara turned from the suitcase and headed toward him, opening her arms wide. Her hair was circled into a bun, and she wore long shorts and a T-shirt that hung past her hips. But even dressed casually, she made his breath freeze in his lungs. Sara was lush curves and soft creamy skin from head to toe.

They came together for a long hello kiss, their arms encircling each other to hold tight. They had lived together for nearly eight months, and Jack wouldn't trade it for anything. Some adjustments had been needed at first, but as they settled into a domestic pairing, both had learned to accept the other's quirks and foibles. Like her terror of spiders, which came into the house to escape the rain. He got a kick out of smashing them for her, but sometimes he set them free outside instead. He kept that to himself.

"I'm afraid I have a little repair for you," Sara said, then bit her bottom lip. It only made her more adorable, so his irritation at yet another project was minimal. And his ire wasn't directed at her anyway.

"What would that be?"

"I could hardly get the kitchen door open to go onto the back porch. The doorknob keeps slipping. Could you look at it?"

Dammit, Calvin.

Jack had worked out an arrangement with the older man where anytime Jack repaired something, he subtracted the amount from their monthly rent and included a receipt for the repairs. "Of course. Shouldn't be too hard to fix." He had no idea his background in residential construction would prove so beneficial.

Jack kissed the tip of her nose, then moved to the open suitcase. He had placed his clothes in it that morning, and Sara was busy filling up the rest of the space. He smiled at the six flat wrapped boxes, her Christmas presents for his family, and shook his head. "I wish you'd stop being so worried about this. How could anyone in my family resist you?"

"Maybe it's partially because of what Heather and Robert just went through."

Their co-workers at the resort had been through quite an ordeal before Robert's traditional island family accepted them as a couple.

"Our situation is completely different," Jack said softly. "And everything worked out fine for them, didn't it?"

"I know. I have to remind myself you didn't have the easiest time believing you fit in with my family either."

Jack couldn't resist a smile. "Why? Just because your sister owns the resort where I have my dream job and your brother-in-law could break me in half with his pinky finger? What's intimidating about that?"

Sara slid an arm around his waist. "Yet here you are. Not only hasn't Alex broken you in half, you're friends. And Hope thinks you're terrific."

"My family will think the same of you."

"Let's go to Galveston. After you fix the doorknob."

Chapter Four

SARA STARED out the window of the rental sedan, fascinated by the flat expanse before her. The sky was a muted blue with thin wispy clouds, and a dull haze hung over the horizon. Her and Jack's flight to Houston had been uneventful, and they were now halfway through the drive to Galveston.

Forty-five minutes until showtime!

Well, not exactly.

First, they'd check into their hotel, then head over to Jack's family home. She couldn't deny that the hotel room was a major relief—around-the-clock family dynamics might be a bit much on a first meeting.

Jack was completely relaxed as he drove, one hand loosely holding the top of the steering wheel. His posture was that of someone driving a road they were highly familiar with and eager for where it would end.

"Let me run through your family again," Sara said. "Just to make sure I've got it."

Jack grinned. "Go for it."

"Your father is Joe and he's an orthodontist. Your mother, Patricia, is a dental hygienist at his office."

"Mama goes by Trish, and she didn't work on patients very long. She's been the office manager as long as I can remember."

"Is that how they met?"

He nodded, his smile widening. "Yep. Love bloomed over people's braces."

"And we met at work too, continuing the family tradition. Moving on to siblings, your oldest sister is Mary and she's the oral surgeon. One brother is a dentist, right?"

"Henry."

"Right. Your other sister is Amber, who's a barista. And of course, your brother Will, the park ranger. That's everyone, right?"

Jack's grin widened. "Nope. You forgot Gregory. He's a petroleum engineer in Houston."

Groaning, Sara let her head flop against the headrest. "I'll never keep it straight."

He reached over and clasped her hand. "Of course you will. You just need to match the name to the face, then it will be easy. Besides, I don't think everyone's coming this year. Last I heard, Greg was on an offshore rig out in the gulf."

Sara recited the names silently in her head, counting off on her fingers. Then something occurred to her. "All of you have formal, traditional names—Mary, William, and you're John. How come your parents broke tradition with Amber?"

"She's the youngest of the family, and I think they just threw up their hands and went with a popular name when baby number six came along. She's twenty-two."

"Can't blame them there." Sara smirked. "I can just picture you all when you were a boy, clustered around the television as you watched Rudolph the Red-Nosed Reindeer. But not because of poor Rudolph. I bet you were all more interested in Hermey wanting to be a dentist."

Jack's short beard didn't hide the red flush that crept over his face. He adjusted his hand on the wheel as he muttered, "There's nothing wrong with that. We enjoyed the other parts of the story too."

Sara threw her head back and laughed, Jack joining her.

Returning her gaze to the broad, flat terrain around them, she grew contemplative. During one of the restless nights Sara had spent worrying about this visit, she'd had an important epiphany. One that had startled her greatly. Namely, that the reason she was so worried about meeting Jack's family was because she wanted so badly to be accepted by them. Maybe even loved by them someday. After years of not wanting to be tied down, she'd laid there staring at their ceiling, stunned that she wasn't carefree Sara anymore. Her experience of moving to St. Croix and reuniting with Hope had kindled a sense of what it meant to *belong*. Moving in with Jack had only solidified that feeling more.

Once they reached downtown Galveston, Jack turned down a broad avenue lined with stately buildings. Trees and ornamental streetlights lined the streets. Sara craned her head to see better. "How pretty! It kind of reminds me of Charleston—without the Spanish moss."

"Downtown is hopping during Christmas. We should have plenty to keep us busy. The hotel is just ahead."

Past the next traffic light, a brown brick structure loomed as it took up an entire block. Several vans were lined up on the street, *Galveston Restoration* painted on the sides. Midway down the block, they passed the entrance of the Galveston Grand Hotel, a uniformed doorman standing in front of double glass doors as a burgundy canopy arched overhead. Jack continued around the block before descending into a parking garage.

They shut the car doors, the sound echoing around the dark cement structure, and Jack lifted their suitcase out of the trunk.

They took an elevator to the lobby, emerging onto a plush tan carpet. A quiet hum sounded around them, groups of people talking, and the entire lobby was decorated for Christmas. A twenty-foot tree rose in one corner, white lights blinking, and soft Christmas music played overhead.

As they made their way to the polished wood check-in counter, they paused to let three men in white coveralls pass, each carrying an industrial vacuum. Jack smiled at the check-in agent, a middle-aged woman whose brown hair was slipping from her clip and her glasses slightly askew. She looked up and took a deep breath when she met Jack and Sara's eyes. "Good afternoon. What can I do for you?"

"We're checking in. Reservation under Jack Powell," he said, setting the suitcase on the floor.

The woman's eyes tightened as she typed on her keyboard. Then she placed both hands on it and took a deep breath. "That's what I was afraid of. We're completely sold out."

Sara's heart skipped a beat. "How can you be full? We have a reservation."

The woman flinched. "I know, and I'm terribly sorry. We had a major plumbing leak this morning and it's shut down several floors. We've got crews working non-stop to get it cleaned up, but our capacity just got cut by a third."

Another jumpsuit-wearing crew walked through the lobby, *Galveston Restoration* embroidered on their backs, and Sara recalled the vans sitting out front.

Her heart sank into her shoes.

The agent returned her gaze to the terminal. "We have a note on your reservation that we tried to find you an alternate room at another hotel. But it's Christmas, so everyone is full. I'm so sorry. If you look farther out of town, I'm sure you can find something."

Sara stiffened, nerves dancing in her gut. "Wait a minute. Are you saying there are no rooms anywhere?"

"None in town. Of all the times for this to happen..." Another lock of hair fell out of the woman's clip, and her appearance now made sense.

Sara turned her gaze to Jack. He stared at her with a small smile playing around his lips. "Good thing there's a place we can stay, huh?"

His eyes were beseeching, and she returned his smile with the bravest one she could manage. "Christmas at the Powells, here we come."

Jack pulled out of the parking garage and back onto the main avenue. "My folks live out of town a bit. We'll be there in ten minutes." Jack placed a call over the car's Bluetooth to his mother, who quickly answered.

"Jacky!"

Momentarily forgetting the wave of dread building within her, Sara whipped her head to him, a grin spreading across her face as she mouthed, "Jacky?"

He shot her a warning glance and shook his head, which only made her grin more.

"Hi, Mama. We're here and on our way to your house now."

"Wonderful! That was quick. You're already settled in at The Grand?"

"Not exactly..." Jack gave her a quick update and asked if there was a guest room available.

"Well, of course. You know I wanted you two to stay here all along." Trish spoke with a warm voice, her Texas accent faint but distinct. Just like her son's. Sara liked her casual mention of the word two.

"Thanks. Sara's here with me in the car. Say hello, Mama."

"Oh, I'm so looking forward to meeting you, Sara! I already admire you for taking all of us on at once."

Sara's smile lingered, and the hot ball of anxiety she'd been carrying for weeks loosened a little more. "Thank you, Mrs. Powell. I'm looking forward to spending Christmas with all of you."

"Oh, please call me Trish!"

Jack made a right turn onto a smaller road. "We're getting close, Mama. See you in a few minutes." After disconnecting the call, he turned to Sara. "See? Nothing to be afraid of."

Sara nodded, but couldn't help the thought that formed. *I sure hope not. Because for the next three days, I'm going to be with them twenty-four hours a day.*

After several more turns, Jack rolled down an elegant street filled with considerably large houses. Each was on a spacious lot, manicured green lawns separating each house. Jack pulled into an asphalt driveway and stopped before a brown two-story brick house with a black roof and a three-car garage. Tall columns flanked the broad entry door. As they exited the car, Sara gaped at the structure. "This house is huge!"

Jack lifted one shoulder. "It's not a mansion, but with six kids, the space came in handy."

He retrieved their suitcase, and they walked up a brick entryway lined with black solar lanterns. Sara stayed a step behind, her heart kicking into a gallop as Jack led.

Instead of knocking, Jack twisted the doorknob, walking straight in as he called out, "Ok, the party can start now. We're here!"

Chapter Five

JACK SHUT THE DOOR, and Sara's stomach writhed as the sound of hurrying footsteps came toward them. Wrapping an arm around her shoulders, he pulled her tightly to his side.

God, I love this man.

They stood inside a two-story foyer. A library sat to Sara's left, and to her right, a sweeping staircase curved up to the second floor. Lit green garland wrapped around the banister. Before them lay a hallway, and four shadowy forms hurried toward them.

The quartet stepped into the bright foyer, led by a plump woman with dark hair cut in a long shag. Just behind her was a man about Jack's height with steel-gray hair, but his eyebrows were still a medium brown, as were his eyes. Both wore identical giant smiles, and the woman reached out to Jack, who disengaged his arm from Sara's shoulders. The woman fell into Jack's arms as he laughed and patted her back.

"Oh, Jacky! How I've missed you."

"Me too, Mama."

Jack let go to shake hands with his father, then pulled Sara tight again. She met Jack's gaze and nearly melted at the happiness and pride in his eyes. He turned back to his parents. "Mama and Dad—I'd like you to meet Sara Collins."

Giving Sara a warm smile, Trish took both her hands, squeezing softly. "Welcome to our home. We're happy to finally meet you."

Joe reached out with a handshake, grasping her hand gently. "Glad you could make it. I heard there was a little mix-up at The Grand."

"Yes, there was," Sara said, some of her butterflies settling. "Thank you so much for letting us stay. Apparently, all the hotels in Galveston are sold out."

"Oh, I'm sure they are," Trish said with a wave. "Not exactly easy to get a hotel room on December 23rd, is it?"

Movement behind the couple diverted Sara's attention to the two people standing behind them, obviously Jack's siblings. Both looked in their twenties and had the same dark-brown hair. The man's shaggy mane curled at his neck, and he had a friendly, somewhat long, face. The woman's hair was pulled back in a ponytail and she wore no makeup on her heart-shaped face. Slightly taller than Sara, she was dressed casually in capris and a long-sleeved T-shirt.

"Come on, guys," Jack said, beckoning them forward. "You can't hide back there all day."

"We were hardly hiding," the woman said with a frown, folding her arms over her trim stomach. "We just didn't want to bombard poor Sara all at once." She stepped forward and surprised Sara by giving her a warm hug. "I'm Amber, and this is Will. Don't worry, he's been ordered to be on his best behavior."

Will gave her a crooked, but charming, smile as he shrugged. "That's never worked before, and probably won't this time. Nice to meet you."

"You, too. I'm happy to be here."

Ok, only two siblings for now. I can do this.

"Are you two hungry?" Trish asked. "I've had pulled pork going in the Crock Pot all afternoon."

Fifteen minutes later, they sat around a rectangular table in an alcove off the bright kitchen. On the other side lay a family room, a large-screen television hanging on the wall. In one corner, the base of a Christmas tree was stuffed with presents. A panel of windows gave a view of the neat back yard where a cement patio surrounded a covered swimming pool.

Sara swallowed a bite of her sandwich. She hadn't realized how hungry she was, but so was everyone else. Their arrival had coincided with dinner time.

"So, Jack tells us you're in charge of quite the construction project," Jack's father said.

Sara wiped her mouth with a napkin. "Yes. My sister and I are designing a new spa for the resort. My plans might have been a bit too ambitious though. We've been plagued by construction delays."

Jack explained the water design for Aqua. "There's been a few hiccups, but it will be one of the best spas on the island when it's done."

Amber stared at him, a smile lighting up her face. "I don't even need to ask if you're good at what you do, Sara. I hardly recognize Jack. Not only the beard—his hair looks great. He's almost handsome."

Jack gave her a deadpan look as laughter broke out around the table.

"He's an easy subject to work with," Sara said, their eyes meeting for a long beat. "It's not too hard to make Jack look good." She turned back to his siblings. "Do you both live here in Galveston?"

"I live in Austin," Amber replied. "But I'm staying here for Christmas."

"I've got an apartment on the other side of town," Will said. "It's closer to the state park where I work."

"Will is still trying to find the career that suits him best," Trish said, turning a smile to her youngest son, but Joe's face was carefully neutral. Trish looked at Jack. "You seem to have settled in St. Croix well."

"I have," Jack said. "I love being a divemaster and have plenty of work now. Just before we left, the dive manager asked if I was interested in becoming an instructor. So I might have a promotion in the future. You been diving lately?" he asked Will.

"Yeah. I've been going with a guy I work with, diving the oil rigs on our days off."

"Oil rigs?" Sara asked.

Jack nodded. "That's the main type of diving here. The rigs become artificial reefs, and some are really spectacular. Not all are open to divers though. If we had more time, I'd take you to dive one of them."

Dinner was an easy, comfortable meal and Sara relaxed in her chair. Under the table, Jack reached over to squeeze her knee, and she placed her hand over his. When it came time to clear the plates, she jumped up to help, wanting to make a good impression. Trish set a plate of chocolate chip cookies in the middle of the table and the conversation continued.

Sara ate one to be polite, but was conscious of her full figure, even though Jack accepted her just as she was. There was no judgement or condescension from his family either. She raised a hand, trying to stifle a yawn, but Jack saw it.

"It has been a very long day for us, and we still need to unpack," Jack said. "Did you make up Mary's old room for us?"

"Yes," Trish said. "It's all ready to go."

"Lucky you," Amber said with a laugh. "I got my old room with the tiny bed and pink Hello Kitty wallpaper, and you get the suite with attached bath."

"Jeez, Amber," Will said, smacking her in the head. "You think it should be the other way around?"

"Oh, quit fighting, you two." Joe said, smiling, then turned to Sara. "We've made over a couple of the kids' old rooms into guest rooms, but Mary's is the only one with a private bath."

"Everything sounds perfect. Thank you."

Jack scraped back his chair and stood. "Come on, darlin'. I left the suitcase by the front door. Let's get settled in."

Following Jack back down the hallway toward the foyer, Sara enjoyed the warm, lived-in vibe of the house. He turned to her after picking up their bag. "You doing ok?"

She stood on her tiptoes to give him a quick kiss. "Yes. I like your family a lot, though I'm glad only Will and Amber are here tonight."

Jack took her hand. and they ascended the curving staircase. "I admit, all six of us at the same time can be a bit overwhelming."

A broad hallway stretched in both directions at the top of the staircase and Jack turned left, following the hall to the last door. He opened it, and Sara stepped into a large bedroom painted a serene blue. The room contained a queen-sized bed with a navy-blue bedspread, a long dresser on the opposite side. Two doors lined a third wall, the bath visible through one. With a happy sigh at being with only Jack again, she got to unpacking.

Sara wore a long white nightgown to bed, slipping between sheets that still smelled of fresh laundry. Jack curled up behind her and wrapped an arm around her waist. She took his hand and kissed it.

"There's a big winter festival downtown at The Strand," he said, his voice already becoming sleepy. "I thought we could head down there tomorrow. It will be in full swing Christmas

Eve, with shops and entertainment. Maybe we can get Will and Amber to join us."

Sara wiggled her toes, letting his solid warmth complete the process of relaxing her body. "That sounds like fun. It'll be nice to spend more time with Will and Amber."

A smile came to her face that she wasn't just saying that to make Jack happy. She really did look forward to it.

THE STRAND WAS Galveston's historic district, a broad avenue flanked by picturesque buildings constructed in the eighteenth and nineteenth centuries. At the moment, though, it was taken over by Christmas carolers and various celebrants dressed up in their best Charles Dickens attire. Jack had always avoided it in the past, thinking it touristy. But he was enjoying it now—because Sara was. Will and Amber had joined them, and the quartet spent several hours exploring the festival.

A surprising number of shops were open on Christmas Eve. The day was sunny with the temperature in the mid-sixties, chilly compared to St. Croix. Jack was comfortable in a T-shirt and jeans, but the temperature had prompted Sara to wear a cardigan sweater.

They were standing on the sidewalk in front of a pottery shop when Will grabbed Amber in a horse collar hug, causing her to shoot him a dirty look. "Come on, sis. Let's give the love-birds some time alone."

"Oh, is that why you insisted we drive separately?" Amber asked him.

Will winked at Sara. "You get major props from me. I'm impressed you didn't kick Jack to the curb when he wanted you to meet us all at once, and on Christmas."

"Oh, that never even crossed my mind," Sara said, then

burst out laughing when Jack turned to her, his mouth dropping open.

Then he broke into laughter too. "Yeah, I might have gotten my ass chewed a little. I kept telling her she'd be a giant hit, and I was right."

Amber disengaged herself from Will. "He is—we're glad you're here, Sara. We'll give you a little time alone. See you back at the house."

After they left, Jack took Sara's hand as they strolled along, enjoying the simple pleasure of being part of a couple. Especially since he'd never felt this *invested* before. They passed an expensive-looking boutique gym where people were running on treadmills and doing floor workouts. "I love you, you know."

"Well, I love you too." Sara smiled at him, gloriously curvy in a long, brown, tie-dyed skirt and a peasant blouse. Her hair fell in glossy curls down her back and shoulders, and she'd given herself lighter highlights. She took his breath away.

"You have a nice family, Jacky." Sara bit her bottom lip, trying not to laugh.

Jack sighed. "Only Mama gets to call me Jacky, ok? I tried for years to get her to stop, but it's a lost cause. So don't you start with it!"

She only laughed harder, and he couldn't stop the answering smile that rose on his own face.

Just past the gym, a group of carolers passed by, and they paused to listen. After the singers moved on, Sara turned to face the window display of an antique store, studying an ornately carved chair. He turned with her, admiring the workmanship.

"Well, hello there, Jack," said a woman behind him. "Word on the street is you moved away. Did you miss something and decide to come back?" His blood turned to ice, recognizing the voice instantly.

Sara was already turning around, so he had no choice but to

do the same. Diane stood before them. His ex-wife was dressed in tight, athletic capris and a skin-tight pink performance shirt. Her almost-black hair was pulled into a tight ponytail. A visor shaded her face, which was thinner than he'd last seen it, though her lips were bigger.

"I have moved away," he said evenly. "We came home to visit my family for Christmas."

The slight emphasis he'd put on *we* caused Diane to turn to Sara, inspecting her from head to toe. The last thing Jack wanted was to introduce these two women, but he couldn't see a way out of it. "Diane, this is my girlfriend, Sara. We live on St. Croix." Again, he put an emphasis on *we*.

Sara stiffened beside him, and her hand tightened in his, but she nodded politely. "Hello."

"Well, aren't you two the cozy little couple?" Diane's eyes danced, but there was a slightly malign spark in them. "I was just working out at the gym next door. What timing we have!"

"If you say so," Jack said. "We were just heading back to the house." He had absolutely no desire to have any conversation with his ex. "Goodbye, Diane." He let go of Sara's hand and wrapped his arm around her shoulders, turning her as they walked away.

"Have a lovely Christmas, Jack," Diane called out behind them, her voice almost excessively friendly. "And you too, Sara. There's an incredible bakery on the next block. I'm sure you can find something special for tomorrow morning. You look like a woman who knows her way around a bakery."

What the hell is that supposed to mean?

But Jack ignored Diane, and so did Sara, though she stiffened under his arm. The day was now less bright, and he looked up, surprised there were no clouds dimming the sun's light.

What in God's name did I ever see in that woman?

Chapter Six

RED-HOT ANGER KNIFED through Sara as she walked beside Jack. She inhaled a long breath, forcing herself to relax. But that idea was thwarted when they turned the corner and passed the bakery Diane had referred to.

Bitch, bitch, bitch...

Sara repeated the mantra in her head, timing each word to her footfalls. *I may not be a rail-thin, collagen-lipped exercise fanatic, but at least I'm a decent human being.*

"Well, she was the last person I wanted to see," Jack said. "Why the hell was she interested in us buying something at this bakery?"

Sara whipped her head toward him, but his expression only held befuddlement.

He has no idea she said that to insult me!

Her anger melted away, replaced by a warm fuzziness that slowly spread through her chest. *Oh, my sweet, loyal Jack.* A tiny smile cracked her face, but it fell when she saw the tight set to his jaw. Diane had broken his heart. Seeing her again must have affected him strongly.

She wrapped an arm around his waist. "Are you ok?"

He stretched his jaw open, forcing himself to relax. "Yeah. It was a bit of a shock though."

"I'm sure it was. Don't let it ruin your day."

"Oh, I have no intention of that. She sure was nasty, though. I didn't like how she looked at you—I wanted her to know we were a couple."

"I know you did, and that meant a lot to me. Let's put your ex-wife behind us. We've got Christmas to celebrate."

This time, when they pulled up to the Powells' large house, Sara was more at ease. Oddly, the encounter with Diane was partially why.

He's with me, not you, bitch.

THE NEXT MORNING, Sara and Jack woke up early. She took a shower and got ready before heading downstairs, wanting to be prepared for the festive chaos to come. Jack's oldest sister Mary was coming with her husband and daughter, and his brother Henry would be there with his wife and three children. Sara picked out a long dress with a swirling pattern of pink shades. Small streaks of dark red lent it the proper Christmas tone without being too over the top. As she flat-ironed her hair, she savored the silence—likely the last quiet she'd experience for the rest of the day.

Her light-brown highlights were even more striking with her hair straightened, and as the light glinted on her hair, she liked the look. Dressing nicely always gave her confidence a boost, and she needed that today. After breathing out a deep sigh, she attached a pair of long earrings. Sara returned to the bedroom, where six flat wrapped boxes sat on the bed. Five were eight by ten, and the sixth was slightly larger. All were her presents for Jack's family.

She made her way to the family room, where the large Christmas tree blinked in its corner. Jack was drinking coffee at the island and saw her armful of gifts. He hurried over to help her place them under the tree. She'd thought hard about what to give his family and was proud of her choice.

As they returned to the kitchen, Trish poured Sara a cup of coffee and slid it over the island. "Merry Christmas! You look incredible. You put me to shame—that's for sure." She indicated her black sweater with a gold Christmas tree and khakis.

"Oh, hardly," Sara said, adding milk and sugar to her mug. "I just like wearing dresses. And Merry Christmas to you too."

Amber walked into the kitchen from the hall, yawning and wearing reindeer pajamas. She stopped short, widening her eyes at Sara. "Oh, crap. How do you look so good first thing in the morning?"

Jack grinned and pulled Sara against his side. "She looks good all the time."

That made her feel better. She had begun to worry about being overdressed. But Jack wore a dressy sweater and neat jeans, and she relaxed.

Trish looked toward the tree and frowned. "I hope you didn't feel you had to get us gifts. Goodness—just meeting us all at Christmas is pressure enough."

"Not at all."

"Wait until you see what she brought, Mama," Jack said. "You'll be happy she did."

Trish gave Sara a warm smile. "I'm sure we will, dear. Thank you."

Sara's heart melted at the simple statement and the feeling of acceptance it brought.

Jack's mother moved to the counter. "I baked a coffee cake. Let's dig in and enjoy some peace and quiet before the chaos arrives."

Will walked into the kitchen, wearing jeans and a buttoned-up long-sleeved shirt. He brightened at Trish's words. "Looks like my timing was impeccable." Then he inclined his head to Sara. "I have to admit, Mom's coffee cake probably has my welcome cake beat."

Sara laughed, her smile lingering. She already liked Will immensely. He had a long face and casual, endearing personality that reminded her of a dark-haired Owen Wilson. The previous evening, he had welcomed her to Galveston by baking a sheet cake just for her. She and Jack had sat on bar stools facing the work area of the kitchen as he prepared the ingredients. The batter had looked a bit thin when he placed the pan in the oven, but Sara wasn't about to question it. She was about as far from Betty Crocker as you could get.

But twenty minutes later, when Will pulled the pan with its flat, lumpy contents from the oven, something was obviously very wrong. He crossed to the recipe and studied it. "Oh, I see what I did."

"Did you leave out baking powder?" Sara asked, trying to remember if that was the ingredient that made baked goods rise.

Will sighed. "No. I left out the flour."

Jack burst into laughter, slapping his hand on the granite counter. "The *flour*? How could you forget that?"

Will stared at him primly. "I never said I was a professional, now did I?"

Now he ambled over to Trish's coffee cake and took a deep sniff, smiling. He glanced at Sara and nodded. "This one has flour. You're safe."

Two hours later, the atmosphere in the family room couldn't have been more different. The four children ranged in age from six months to ten years, and the older ones were ecstatic over the contents of their stockings. The chocolate in them only added to the volume in the room. All of Jack's siblings were there except Gregory, who was spending Christmas on an oil derrick in the Gulf of Mexico. Sara sat on the couch next to Jack, blinking at the level of noise. A high-pitched squeal rose above the general din and Sara tried not to wince.

"Courtney! Keep it down," Mary said, laughing at her daughter's reaction to the latest toy craze, an egg that hatched into a dinosaur. Each one was unique, and some had become highly valuable. Mary was an oral surgeon and the eldest of the Powell children. Nearing forty, she had light-brown hair and a confident, yet reassuring manner, which had to be a huge asset in her job.

Henry and his wife Alana spent much of their time trying to keep their two older children in line. The boys were two and four, and their baby girl Sophia was currently sleeping in Alana's arms, apparently used to the volume.

There was a momentary diminishing in the cacophony, and Jack spoke up, smiling at Sara. "You want to hand out your presents?"

"Sure." She rose and gathered her boxes, handing one to each of Jack's siblings and the larger box to Trish and Joe. The extra, Greg's, she returned to the tree.

"These are just from Sara?" Will asked Jack, a gleam in his eye. "You let her do all the dirty work, huh?"

"I thought my presence here was enough of a gift," Jack said, then grinned at the moans that went around the room.

"Any particular order we should go in?" Joe asked Sara.

"No. You can all open them at the same time if you want."

The sound of tearing paper filled the room, and Sara held her breath. She swept her gaze around and stopped when Trish got all the paper off and studied the painting before her. "Oh!

This is beautiful. What a serene image—that cove looks heavenly." Then she squinted. "Wait. Is that your name in the corner?"

Oohs and aahs came from the others.

"Sara's an artist," Jack said, pride evident in his voice. "She painted all of them."

"Thank you," Amber said as she trailed a finger over the surface. "You're really talented."

"I don't know about that, but you're welcome. I love painting watercolors and thought you all might enjoy a little taste of St. Croix. Some of them are of the cove near our house, the others the resort where we work."

Strong emotion filled Sara at their expressions. There was pride in seeing her works accepted with enthusiasm, but also something deeper. A sense of giving a meaningful gesture and her intention being understood.

Joe and Trish murmured together, then Joe nodded. "There's a perfect spot for this at the office. That way our patients can enjoy it too."

Tears filled Sara's eyes and a soft touch lighted on her forearm. She turned to Jack, who winked at her, then took her hand. She clasped his tightly and swallowed past the lump in her throat.

It was noon before all the presents were opened. Trish circulated around the room, rounding up the discarded wrapping paper that lay in heaps as the children played with their new treasures on the floor. Sara was pleased that no one felt obligated to give lavish gifts. The morning had been casual, yet exciting, and she smiled at the figurine in her hands from Joe and Trish. It was a charming ceramic figurine of several tropical fish with a branch of coral behind them. It was perfect for their cottage, and she loved it.

Jack leaned close. "Still wish we hadn't come?"

She shook her head. "I'm really glad we did. Thank you."

He stared back, his enormous liquid eyes making her breath catch in her throat. "No, thank you, Sara. This was perfect."

Henry's wife Alana was trying to manhandle a Lego set into a bag while she balanced Sophia in one arm. As she neared Jack and Sara, she looked up, and her eyes widened. "No, Colton! Don't put that in your mouth. Here—" She turned and thrust the baby into Sara's arms as she ran across the room to dislodge an action figure from her son's mouth.

Stunned, Sara stared at the bundle in her arms. Sophia stared at her benignly and stuffed her fist into her mouth, not at all put out by being thrust into a stranger's arms. Several of Sara's friends had become parents, so she wasn't unfamiliar with holding a baby, but couldn't help the panic rising in her stomach. She glanced up at Jack, who was grinning broadly, so her inner reaction must have shown on her face.

The subject of children had come up between them a time or two, and Jack hadn't hidden the fact that he'd love some of his own. And his warm, easygoing personality ensured he would make a fantastic father. But as a recovering commitment-phobe, the warm, soft weight in her arms aroused a combination of curiosity and absolute terror in Sara.

"Don't worry," Jack said, his smile getting bigger. "You have the privilege of handing her back when you want to."

Sara was trying to formulate a proper response when Alana returned and took the baby from her. "Sorry about that. Never a dull moment. I have no idea what possessed us to have three children within five years."

"Oh—it's no problem. She didn't seem to mind."

But Jack was right. Handing Sophia back was a relief, though Sara couldn't resist stroking a finger down the baby's impossibly soft cheek as she transferred her into Alana's arms.

SARA CLIMBED INTO BED, worn out and grateful. A perfect way to end Christmas day. The house was silent again, but the presence of a happy family lingered. Dinner had been a casual, boisterous affair, and Sara had even helped with the preparations. Despite warning Trish about her lack of culinary skills, she had successfully boiled *and* mashed the potatoes.

She'd had a chance to speak with each of Jack's siblings and enjoyed meeting them all. But her favorite was Will. He had a laid-back, somewhat bewildered outlook on life that made him extremely likeable. They'd had a few moments alone after dinner when she'd been able to find out more about him.

"So you're a pastor without a church?" Sara asked.

Will shrugged. "I discovered the formal church scene wasn't for me. I understand why a church building is important to people, but I don't think you need a building filled with wooden pews to understand God. He's all around us, in the sand and the trees, and the people that surround us."

"What a beautiful thought. I've never been religious myself, but I can understand what you mean. I can also see why you'd be drawn to being a park ranger."

Will nodded. "I like working outside in nature, and with people too. I'm still trying to figure out how to work my ministry into the whole thing."

"Maybe you'll find a way to do both at the same time."

Now, Sara settled in on her side, and Jack scooted over in the bed, tucking behind her. He nuzzled her ear. "The visit went fast. You were a huge hit in case you didn't realize. Not that I had any doubt."

She brought his hand up to her mouth and kissed it, closing her eyes. "You always have faith in me. And dinner wasn't nearly as scary as I thought it would be. Since so many people were there, it actually took the pressure off. I just blended in, which was kind of wonderful."

"I'm glad you feel that way." He wiggled against her butt. "Only one thing could make this Christmas even better."

Sara's eyes flew open. "What? Are you serious?"

He pressed his hips against her. "Isn't that rather obvious?"

"Jack! We are *not* having sex in your parents' house. Your mom will change the sheets after we leave, for God's sake!"

"We can get a towel, then."

"No, Jack." She scooched forward a bit.

He spooned behind her again. "Didn't realize you were so prim and proper."

"In your parents' house—yes, I am. End of story. We'll be home tomorrow night!"

Jack laughed softly behind her. "Ok, fine. Destroy my dreams."

Sara couldn't help smiling, then bit her lip, closing her eyes again.

"Can we at least stay snuggled together like this?"

Laughter bubbled out. "Absolutely. This is wonderful. But no more, so settle down."

"Merry Christmas, darlin'." He said the words slowly, drifting off.

Her smile remained, the Carpenters song running through her head. "You, too. I love you, Jack."

His only answer was a light snore. But coupled with being wrapped up in his arms and his love, it was more than enough.

Chapter Seven

"IS SARA USUALLY A LATE RISER?" Will asked Jack as they sat in the family room the next morning. Will sprawled on the couch while Jack sat in a recliner. It was after 9 a.m.

"Not usually. She was pretty tired after yesterday."

A grin spread across Will's long face. "Yeah. I can imagine that was a bit to take in."

"She did great though. I'm proud of her."

"Her paintings were a big hit. That was a good idea."

Jack raised a brow. "You gonna hang yours?" He knew what Will's apartment looked like. The beautiful beachscape Sara had painted him would probably have shirts hanging from it within days.

"Nah. I'm going to keep it wrapped in plastic. Then when Sara's super famous, I'll sell it and retire."

Jack laughed. "Little young to be thinking about retirement, aren't you?"

"Never too young!" Then Will became pensive. "When I went to seminary school, I was so sure I'd found my calling. But the thought of standing in front of a huge group of people scared the crap out of me. And I can't stand being cooped up inside."

"Dad getting a little impatient with you? I noticed he sent a few barbs your way."

"He wants me to make up my mind. Says that what's cute at eighteen isn't quite so great ten years later." Will studied Jack, eyeing him steadily. "Your new career seems to have worked out pretty well."

Jack thought of Sara, and a soft warmth spread inside his chest. "Very well. Though I went through some bumps before finding my stride."

Just then, Sara walked into the kitchen, dressed in jeans and a long-sleeved Half Moon Bay Resort T-shirt. "Morning, you two." She crossed to the coffeepot and poured herself a cup before joining them. "I'm surprised I slept so late. You should have woken me, Jack. Has Amber left?"

"You needed the extra sleep. Amber took off early. You two said goodbye last night, but she wanted me to tell you how glad she was you came. Mom and Dad are in the back yard."

"Little quieter this morning, huh?" Will asked with a smile.

"Yes. I've never experienced anything like that. I loved it, but I have to admit I'm feeling the need for a little quiet." After a sip of coffee, she turned to Jack. "Did you get enough time to catch up with everyone?"

He nodded. "As much as we could, anyway. It's always hard to talk with Henry—he's distracted by the kids all the time. Will and I were catching up just now."

Sara nodded. "I was thinking about taking the car and driving back downtown. I'd like to do a little more shopping."

Jack straightened. "Sure. We can head down there together."

Sara shook her head as she stood. "Stay with Will. I know shopping isn't your favorite thing, and a little solo trip is just what I need."

He stared at her, understanding she was giving him time

alone with his family, but slightly put out she was exploring without him. "You want some hints on where to go?"

Smiling, she came over and planted a kiss on his lips. "Nope, I want to explore. I'll start out at The Strand and go from there. See you two later."

She walked out of the room and Jack followed her with his eyes, frowning.

Will laughed. "Poor Jacky's getting left out?"

"Don't call me Jacky," he said absently. Then he turned back to his brother and shrugged. "She doesn't want to be in the way, even though she's not."

Will crossed his feet at the ankles, adjusting the throw pillow behind his head. "I think Sara's good for you. It just proves what I was saying before she came down. That moving to the Caribbean was good for you."

"No argument there. I love being a divemaster."

"I can see why. Who wouldn't want to spend all day frolicking in the ocean?"

Jack laughed. "Watch it. The job isn't all fun and games, you know. There's a lot of hard work most people never see."

"Can't be that hard if you're doing it."

Jack threw a small pillow at him, and Will caught it, bursting into laughter. "When do you guys leave for the airport?"

"Around noon. That should give Sara enough time for her little shopping trip."

SARA STROLLED ALONG THE SIDEWALK, enjoying the calmer atmosphere of The Strand. Though still decorated, the area now had a business-as-usual vibe. The morning was warmer than Christmas Eve, and her long-sleeved shirt and leggings were perfect. She carried two shopping bags in one hand, then glanced at her watch. It was nearly eleven, and she should head back soon. But one appealing clothing boutique had been closed her previous visit. It was next to the antique store, which brought back the memory of meeting Diane, and Sara quickly pushed the recollection from her mind.

Initially, she had thought of venturing off The Strand, but with so many interesting stores and boutiques lining the street, she hadn't needed to. She stopped before the boutique's display window, admiring the pencil skirt and fitted vest the mannequin wore.

Oh, if only I had the figure for that.

But Sara knew how to dress to emphasize her assets, though she'd decided on casual that day. Her present outfit would be perfect for the plane trip home.

A shadow rose as someone stopped next to her. Sara turned to see Diane next to her, once again dressed in tight, neon-colored athletic apparel. Sara's stomach lurched.

Jack's ex-wife smiled, and once again, there was something slightly vicious in it. "We need to stop meeting like this, though I doubt you're on your way to the gym. What was your name again?"

"Sara," she said evenly, staring Diane straight in the eye. "And meeting again shouldn't be a problem. Jack and I are flying home today."

"Ah. To your island paradise?"

Sara cocked her head. "Actually, yes. We live in a cottage on our own beach." Hoping Diane would just leave, she turned back to the display.

"I shop here all the time. You know, there's a sporting goods store across the street. I'm sure you could find something in the tent and awning section that would fit you."

Sara inhaled sharply as her heart thudded in her ears. But

she wasn't about to let this bitch see she'd hit home with that remark. She slowly turned to Diane, putting some iron in her voice. "I saw it. And of course you'd know where the sporting goods store is, since it's right next to the silicone and Botox clinic. I imagine you walk by it all the time."

Diane couldn't hide a flinch, and Sara let a gleam of triumph enter her eye, even as acid burned through her stomach.

"Listen, you fat little shit." Diane stepped closer. She stood several inches taller, but Sara held her ground, staring back. "I could have Jack back anytime I wanted. All I need to do is snap my fingers and he'd come running."

The deeply insecure Sara she'd spent so much time overcoming suddenly woke up, and she did her best to ignore the phantom, standing as tall as possible and raising her chin. "You really think so? I don't. He's not some dog you can order around. Now I understand why your marriage broke up. You blew it, Diane—he's with me now."

An ugly smile rose to Diane's face, and Sara couldn't help stiffening. "Yet neither of you is wearing a ring. I've been looking around for a new project. I might just have to think about this for a while. Have a lovely plane trip home, Sara." With that, Diane whirled on her heel and sped away, her head held high.

The breath Sara hadn't realized she was holding exploded out, and a cold sweat trickled down her back. She took several deep breaths, trying to calm herself, then turned around and headed toward her car.

She's just trying to stick pins in me. As if Jack would have anything to do with her. My God, was she like that when they were married? How could he want to stay married to that?

A small, quiet voice answered. The one she'd been trying to

suppress. *Because he's the most loyal, committed man you've ever met. Why wouldn't she want him back?*

───────

THE PLANE FLEW through a cloud bank, sending the fuselage into twilight. *Kind of like the end of our trip*, Jack thought. Sara had come back from her shopping expedition later than he'd expected and been quiet as they finished packing their things. She'd been warm and effusive when she'd said goodbye to his parents and Will, but he could tell something was wrong.

Though his concern had at least distracted him from the emotional farewells to his parents, especially his mother. On the trip from Galveston to Houston airport, he'd asked Sara casually if everything was ok, and she'd assured him it was.

With a big worry line in between her brows.

The plane banked into a gentle turn. One side of the aisle only had two seats per row, allowing them a little privacy. Jack reached over and took Sara's hand. She had been staring out the window, but turned to him with a tiny smile.

He didn't smile back. "Are you sure you're ok?"

"It's nothing. Let's just remember what a wonderful Christmas it was."

"Sara, we've had some problems communicating in the past. Me more than you. But we also promised we'd improve on that. Please tell me what's wrong."

Her gaze drifted to the seats in front, and she spoke softly. "When I was in town this morning, I ran into Diane again."

Shit!

He didn't need to ask if it had been a pleasant meeting, and a roaring filled his ears that had nothing to do with the airplane. "What did she say to you?"

Sara hesitated, her eyes filling with tears. He didn't think she was going to answer when she said in a heavy voice, "She called me fat and dumpy, then said she could get you back any time she wanted."

His jaw fell. He was aware of Sara's insecurity about her weight, and he also knew Diane could be vindictive. "None of those things are true. You understand that, right? Sara?"

Her head flopped back against the seat. "I should have just told her to go to hell and walked away when she first showed up. It's not like I didn't know how nasty she could be after that bakery comment."

"She's jealous. Even if she wanted to get back together with me—which I don't believe for a second—she'd never succeed. I love you, Sara." He raked a hand through his hair. "I don't even get why she wanted us to get pastries."

Sara started laughing. There were some tears mixed in—it was one of those outpourings of emotion you can't quite control. So he let her have her moment. Eventually, laughter won out, which pleased him, even if he didn't quite understand it.

"Oh, Jack. I love you so much. You really don't know, do you?"

He got that sinking feeling, the one when he was missing something important. "No, but I think you'd better tell me."

"It was just her not-so-nice way of telling me I was overweight."

He sat there blinking out the window until the comment made sense. Then the roaring came back. "That *bitch*! Sara, I never would have let her speak to you that way if I'd known. I'd have lit into her in no uncertain terms. I'm so sorry."

She was still smiling and lifted a hand to his face. "I know. I normally don't put up with crap like that, and today I got my shots right back at her. But the other day I was just so shocked I couldn't reply. Let's just put it behind us."

Jack kissed her, brushing a soft, feathery kiss across her lips, then held her gaze. "Diane means *nothing* to me. You're not only my present, Sara. You're my future."

She settled against his shoulder and closed her eyes. Jack stared absently at the lavender clouds racing by as the plane flew into the evening. He kissed the top of her head, then leaned his cheek against it as her breath deepened. Closing his eyes, Jack eased out a long sigh, letting the strife with Diane go. He and Sara were going back to their life. The one they had created together and would continue to build.

Chapter Eight

JANUARY...

SARA CIRCLED her hair into a bun as she stepped onto the back porch. A short storm had rolled through the previous day, but that morning had dawned clear and calm. She and Jack arranged their schedules so they regularly had a day off together, and diving the reef inside their cove was one of their favorite activities.

Jack was bent over two scuba tanks. He finished attaching her regulator and straightened. "Ready?"

"Yes! I'm looking forward to seeing my babies." *Even better, these babies are a whole lot less work than Sophia.*

After returning from Texas, Sara had entered Aqua and been surprised when the workers were installing a full water-proof liner in the canal. She had joined Hope, who was reviewing the project's progress.

"I made an executive decision while you were gone," Hope said. "The leaks just brought home that these channels have to be as watertight as possible. So I added the cost of a liner to the budget."

Sara wholeheartedly agreed, excited to see the spa coming together at last. Soon the flattened river rock would be installed, and the long-delayed stacked stone for the feature wall was rumored to be arriving the following week.

Now, Jack held up her tank so she could slide her arms into the BCD.

"Let's get to it, then." She gave him a wink as she closed her buckles.

The ocean hardly made a splash as it reached the beach, perfect for a shore dive. Sara tucked her fins under one arm and carefully descended the stairs. The tank and weights in her BCD added nearly sixty pounds and made walking across the beach taxing. The sand continued at an easy grade underwater, the entry presenting minimal difficulty.

"Can't ask for a better shore dive," Jack said. "This is about as easy as it gets."

"Especially when you have your own private divemaster. Soon to be an instructor!"

He shrugged, but a smile lit up his face. Alex was talking to several people running IDC courses but hadn't made a choice yet.

Sara placed her second stage in her mouth and gave him the ok signal, then they descended. Several isolated coral heads were scattered across the sandy plain, but the one Sara was most interested in was an oval-shaped structure, about six feet long. Encrusted with soft and hard corals, the bommie was covered with small sea fans, which waved back and forth in the gentle surge. The water was only fifteen feet deep, so the sunlight made the formation nearly glow with color.

Sara finned to the far end, with Jack just behind. Her destination was a section of the structure half a dozen juvenile yellow-tailed damsel fish had designated as their home. Shortly after moving in, she and Jack had dived the reef, and Sara had been entranced by the brilliant fish at first sight. At that time, the young fish had only been two inches long, and a bright royal blue. But their crowning glory was the turquoise spots scattered across their back, so bright they looked fluorescent.

The fish had grown steadily over the months but retained their bright coloring. As she peered at the coral, Sara was pleased to see all six were still there. She gave a delighted gasp that several were also developing a dusky yellow shade on their tails, hinting at the bright color it would become as adults, which gave the fish their name. She turned to Jack and pointed at them, and his eyes softened behind his mask—he'd noted the change too.

After getting her fill, Sara continued swimming around the formation. Several other juvenile fish species also lived in it, as well as a few small moray eels. She had worried about her fish getting eaten. But apparently the eels were as worried about becoming dinner as the young fish and hadn't bothered them.

From the coral formation, they continued down the sandy slope and eventually reached the vibrant reef that led out to the edge of the cove and beyond. They leveled off at seventy feet. Sara had taken an advanced scuba class with Hope and Zach, and one of the requirements had been a deep dive. Alex had taken them to 110 feet, and watching the reef had been fascinating. As their depth increased, the vivid hues became muted as colors other than blue slowly filtered out, leaving the coral reef a drab, monochromatic color.

Alex had brought an empty plastic water bottle with him, and all three students had been astonished when he produced it from his pocket at 110 feet. The bottle was completely smashed together, the pressure of the water condensing the air inside the bottle nearly to nothing. When they had surfaced afterwards, it had been back to its usual shape.

Happiness filled Sara as she swam side-by-side with Jack, watching the busy reef teeming with fish and corals. She took his hand and they smiled at each other before continuing on. Jack had a specific destination. If the young damsel fish were her favorites at this site, his was a specific whitemouth moray eel, which tended to stay in one general area at around seventy feet of depth.

Jack's head swept back and forth as he searched. It astonished her how well he could pick out highly camouflaged animals. Sometimes he had to point directly at a creature before she saw it.

"Ha!" Jack's exclamation came through clearly, and he stopped, pointing to a sheltered crevice. The eel was nestled within, its head pointing out of the hole. The eel breathed by opening and closing its mouth. The pure white interior which gave the creature its name made it easily visible while inhaling water. Then the white-spotted eel nearly disappeared when it closed its mouth again, blending into its surroundings.

Sara suspected Jack wanted the animal to come out and interact with him, but so far, the eel hadn't done so. When they had first dived the site, it had withdrawn into its hole as they admired it. Now the creature must be getting used to them, because it didn't react as they crept closer. But there was no denying the needle-like teeth the eel possessed, and Sara had no desire to know it on a closer inspection. Jack grinned at her and tipped his head, indicating they should continue.

An hour later, they stood at the water's edge. One benefit of having their own dive site was not needing to keep to a set schedule. They could stay down as long as their air supply lasted, though Sara was a long way from matching Jack's air consumption.

Of course, I don't do this for a living, either.

"You've turned into a great diver," he said. "Seventy-five minutes is a really long time."

"Thank you. I've come a long way." She wasn't the careless diver who knocked over the resort's coral-restoration project. Which was a good thing.

He helped her off with her gear and they disassembled it, leaving the tanks by the stairs. Jack would refill them back at the resort. Both tanks sported a large green and yellow NITROX banner, filled with enriched air that allowed them to extend their dive times, since the mixture contained less nitrogen.

Sara unzipped her wetsuit. "Shower time. I can't wait to get the saltwater out of my hair." She didn't even try to brush out her long locks after diving. Instead, she carefully separated it in the shower, shampooing thoroughly to clean it without damaging it. A stylist was expected to have nice hair, after all.

Jack appeared and stepped close, making a deep rumbling in his chest as he gathered her in his arms. He nibbled a line up the side of her neck to whisper in her ear, "Care for some company?"

"Mmm. As long as you don't mind if it takes me a while to wash my hair."

"Don't mind at all. I like to watch."

Sara led him by the hand through their bedroom and into the master bath. She reached behind the seashell curtain to turn on the faucet. Unfortunately, their shower wasn't the type featured in home improvement shows—unless it was the *before* part. A simple ceramic tub with beige tile didn't give enough room for too much amorous activity. The grout was a bit stained, and some of the tiles were broken, but the bathroom had two sinks and was perfectly serviceable.

Sara peeled off her one-piece swimsuit and stepped under the stream of water, closing her eyes as the water poured over her. She unfurled her hair from the bun, letting the flow stream down her back. The curtain rustled as Jack joined her. Eyes still closed, she leaned her head back. She was enjoying the warm sensuous water when Jack's warm hands cupped her breasts, his thumbs softly brushing back and forth.

She smiled. "I thought you were watching me wash my hair."

"Believe me, I am."

Opening her eyes, Sara reached for the shampoo, and couldn't help noticing he was obviously enjoying watching her.

Leaning forward, Sara kissed him deeply, slowly circling her tongue around his and reaching behind him to stroke the soft swell of one cheek. Then she poured out a healthy palmful of shampoo and sudsed up the mass of her hair.

As she backed into the shower spray, she darted her eyes to Jack's. He watched her steadily, his ribcage rising and falling with each deep breath. She closed her eyes and rinsed, then thoroughly coated her hair with conditioner.

Tipping her head, Sara arched her back as she rinsed, knowing exactly where Jack's eyes were. Then his hands were stroking both breasts and she gasped, leaning into his touch. She kissed him again, rubbing her full breasts against his torso. She was incredibly sensitive, which Jack picked up on, slipping his hand between her legs. Groaning, Sara wrapped her hand around the length of him, stroking slowly.

Jack broke the kiss. "Let's trade places so I can wash off."

They pivoted around each other, the movement not quite as sexy and easy as Sara could have wished for. The tub was narrow, and calling 911 after falling out of the damn thing was *not* on the agenda.

Jack washed his hair, and now it was her time to watch. He was thin and had a masculine build without being overly muscular. A fine scattering of dark-brown hair covered his chest, and she ran a hand across it. He smiled, then stepped back into the stream to finish rinsing off. He ran a hand over his face, wiping away the water as he stepped forward and kissed her again. He pulled her tight against him, brushing one hand down her back and over her ass, sending a shudder through her.

"Guess I'm not the only one who likes to watch, huh?" he whispered.

"No. Let me show you. Let's go."

The sheets were smooth and crisp against Sara's naked skin as she slipped into bed. But Jack's body was anything but cool. He came to her with hot urgency, pinning her on her back as he rolled half on top of her. Kissing his way down her neck, he softly bit one breast, making her cry out. As he resumed using his tongue, he slid his hand over the curve of her stomach, tracing circles around her navel. She wanted to grab his hand but resisted, enjoying the teasing. Finally, Jack brushed his fingers down her abdomen and stopped between her legs, caressing her in long, deliberate movements.

Sara gasped at his touch, moaning.

Jack smiled, pulling away to watch her face. "Maybe I'll watch some more."

"Oh, shut up and come here."

She urged him fully on top of her, and he laughed softly. Then his smile disappeared, and he smashed his mouth to hers, probing his tongue deeply into her mouth. He entered her with one forceful thrust, and she gripped his shoulders. Her breath came faster and faster, and she pressed her forehead into his shoulder. "Oh God."

Neither of them was in the mood for tender, gentle lovemaking.

They pounded together, Jack using long, deep thrusts. Then Sara rolled them over and sat up, straddling him. Jack reached up to cup both breasts. She arched her back, closing her eyes as she rose up and slid back down, drowning in each second. He slipped one hand down, circling with his thumb. Sara leaned into his touch, and he went faster, making her gasp. Her climax rose and flooded over her, and she slid both hands to her breasts, abandoning herself completely.

Still exquisitely sensitive, Sara bent down and took his bottom lip between her teeth, pulling slowly. She held his eyes, still sliding up and down him, until Jack took a handful of her wet hair and pulled her face toward him, giving her a hard, bruising kiss as he thrust into her. Then, breaking the kiss, he swept his mouth to her ear, calling out her name.

BOTH OF THEM fell asleep afterwards. Sara woke just after noon. But instead of the groggy confusion a nap can bring, she remembered everything. Jack breathed deeply on his back, and she curled up beside him with her head in the hollow of his shoulder. She turned her head and pressed her lips against his soft skin. "I love you, Jack Powell."

His breathing changed, and he moved one arm to stroke her side. Then he embraced her fully, pressing their bodies together. "I love you, too. More than you know."

Chapter Nine

THE SUN KISSED the horizon as Jack walked through the wrought-iron gate and peered around the buzzing patio of Frederiksted's The Refinery. Spotting Alex and Robert at an elevated table, he joined them and ordered a beer to add to theirs. "So, how's it feel to be slumming with us again?"

Robert flashed the smile he was known for. He still wore his Half Moon Bay Resort staff polo, and its light-blue color contrasted strikingly against his dark skin. "It was great to be back in the water. I'll always love divin'. And I need to work once in a while to show you two how it's done."

Alex shot him a grin. "I'm surprised the guests weren't asking for your autograph."

"Oh, knock it off."

Laughter rang around the table. "Have you finished your pictures for the Tourism Board promotion?" Jack asked.

Robert, a long-time divemaster turned professional photographer, had just landed two major opportunities. Besides being the featured premiere artist at Ember, the St. Croix Tourism Board had chosen him to photograph the island for their new international campaign. His eyes became round as he rubbed a hand back and forth over his shaved head. "Yeah. I handed in the last of them a couple of days ago. Beatrice at the Board said I should get the final payment within ten business days. I still can't believe it."

"Your life's taken a turn for the better, that's for sure." Jack said. "Your father is doing ok?"

Robert's eyes softened. "He's doin' great. That heart attack was a wake-up call for him. He's hangin' out on the fishin' boat a couple days a week, but Eddie says he just sits on the deck, enjoyin' bein' out on the water." His younger brother Eddie was now the senior captain of Davis Fishing, outranking even the captain of their other boat.

Alex nodded. "I can identify with that. And your folks are still getting along better with Heather?"

"Much better." Robert glanced at his watch. "Which reminds me, I need to get goin'. I'm pickin' up Heather from Ember and we're havin' dinner at my parents. Mother is goin' to teach her how to make conch fritters." He stared at Alex and Jack. "No *way* am I missin' that. My Mom's conch fritters are out of this world."

Jack lifted his bottle in a toast. "Don't let us hold you up."

After Robert left, Jack swept his gaze over the brick patio, his eyes momentarily pausing on an empty table in one corner. "I don't see any local tycoons or henchmen in here this time, so that's good."

Alex took a swig of beer before grinning. "Have you been here since we had our little chat with Wayne Timmons?"

Jack shook his head. "Robert and I usually go to Breakers, since it's closer to the resort."

"I like this place. And I'm not about to let the memory of that idiot Timmons change that. I haven't heard a word about him or Beavis and Butthead since we had our confrontation."

Jack swallowed. Alex referred to an altercation Jack and

Dexter Ridgeway had with the three men, Timmons and his local muscle. Things had been about to turn violent when the former SEAL appeared at Jack's side—holding a large pistol. The situation fizzled rapidly at that point. Jack still had some unsettled *what-if* moments, but no doubt Alex could be more sanguine, having faced situations far more perilous.

He still had no idea how Alex had appeared out of the blue. "Where did you come from, anyway? One second, I was all alone about to get the shit knocked out of me, and the next you were there."

Alex shrugged one shoulder and gave him a tiny grin. "I was there before any of you arrived. You all walked right past me when you walked down the path to the shore."

Jack stared at him blankly. "You're kidding!"

Alex's face broadened into a grin. "Jack, I'm pretty good at being invisible when I need to. My life depended on it for almost twenty years. I followed you and hid in the brush until things got a little tense."

"Your appearance did the trick," Jack said. "They backed right down. I'm happy to have all three of those guys in the past."

Alex sobered, eyeing Jack as leaned forward in his chair and rested his arms on the table. "It's the future I want to talk to you about. I've been looking into an IDC for you. Still interested?"

Jack straightened. "One hundred percent. What do you have in mind?"

"I couldn't find what I wanted in St. Croix, but there's a dive shop on St. Thomas that's exactly what I'm looking for. You'd be there for about four weeks, rooming with another guy near the dive shop. Since its work training, Half Moon Bay will pick up the tab."

Jack's mind flashed back to the first six months after he'd left

Galveston. He suppressed a shudder. "It's not Bubbles Forever, is it?"

Alex shook his head. "The operation is called Seascapes Diving. Is the other one where you used to work?"

Jack scratched his beard. It itched in the heat, but Sara loved it, so he kept it for her. "Yeah. That job was kind of a nightmare. Nothing but cruise-ship tourists with no experience, and the shop didn't care. All they saw were dollar signs."

"St. Thomas has plenty of those kinds of dive shops, and St. Croix has a few too. Seascapes takes training seriously. I talked to the IDC instructor personally and we meshed pretty well. I want you to be well prepared, Jack—it won't be a walk in the park."

"Is there going to be a Hell Week?"

Alex burst into laughter and leaned back again, crossing one ankle over his knee. "Don't worry, nothing like that. I didn't say anything about my background, but Scott, the IDC instructor, indicated he knew who I was."

Jack grinned and took a drink. He hadn't been worried, but was pleased to be comfortable enough around Alex to poke fun at him. "When does the class start?"

"Next month. I have a feeling my sister-in-law might not be too happy with me."

A pang ran through Jack's stomach. "Probably not. A month is a long time to be apart."

"St. Thomas is only a twenty-minute flight. If you pine away for each other too much, I'm sure you two can manage something."

Jack's smile lingered. "Such sarcasm! How would you like to be separated from Hope for a month?"

Alex's smile remained, but his eyes became hooded, hiding his thoughts. He tapped his left ring finger against the wooden table, his wedding ring softly clinking against it. "No comment. We're not talking about me, are we?"

Jack sobered, staring at Alex. "Thank you. I really enjoy teaching, and I've wanted to become an instructor for a long time. Working with new divers is one of the best parts of the job, as far as I'm concerned."

Alex laughed again, deflecting the serious moment. "You haven't been doing this long enough then. And you're welcome. I wouldn't suggest this unless I thought you'd be a great instructor." He finished his beer. "Let's get out of here so you can get home. You've got a few weeks before you need to leave, so I'm sure you'll make the most of it. And Sara will have plenty of time to sharpen the knives she'll want to use against me."

WHEN JACK GOT HOME, Sara was on the back porch, painting the cove as the sun set in the distance. The green trees and bushes extended halfway out the arms of their little cove, then gray rock took over until it disappeared into the water. The western horizon still displayed an unusual rose-orange color, and Sara had mixed her paints to capture it. Jack shut the door behind him with a slight scree of rusty hinges and reminded himself to oil them.

He stopped behind Sara and rubbed her shoulders. She leaned back against him with a groan, resting her head back against his shoulder. "That feels fantastic." Turning her head, she gave him a quick hello kiss. "Did you have a good time with the boys?"

"I did. Robert and Heather seem to have worked out all the issues with his parents, and his dad is recovering from his heart attack." He studied her canvas. "I really like that painting." She had painted it in abstract swaths of color, which only made it more alluring.

"Thanks. I like this one too. The colors were really different tonight." She put a final dab of orange against the setting sun, then swirled her brush in a glass mason jar filled with water. "Done."

Jack led her by the hand to a nearby couch, and they settled into the soft cushions. "Alex had some news for me. He found an IDC."

Sara turned toward him, widening her eyes. "That must have made you happy!"

A tiny smile twitched on one side of his mouth. "It did. It makes me feel good that Alex has enough faith in me to pay for instructor training."

"Well of course he does. He knows how good you are. When does the course start?"

"Next month. Here's the thing... The dive shop is in St. Thomas."

Her face fell. "Oh. I guess we can live without each other for a little while. I can't imagine this will take too many days, will it?"

Jack exhaled the breath he'd been holding. "Close to four weeks."

She sat there, blinking. "What? I thought it would be less than one!"

"IDCs are very involved. Plus, Alex wants me to stay a little longer to get some advanced instructor endorsements and experience. It's a good plan."

He could see the struggle on her face as she tried to be happy for him. "You're telling me there isn't a single instructor course on St. Croix?"

Jack tipped his head to the side in a so-so gesture. "None Alex is satisfied with. His reasoning is sound, Sara. St. Thomas is much busier than St. Croix—I'll get a lot more exposure to students there."

She stuck out her bottom lip and he had to resist kissing it. "You're the only thing keeping me sane right now with all the Aqua delays."

"Then you'll have to come visit me. I'm going to miss you too."

Her jaw tightened and a familiar spark ignited in her eyes. "Alex is going to hear about this. Don't you worry."

A slow smile lit Jack's face. "I think he's already expecting it. Besides, you've got Hope and the other girls to keep you company. You won't even notice I'm gone."

She slid closer, and he took a deep breath of her wonderfully scented hair. "Of course I will—I depend on you. Besides, who's going to kill the bugs while you're gone?"

Chapter Ten

BRIGHT SUNLIGHT FILTERED through the windows of
Hibiscus, making Sara grateful for the air conditioning. Selena
Allen's massage client signed her room charge, then walked out
the front door. Though she only held it open a moment, a warm
wave of air washed over the room. Selena's voice drifted in from
the private covered deck they used as an outdoor massage area,
saying goodbye to her client.

Moments later, Selena rushed through the glass door, a ball
of used linens wadded up under one arm. "Hoo boy," she said,
pulling her light-blue polo shirt away at the neck in an attempt
to cool off. She waved a dark-colored hand in front of her face.
"It's a hot one today, though that woman didn't mind. I can't
wait until Aqua opens, and we have the new air-conditioned
treatment rooms."

Sara gave her a sympathetic smile. "I'm sure there will still
be plenty of people who want one of the outdoor pavilions too.
You have to admit, listening to the ocean during your massage is
rather relaxing."

"I don't deny that, but I think plenty of clients will want to
stay where it's nice and cool *and* they get the view. Oh! That

lady said there was a big delivery truck up by Aqua. I wonder if the stacked stone is finally here?"

Sara gasped. This was what she'd been waiting for! Her fingers flew on the keyboard as she brought up the schedule. "I've got a color and highlight that's going to take up most of the afternoon, but she's not coming until 1:30, so I've got plenty of time to run up to Aqua. You want to come with me?"

Selena shook her head. "I've got another massage in fifteen minutes. Give me the scoop, though."

Sara rushed down the stairs to the pier, barely noticing the dive boat as it approached the dock. She hurried up the beach, scrutinizing Aqua in the distance. But no large delivery trucks were parked in the lot, meaning the mystery arrival must already be inside. She climbed onto the brick patio and entered through the glass doors.

On the far side of the lobby, George and several other workers stood around two six-feet-tall pallets wrapped in plastic. With a large box knife, one of the men sliced through the thick plastic. The other pallet already had a large slash in the plastic wrapping.

Sara's sandals clicked as she hurried across the cement floor. "George! I heard about a big delivery."

The project manager flinched as he turned toward her.

Just then, the man behind him ripped open the plastic and said, "Uh-oh. This one's the same, boss."

At those ominous words, Sara inspected the partially open cube. Thin pieces of rock were stacked neatly and precisely on the pallet.

Thin pieces of reddish-brown rock.

Sara stumbled to a stop several feet from the men. She swore she could actually feel her head starting to explode. "George? Why am I looking at *red* stacked stone?"

He sighed heavily. "They shipped the wrong color."

Sara marched up to him, parking her hands on her hips. Even though George was much taller, he took a giant step back, so she must have been sufficiently daunting. "Shipped it wrong? Or did you order it wrong?"

Swallowing, George held up a clipboard in one hand. "I was just double-checking to make sure. I ordered one pallet of Smoke Gray, and one of Charcoal. They shipped two of Redwood."

"What are we supposed to do with red stone? The river rock in the canal is gray, plus we're going to have gray couches and gray doors!"

He tucked the clipboard under an arm so he could hold both hands out to her, making placating motions. "We'll send it back and make sure the supplier rushes the correct pallets."

Sara squared her shoulders, letting her voice rise. It echoed around the room. "And how long will that take? We were supposed to receive this in *October*!"

"I'm sure we can get it quickly since it's their screwup."

Sara glowered at the emphasis he'd put on *their*. "Not if they don't have the material!"

"The company said they received all of their back-ordered supply. I know you want to see this wall finished because it's such a focal point, but it isn't structural. We can transfer the crews to work on other parts of the project until the correct stone gets here. The channel is completely done and water-tight." He stepped back and pointed to the basin in front of the yet-to-be-finished wall. "Look. We finished the river rock in the pool too. Swapping out the red stone shouldn't slow down the project finish date."

Sara forced herself to unclench both fists, bunched at her sides. The gray flattened river rock was lovely inside the channel and pool. As much as she wanted to lash out at George, the delay wasn't his fault. She took a deep breath, then let it out slowly, tightening her grip on her temper. "It better not, George. I've had just about all I can take."

Without waiting for his reply, she spun around and pushed through the doors back into the noontime heat. She marched back down the beach, aggravation giving extra motivation to her steps. Jack was working on the coral-restoration project that day, and she was already looking forward to leaning her head on his shoulder after work.

So who am I going to lean on when he's in St. Thomas? For a month!

Hope was skinny, though Sara admitted she had plenty of muscle tone in her shoulders. But no one replaced Jack. She stomped onto the pier, her mood growing blacker by the second. As she passed into the dim tunnel created by Hibiscus spanning overhead, Alex came out of the gear room. He closed the door behind him.

And all Sara's anger and frustration found the perfect target.

"Stop right there. I've got something to say to you!"

Alex leaned against the closed door. What looked like a tiny smile crossed his face before he regarded her evenly. But she had to be imagining that. "Don't you always?"

She stopped right in front of him, nearly kinking her neck to look up at him. "You mean to tell me there's not one *single* scuba instructor course on St. Croix that Jack can go to?"

"None like what I found on St. Thomas, no."

"Dammit, Alex! Are you doing this just to piss me off?"

He rolled his eyes, but there was a definite gleam in them. "If you're going to yell at me, let's go inside. This isn't exactly professional." Jerking his head to the side, Alex turned and re-entered the room he'd just left, Sara hot on his heels.

The scuba equipment room was hot and humid, but well-lit after he flicked on the lights. He opened the single window to let in a breeze. Whatever humor he'd found in the situation was gone now, and his voice was soft and even. "I understand why you're upset, but this isn't about you, Sara."

"You think Jack *wants* to spend a month on another island?"

Alex sat on the corner of his workbench, crossing one ankle over the other. "I think he's willing to sacrifice to get what he wants, and I'm not forcing him to do anything. He looked pretty excited to me."

She sighed, sweeping her hair over one shoulder to give her neck some air. "He is excited."

"My first priority is to find the best instructor for this resort. I think Jack is that person."

"That's not what I'm upset about!"

"I know that." Alex paused, eyeing her carefully. "You know, I have rather extensive experience appraising men and what suits their strengths. I want Jack to be fully confident when he returns here, and this shop will provide that. St. Croix doesn't see anywhere near the divers St. Thomas does, though that's a blessing. The more varied experiences Jack gets in his IDC, the better off he'll be."

Sara frowned, unable to refute his logic. "I hate it when you make sense."

Alex smiled crookedly. "It's rare, but it happens from time to time. Look, it's past noon. Why don't you head to the lobby and have lunch with Hope? You can tell her all about what a terrible person I am."

She nodded, acknowledging the gnawing in her stomach wasn't just stress. "That is an excellent idea. Though she has an annoying habit of defending you."

His crooked smile became full and warm, and Sara couldn't help but thaw a little at the obvious love for Hope on his face. "Maybe she'll make an exception today, just to make you feel better."

"All right. I'll head up there now. I have to fill her in on the latest disaster at Aqua anyway."

As Sara shut the door, Alex was pulling his phone out of his pocket, tapping away with both thumbs. She snorted as she walked up the pier.

I don't need to guess who he's texting.

She entered the welcoming resort lobby, cooled by ceiling fans, and crossed the tile floor, passing by the gorgeous glass dolphin sculpture Hope and Alex had bought on their honeymoon. The resort had two front desk clerks, Martine and Corrine. Sara greeted Corrine, who nodded back, her platinum-blonde hair slicked back into a clip. The tropical sun was brutal on her pale skin, and she'd come to Sara several times for sunscreen and skin care recommendations.

Sara passed by and entered the lobby office, where two desks faced her. The desk belonging to general manager Patti Thomas was empty. Hope sat behind the other and glanced up from her terminal at Sara's entrance.

"Don't bother looking surprised," Sara said. "I know Alex told you I was on my way."

"He did." Hope stood and came around her desk. Wrapping an arm around Sara's shoulder, she steered them out the door and by the front desk. "We're having a sisterly lunch. Hold down the fort, ok, Corrine?"

They sat at Hope's usual corner table in the restaurant. She liked privacy, yet still wanted to be visible if guests had any questions or concerns. The two women placed their orders, then Sara sat back in her chair, eyeing her sister narrowly. "Your husband is trying to make me miserable. I'm feeling distinctly ganged up on, you know."

"By me and Alex?"

"Yes. He just played bad cop, and now you're here to play good cop."

Hope's brows rose skyward. "Was he that awful to you?"

Sara deflated and crossed her arms on the table. "No, I'm just upset. He was very logical, not to mention completely immovable. Did you know about this little plan?"

Hope nodded. "Alex chose the IDC site, but he discussed his reasons for picking that one with me."

"And you didn't try to talk him into something closer?"

Hope's face went blank. "Of course not! Sara, I love you and I think the world of Jack. But this was a business decision. Every person who works here depends on the choices Alex and I make —including you and Jack. When it comes to the dive operation, I wouldn't dream of questioning Alex's judgement. He has specific additional training he wants Jack to receive, and this shop on St. Thomas was very willing to work with him." Hope stared at her. "Alex could have saved a lot of money by choosing another site, you know. But he views the course as an investment, and he wants the best for Jack."

Sara wasn't ready to give in yet. "And the best for the resort."

"Of course. In this case, they happen to be one and the same." Hope glanced around the room, frowning, before meeting Sara's eyes again. "Alex has been the only instructor here since he moved to St. Croix over seven years ago. He's never even considered an additional instructor until now—Jack should be proud of himself. And so should you."

Sara's shoulders fell. "I am proud. He'll be a great instructor. I just wish this class weren't happening while all the turmoil with Aqua is happening. He's always there for me."

"I know it's a long time to be separated. You'll have to fly over to visit."

"Damn right I will."

Hope took a sip of iced tea. "How is Jack feeling about all this? Going to a different island, and having to stay in what's basically a dorm room with a stranger? And he doesn't know the shop at all."

Sara closed her eyes and rested her face in her hands, breaking into a weak laugh. "Hope, you have an amazing talent for being caring and yet sharp as a knife, both at the same time."

Hope laughed. "What does that mean?"

Heat rose from Sara's neck up her cheeks as she looked up at Hope's warm, hazel eyes. "I haven't even asked him. God, what a pity party I'm throwing myself here. Jack is so easy going it's hard to imagine him being worried."

"I'm sure he is happy about it. But he might be a bit nervous too. And I'm positive he's going to miss you terribly." She gave Sara a sly smile as their entrees arrived. "Seeing you like this is kind of amazing to me, you know."

"How's that?"

"Ms. Sara Collins, the woman who refused to be tied down. Yet she can't bear to be apart from her man for a few weeks."

Sara gave her a rueful smile. "Maybe that's part of why this is throwing me for such a loop. I'm coming to the realization I can't live without him."

"That's not such a bad thing, is it? This situation might be good for you two."

Sara gaped at her. "What, being kept apart?"

"Absence makes the heart grow fonder and all that."

"Says the woman who's never been apart from her man."

A cloud came over Hope's face, making Sara regret her words. "Not since we moved in together. Only the night I spent in the hospital after my emergency hysterectomy."

"I'm sorry. I shouldn't have said that. My tongue grows barbs when I get pissed off."

Hope burst into laughter. "I'm the last person you need to inform of that little trait!"

Sara took a sip of iced tea, uneasiness washing over her. "It's an unsettling feeling. I don't like being so vulnerable."

"I can understand that. Is this just about you and Jack? Or are you still stinging from what his ex-wife said?"

Hope was the one person Sara could never fool. "I hate that I'm still thinking about what she said. Even though she's thousands of miles away." Sara shook her head. "I thought I was through being insecure."

"You're human. You can't just shut your emotions off like a light switch. Jack's not going anywhere, and certainly not back to his ex-wife." Hope snorted. "My God. Jack and Diane—I still think it's hilarious."

Sara had to laugh too. "Yeah, I know. But she wasn't so funny in person. My head knows Jack is devoted to me, but sometimes my heart has a hard time believing it. Let's change the subject."

"By all means."

"Though this one isn't much more pleasant. Have you heard the latest about Aqua? The stacked stone?"

"Yes, George called me earlier. He already called the supplier and they're sending the replacement stone right away. It will work out in the end, Sara. Both Aqua and Jack's training course."

Sara groaned, stabbing her salad with a fork. "I hope so. On top of everything else, I turned on the kitchen faucet this morning and it broke, spraying everywhere. So now Jack has to repair that tomorrow on his day off. The house will probably be completely demolished by the time he gets back from St. Thomas."

Hope folded her napkin and placed it on the table. "You told me yourself—he enjoys fixing things. When he comes back here, he'll just have plenty of projects to look forward to. Not to mention reuniting with you. Maybe this separation will be one of the best things that's happened to you two."

Chapter Eleven

THE NEXT MORNING, when Jack walked into the kitchen wearing boxers and a T-shirt, Sara stood looking out the window. She'd dressed for work in a bright purple blouse and black slacks. She tended to wear loose flowing dresses that hid her lush figure, but he loved it when she dressed like this—with her curves on full display. Instead of curled, her hair lay in a flat, glossy sheet down her back. Jack came up behind her, sweeping aside the mass of hair with one hand so he could plant a kiss on the back of her neck. With his other hand, he gave her cheek a healthy squeeze. "Hmmm, seeing you like this makes me want to go back to bed."

She turned around and circled her arms around his neck, giving him a peck on the nose. "Too bad I have to work."

His gaze traveled to the faucet behind her, and he tamped down the surge of ire that wanted to rise. He moved his gaze to her brown eyes once again. "There's always tonight."

"I'll miss you."

"I'm not going anywhere for several weeks yet."

"I know. And you're feeling ok about going?"

Jack broke into a wide smile. The previous evening, Sara

had come home filled with guilt that she hadn't asked how he felt about going to St. Thomas. Then showed him how determined she was to make up for the lapse. "Yes. Like I said last night, the whole thing is a little intimidating, but I trust Alex. He wouldn't choose this IDC if he didn't think it was the best one for me. It's time to take a leap of faith."

"I have no doubt you'll be a smashing success." Sara slung her purse over one shoulder. "I'm off. Have fun with your projects today."

WITH A FINAL HEAVE, Jack pulled the section of siding away from the house and stared at the offending pipe. The afternoon sun shined directly into the exposed hole. He had fixed the leaky faucet right after Sara left, but he hadn't been able to shake the suspicion that there was more to the problem. He'd opened the cabinet below the sink, but the base was dry. The foreboding didn't go away, rolling over in Jack's mind as he'd dived their private reef after lunch. He'd checked on Sara's damsel fishes and his moray, which still remained stubbornly shy.

Later, as the sun passed its zenith, he walked around the outside of the house, discovering a long trail of damp sand leading away from the exterior. The kitchen sink sat directly on the other side of the warped siding. The disquieting twist in his gut dissolved, though the flash of irritation which replaced it wasn't much of an improvement.

Now Jack set the siding on the ground and stared at the long crack in the white PVC pipe behind the kitchen wall. "Goddammit." Pulling out his phone, Jack dialed. "Afternoon, Calvin."

"Hi, Jack," came the rusty reply. Calvin was getting on in

years, which was why their house was becoming more dilapidated.

"We've got a major leak behind the kitchen sink. The siding is ruined, and I need to replace the pipe too."

"That doesn't sound good. I'm sorry to hear that, Jack. Keep a record of your expenses, and I'll make sure to reimburse you."

Jack stood, wiping his hands on his shorts as he tried to keep his irritation in check. "I appreciate that, but it's not enough, Calvin. We signed a lease for a house that was in good repair. So far, this place has been anything but."

"I hear you, son. I'm not as spry as I used to be, and that's why I've hired my niece Selena to manage the property. But she doesn't know repairs. I'll take $200 off per month—how's that?"

Jack's eyes drifted back to the secluded cove. His misgivings about their home were growing, but Sara loved how rustic it was. "That works. I'll send a bill with my expenses and labor. Also, I'm going to be off the island for several weeks. If Sara runs into any problems, I'm going to tell her to get them fixed as soon as possible and have the contractor send the bill to you."

"That'll be fine. I don't want her runnin' into any problems."

"Talk to you later." Jack hung up, still pissed off. So far, he'd only submitted invoices for parts, but not anymore. This would be a major repair, and he was going to get paid for his time. Their house was very isolated, which gave him comfort knowing Sara would be there alone while he was gone. "As long as the place doesn't fall apart around her..."

Returning his attention to the open hole in the siding, Jack was making a mental list of what he needed at the hardware store when his phone rang. He lifted it to see Will's face smiling on the screen, and his bad mood diminished.

"I know it's short notice," Will said. "But you want to get together for a beer?"

Jack's smile disappeared, replaced by a furrowed brow. "How are we going to do that?"

"Well…" Jack could hear the gleeful smile in Will's voice. "Remember when I told you being a beach bum in the Caribbean sounded like a nice life?"

"Uh-oh. Will, what did you do?" Jack walked along the side of the house and sat on the back porch stairs. He had a feeling he was going to need to sit down for this.

"As of yesterday, I'm now an official island resident! So we can get together for that beer."

Jack's mouth dropped open. "You moved *here*?"

"I did!"

"Where are you living?"

"I rented a little studio apartment in town. I still can't believe how expensive it is, and this shithole was the best I could find."

"Which town? There's two here."

"I'm in the western part of Charlotte Amalie."

At first, Jack just froze. Then he closed his eyes, a deep laugh rumbling out of his chest. He leaned against the banister, laughing harder.

"What's so funny? This doesn't look like a shady part of town."

"I'm sure it's lovely, Will. Do you realize Charlotte Amalie is on *St. Thomas*?"

"Yeah. So what?"

"I live on St. Croix, you dumbshit!"

"What? You told me the US Virgin Islands! I distinctly remember that, Jack."

"Yes, that's true."

"I googled it. St. Thomas was the first thing that came up."

Jack breathed out a sigh, still trying not to laugh. "There are three US Virgin Islands."

There was a pause. "Really?"

"God, Will. What are you doing there?"

"Oh!" His voice brightened again. "I got a job leading tourists on walking tours of Charlotte Amalie. I start tomorrow."

Jack started laughing again, his bad mood slipping completely away now. "You got a job as a tour guide, and you don't even know what island you're on. That sounds about right."

"I know exactly where I am. You're the one who can't give clear directions."

"At least I know how many islands there are!"

Will paused. "I swear when you left you told me you were moving to St. Thomas."

"I did. I also informed you when I moved to St. Croix *over a year ago*."

"Huh. Don't remember that part."

Jack snorted, then shifted on the step, ignoring the loud creak that came from the wood. "I can't believe you just up and left Galveston."

"I was bored, and a little lost. I like working outdoors, but I can't figure out what I want to do. I still want to work in a church capacity somehow, and there's a little church near my new apartment. I might pop by and ask if they need any youth group leaders."

Jack considered the notion. "That's actually not a bad idea."

"Don't sound so surprised."

"Yeah, you're right," Jack said, grinning. "The rest of this conversation has been so normal."

"Why should you have all the fun in the family?"

"Why, indeed?" Jack paused as another laugh escaped, not believing the course of this conversation. "You're in luck, little brother. I'm actually going to be spending several weeks on St. Thomas, starting next month."

"There—you see? I knew what I was doing."

"Sure you did." Jack told him about his instructor course.

"Sounds intense."

"I'm sure it will be. I've wanted to be an instructor for a long time, so I'm looking forward to it."

"We'll get to go diving together!"

Jack grinned. "I'm sure we will. Hopefully I won't need to rescue you."

"Please. I already told you—I've got my advanced cert. I'll probably need to save you."

"You wish." Jack glanced back toward the exposed wall and sighed. "I've got a major house repair to get started on, so I'd better get going. I'll let you know when I'm coming over to the island. St. Thomas, in case you were wondering."

"Bite me." Both of them laughed, then Will heaved a sigh. "So does this mean we're not going out for that beer today?"

Chapter Twelve

SARA DESCENDED the staircase from Hibiscus, and a sense of calm flowed through her as she gazed at the placid cerulean water. Then a frown formed as she pictured Jack fixing the broken pipe behind the sink. She felt slightly guilty about how much she adored their Love Shack when Jack had to spend so much time repairing it.

At first, he hadn't minded, enjoying the hands-on work. But his enthusiasm had obviously waned, and he'd muttered several times about performing repairs on someone else's house. After stepping onto the dock, Sara pushed through the dive-shop door. Alex, Hope, and Zach clustered around the glass counter, deep in discussion. All three looked up as the bell above the door jingled.

"Planning world domination?" Sara asked.

Alex grinned, while Hope pressed her lips together. "Hardly. We're planning our rescue diver class. We'll probably start in the next few weeks."

Sara affected a mock-hurt look as she turned to Alex. "You're forking out all this money so Jack can become an instructor, and then doing the class yourself?"

Alex opened his mouth, but it was Zach who answered. "No offense, Sara, but I don't want anyone but Alex teaching me." Zach's hero-worship of Alex had transformed into a mentor-student relationship over the past year as Alex had taught him to dive. Sara wasn't surprised at his response.

"You don't know what you're missing." She turned to Hope. "You've already got an excuse."

Hope winked at her husband before turning back to Sara. "I'm with Zach. No one's teaching me but Alex."

"What about you?" Alex asked. "There's still time if you want to join. The class will happen while Jack is in St. Thomas, so you could use the course as a distraction while he's gone."

Sara had enjoyed her advanced class but didn't feel any desire to continue her diving education. "No, I'll pass. Besides, like Hope, I'll have my own private instructor soon. But that's not why I came in here." She looked at her sister. "We still on for girls' night out tomorrow?"

"Yep. GNO is officially on. We're meeting at 6 p.m. at Charlie's. Cindy's got business in Christiansted, so we picked a more central location."

THE NEXT EVENING, Sara parked her RAV4, Selena in the passenger seat, in the dirt parking lot of the nondescript local hangout in central St. Croix known as Charlie's. They often met at a beach bar called Marimba for GNO, but Charlie's was a good alternative. She opened the heavy front door and entered the brightly lit cavernous room, sweeping her gaze around.

"There they are!" Selena pointed to a corner booth, and they crossed the floor. Sara slid in next to Heather while Selena sat on the other side. Half Moon Bay's former bartender and new gallery director slid over to make room, tucking a lock of dark-red hair behind one ear.

"How's Robert?" Sara asked her.

"Excellent. His project is all finished with the St. Croix Tourism Board and they're completing the campaign."

"Everything's going well with his parents?"

Surprise widened Heather's eyes. "Great! His mother and I are still careful around each other, but the atmosphere is completely different."

Heather's roommate, Cindy, sat next to her. "Yeah, the only problem is whether I'm gonna have to find a new roommate soon."

Heather laughed. "I'm not quite ready to move in with him. But we're very good together. Good *for* each other."

Sara smiled and ordered a glass of white wine. She always looked forward to seeing Cindy. In addition to enjoying her company, Sara had a professional interest. Cindy wore her black hair in small braids hanging halfway down her back. But she liked to dye several which framed her face bright colors. Today, they were a royal blue. "Love your blue braids, Cindy," she said.

"Thanks." Cindy stroked her ebony hand down one of the royal-colored plaits. "I just got it done yesterday."

"I may need to speak with your stylist sometime. I'd like to hire someone experienced with Black women's hair."

April, a part-time divemaster and server, cocked her head at Sara. "You don't braid hair?"

"Braiding hair in that style is a very involved process, and I could never have the same understanding and instincts as another Black woman. We all have our specialties."

"That makes sense." April swept her long, golden-blonde hair forward over her shoulder and picked at the ends. "I need to see you about a cut anyway. Maybe I should try a new color or cut." A speculative gleam entered her eye, making Sara's ears perk up.

"Your color is gorgeous!" Heather said.

Hope slid into the booth next to April. "I agree."

"Make an appointment," Sara said to April. "Some darker highlights would look really good on you." Unable to resist gossip, Sara needed to know if she had imagined the private look in April's eyes. "Any specific reason you're looking to change your hair?"

April bit her cheek and a blush made her freckles more noticeable, causing Sara to break into a wide smile. *I knew it!* "Ok April. Who is he?"

A big round of *ooohs* went around the table as everyone turned to the divemaster.

"Fine. I know better than to keep anything from you, Sara."

"That will only make it worse," Hope agreed.

Sara ignored her sister, twirling her finger in a *go on* gesture to April.

"His name is Brian, and he's one of the other servers at the restaurant where I work. We've only been together a few weeks, but it's going great."

Sara couldn't resist a peek at Hope but wasn't surprised to see only happiness for April on her face, with no hint of relief.

Must be nice to have that much confidence.

She didn't know how Hope did it. Sara knew April well, and she would never stoop to chasing after a married man, but that didn't stop the divemaster from stealing glances at Alex from time to time. Yet not only did Hope not mind her working alongside him, she was friends with April.

Sara had flat-out confronted Alex about the situation once. He hadn't been pleased, telling her to mind her own business. Sara had no doubts that her brother-in-law had eyes for no woman but Hope. Still, April becoming involved with another man was good news for everyone.

"How did you two get together?" Heather asked April.

"We went for a walk one night after our shifts at the restaurant. I'm still not sure how it happened, but we ended up kissing. And things went on from there."

"Now we're getting somewhere," Sara said, leaning forward. "Went on *where*, exactly?"

"None of your damn business," April said with a laugh, and they all joined in. "But I'm sure you can use your imagination." April took a sip of her mojito and frowned. "I've got an appointment with my gyn to go back on birth control. What do you guys use?"

"I've been on the pill for years to regulate my periods," Heather said.

"Before my hysterectomy, I used an IUD," Hope said.

"I use a contraceptive patch." Sara patted her lower abdomen. "Just change it once a week. Easy peasy."

"I'll see what my doctor says," April said. "Lots of options, for sure. How are things at the Love Shack?" she asked Sara.

"We love it. Especially me, since I don't have to do the repairs."

"I feel kind of guilty about that," Selena said with a flinch.

"Why would you feel guilty?" Heather asked.

"My uncle is their landlord, and bein' so close to the ocean, the house has worn down a bit. Jack's had to do a lot of repairs."

"Jack negotiated a rent decrease with Calvin, so things are going smoothly at the moment," Sara said.

Selena sipped her drink. "Uncle Calvin used to own several rental properties around the island. But as he's gotten older, he's sold them off. That beach house is the only one he's got left and it's gettin' to be too much for him." She looked at Sara. "Are you looking forward to your time alone there, or dreading it?"

"Mostly dreading it," she said, then broke into laughter. "But at least Jack will have company while he's gone." When she'd come home from work the previous night, Jack had told her about Will's big move. Now she retold the story to laughs all around. "I really like Will, but his planning skills aren't the best."

Hope was still laughing. "I think it's adorable. He'll have to come visit us sometime."

"I wouldn't be surprised if he ends up on St. Croix. He moved to be closer to Jack."

"Well, he is," Cindy said. "And he even learned there's more than one island in the Caribbean."

Sara sighed at the smiling faces around her. "We might need to do this more often while Jack's away. All the problems with Aqua are wearing me down. With him gone, I need something to keep me distracted."

Heather frowned, staring at Sara. "I'll say it again. Why don't you pick out some of your watercolors to sell at Ember? Or paint new ones? I need a new artist to feature."

"Yes!" Hope said. "That's what I've been telling her too."

Sara pondered the offer. "You guys may be right. That would give me something constructive to focus on besides my loneliness and frustration. I'll paint some new watercolors for you, Heather."

The conversation turned to a marathon Cindy was training for. Hope was considering a half-marathon at the same event, while Sara firmly bowed out of any running activities. But as she studied the women around the table, gratitude filled her to be surrounded by supportive friends. She and Jack would just have to make the most of the next few weeks.

Chapter Thirteen

FEBRUARY...

Sᴜɴʙᴇᴀᴍs ꜰʟɪᴛᴛᴇᴅ through the aquamarine water, and a curious spade fish hovered close to Jack. The large silver fish approached to within inches as he attached the last piece of brain coral to the frame of the resort's coral nursery. The large structure had once been the roof of Alex's apartment until a hurricane blew it to its present location forty feet below the ocean surface.

Jack back-kicked a few feet and examined his work, satisfaction rolling through him like a warm wave. Brain coral was one of his favorites, and he had established several areas of new growth on the frame. Since Alex was busier leading classes, Jack had taken over much of the day-to-day work on the coral-restoration project.

Hopefully that doesn't change once I get certified to teach too.

But he could hardly complain if it did. Alex had started the project and lent his expertise as a marine biologist anytime Jack had questions.

Turning around, Jack swam back to the pier and climbed onto the wooden dock, enjoying the late-afternoon sun. When he walked into the gear room, Alex sat at his workbench in the corner, working on a regulator.

He looked up as Jack entered. "Did you get those brain coral fragments situated?"

Jack crossed the room and placed his pony bottle, the extra air source used when diving alone, in the corner. "Yeah. I have ten of them going. The first ones I started might be ready for transplanting."

"Good. I'll take a look while you're gone." Alex unfolded his long frame and stood, taking Jack's regulator. "You ready to leave tomorrow?"

Jack's gaze drifted to the neat pile of his personal scuba equipment near the door. Today he had used the resort's gear. "Yeah. Just need to finalize my packing. Will you watch out for Sara while I'm gone?"

Alex had coiled the regulator and was hanging it on its hook when Jack's words made him freeze. He turned his head and met Jack's eyes squarely. "Count on it."

"It feels weird to leave her at the house alone for several weeks. The area is safe, but I'd feel better if someone was checking in on her from time to time."

Alex raised one side of his mouth. "For what it's worth, I asked if she'd be interested in staying at the house with us, but she... declined."

Jack laughed. Actually, Sara had come home raging that Alex thought she was completely incompetent and incapable of taking care of herself. He loved that Sara was fearless where Alex was concerned. Hell, she was fearless where most things were concerned. He was one of the few people who got to see her less-confident, hidden side. Also something he loved. "She doesn't want to look like she can't manage on her own."

"Hope has mentioned staying at your place a few nights while you're gone. If she does, I'll make sure she takes Cruz with her. He's super protective."

"Thanks. I appreciate it."

Alex crossed the room and held out his hand. "Good luck, but you'll do great. Just lean on all the experience you've gained the last couple years, and you shouldn't have any problems."

Jack shook his hand, then moved forward to give Alex a hug. "Thank you for this. It means a lot to me."

"You're welcome. It's not all altruistic, you know. I've got Nitrox classes coming out my ears—I'm looking forward to giving some to you." Alex nodded, and the two men walked out the door together. The former SEAL headed up the pier and home while Jack returned to the dive shop.

He crossed the room and entered the classroom. Several lockers lined the wall, and his text tone went off from inside one. Opening the door, he grabbed his backpack and placed it on a table. Jack pulled out his phone and nearly dropped it, as if it were poisonous, when he saw who the text was from. Grimacing, he opened the message app to make sure he wasn't seeing things. He wasn't.

Diane: How's life in the tropics? I've been missing you lately.

He was strongly tempted to just delete the message—his ex-wife was the *last* person he wanted to converse with. Prior to Christmas, they hadn't talked once since he moved to the Virgin Islands. But he needed to send an unequivocal message.

Jack: We don't talk to each other. Leave me alone. I mean it.

He rammed the phone into his back pocket and stomped out of the shop.

Dammit, I'm not going to let her ruin my good mood. I need a distraction.

Inspiration struck as he grabbed his duffel of gear. He pulled his phone out again to call Will. "How's it going?"

"All settled in," Will replied. "I like it here. There's plenty of action."

"Your tour-guide job going better now?" Jack grinned, his mood already improving. Will's first day in an area he knew nothing about had been rather difficult, and he'd made zero dollars in tips. But he was one of those people who could talk his way out of anything and had quickly picked up what he needed to know.

"Yeah. It covers my rent, but not much else. The gig with the church youth group didn't pan out though. I'm still looking for something else."

Jack tossed the duffel in the back of his truck and entered, starting the engine. "I'm sure you'll find it," he said, transferring the call to his car's Bluetooth.

"I do have some news though. The other night, I had a beer with this guy who's doing an internship at a dive shop. He doesn't have to pay for his classes—he'll work for them after he's licensed."

Jack frowned. He knew all about that business model, though most internships were geared toward prospective dive professionals. His brother wasn't that experienced. "Be careful, Will. Some shops that do internships run good programs, but more are just indentured servitude. The end goal is divemaster. They slam you through the course as fast as possible, then push you to lead groups—whether you're ready or not."

"Relax, man. This is a good one. I've already talked to them, and they don't require students to stay on if they're not happy, but most do. Here's the news—I'm in their divemaster program!"

Jack's mouth dropped open. "What? You don't even have rescue diver!"

"Yeah, but I'm doing that now. It only takes a day."

A day??

"How many dives do you have, Will?"

"Thirty or so. But I'll have plenty by the time I get my divemaster cert. Why, how many do you have, hotshot?"

"After two years of being a full-time divemaster? Thousands. And I had hundreds before I became a divemaster." Jack gripped the wheel. "If you need any extra help with skills, you can come to me, ok? I'll find a way to work it in."

Will sighed, the sound loud inside Jack's truck. "You're such an old woman, big brother. Scuba diving isn't rocket science, you know. But we absolutely will go diving together while you're here."

SARA BREEZED out of their bedroom, freshly changed after work into a tank top and shorts. She headed toward the refrigerator and was pulling her hair into a ponytail when Jack walked in the front door, deep lines etched into his forehead. She pulled two beers out and greeted him with a kiss.

He kissed her back fiercely, then abruptly pulled back and slid his backpack off and laid his phone on the counter. "Thanks for the hello kiss. I needed that."

"Is there a problem with your flight tomorrow?"

A tired smile rose on Jack's face. "No, that's all fine. It's Will. I was just talking to him, and he's signed up for a rush divemaster class."

"I take it you don't approve."

"They're called Zero to Hero courses. Will always jumps into things without thinking them through."

Sara laughed. "I can't imagine him doing that."

Jack's reluctant smile turned into an answering laugh. "You're right. This is exactly like him. If anyone can find a way to make it work, it's Will." He kissed her forehead. "You always cheer me up. Thanks, darlin'." He took the offered beer and drank a long swig as he crossed the room again. "I need to get my duffel out of the truck bed. I'll be right back."

Smiling, Sara leaned a hip against the counter and took a drink of her own. On the counter, his phone chimed with a text, and she glanced at the screen without thinking about it. The name on Jack's lock screen sent her stomach plummeting to the ground.

He's been texting with Diane?

Hairs rose all over Sara's body, and her blood chilled inside her veins. Because Jack's phone was locked, all the screen displayed was Diane's name—the message content was hidden. But Sara knew his password. She hesitated, not wanting to invade his privacy. But bile filled her gut.

I need to know what this is about!

She was saved from her ethical conundrum when Jack returned through the front door and set the heavy bag next to it. He wore a wide smile as he walked to her, but it disappeared as he neared. "What's the matter?"

Sara opened her mouth, but no words came out. Then his phone chimed again, and she looked at it, almost against her will.

A second text from Diane.

Slowly, Sara raised her eyes to stare into those brown ones she loved so much. "Why are you texting with Diane?" She hated how soft and timid her voice was, but couldn't help it. She was dizzy from the rush of emotion overtaking her.

Jack's concerned expression tightened into raw anger, so out of place on his face. He gritted his teeth and spat out, "That bitch! Did she text again?"

"Again?"

There was a dull rushing noise all around her, but Sara could still hear Diane's nasty words loud and clear. *"I could have Jack back anytime I wanted. All I need to do is snap my fingers and he'd come running."*

"Jack, how long has this been going on?" Sara's heart raced. Nausea fluttered through her stomach, leaving an oily taste in her mouth.

Jack's face softened and he softly grasped both her upper arms. "Nothing's going on. Diane texted me earlier this afternoon, and I thought that was the end of it. I guess not."

"Why did she text you?"

Jack grimaced and rubbed a hand over his beard. "I think she's trying to cause trouble. I guess seeing me again put me back on her radar."

Sara was still numb all over. Her last relationship had ended when her boyfriend cheated. She had reacted with fury, throwing his things out her apartment window.

But this relationship was different. Jack was different.

What she felt now was more of an existential threat, deep in her soul.

Raw fear.

Her shock must have shown on her face because Jack picked the phone up off the counter. "We'll look at the texts together, ok? There's nothing going on."

He opened his phone, and her eyes immediately went to the two messages Diane had just sent.

Diane: Don't be that way. We can still be
friends. I love the beard, by the way.

Diane: Maybe friends with benefits…?

Sara swallowed hard. Her throat felt constricted, and the roaring wasn't getting any quieter. "My God. This is the first time she's contacted you?"

Jack glowered at the phone. The fierce, angry expression was so out of place on his handsome face. "Yes, until earlier today." He scrolled up to show her the messages from earlier that day, and the tightness in her throat lessened when she read Jack's response. "I've never heard a word from her since I left Texas." He hissed through his teeth, meeting Sara's eyes again. "This ends here. Diane means nothing to me." Then he typed quickly.

Jack: I told you before. I want nothing to do with you. This is the last you'll hear from me. I'm blocking your number as soon as I send this.

He sent the message and opened Diane's contact, blocking her number. Then he completely deleted her from his contacts. "I should have done this years ago, but it never occurred to me."

After setting the phone back down, he returned his enormous brown eyes to Sara's. The anger in them was gone, and now they only held concern. Then something else flickered through them—fear.

Sara's pounding heart finally slowed.

Jack stroked a hand down her hair, gently closing his fingers around a thick lock. "That's it. Diane's gone for good. I'm looking at my future right now—you're the love of my life, Sara. Do you believe that?"

She briefly squeezed her eyes shut. "Yes, and I feel the same way about you. When I found out Todd was cheating, I reacted so differently. Because that was a casual relationship. Ours isn't."

"I never want another woman in my life. Only you."

She slid her arms around him, and they held each other tightly. "I wish you weren't leaving tomorrow."

Jack pulled back and cupped her face with both hands. "I can postpone my IDC."

Sara shook her head softly enough it didn't dislodge his hands. "This class means everything to you. Both you and Alex went to a lot of work to set it up."

"It does not mean everything to me. You do."

Finally, she smiled and the horrible ache in her soul washed away. "You mean more to me." She slid her arms around his waist, snuggling her head into the hollow of his neck. "Casual relationships were easier on the emotions, you know."

Jack laughed, his chest shaking under her head. "Maybe, but how can you expect to hold on to someone else's soul without giving up a piece of your own?"

"Good point. This is the first time I've ever done that." She pulled back, giving him a mischievous smile. "So, you'd better treat my piece of soul well, buddy."

His eyes remained warm, but his smile faded. "I'll do my best. I know this is new territory for you, and a bit uncomfortable."

"My mom loved Dad desperately and did everything she could to please him. But he left anyway. Of course, he was an asshole, and we were better off without him. But that really gave me a screwed-up vision of what a committed relationship was. I've always thought of marriage as a dirty word."

Jack raised a brow, a ghost of a smile appearing. "And that's changing?"

"Yes." Then she sharpened her gaze at him. "Slowly... and the thought of kids still scares me to death."

He laughed. "You looked pretty terrified at Christmas when Alana dropped Sophia in your arms. But you didn't break her, did you?"

"No. What an incredible responsibility, though. Raising a whole new human being."

"I'm sure most parents figure it out as they go along."

"I made sure I was replacing my contraceptive patch like clockwork after that."

Jack kissed her forehead. "One step at a time. That's all we can do."

"You're incredibly patient with me."

His eyes softened. "It's not so much. And I love you."

She sighed and leaned into him again. "It's going to be a lonely four weeks."

"Not if you come visit me."

"Oh, I plan to visit. If nothing else, it will give me an escape from wanting to kill George when the next setback at Aqua happens."

Jack laughed again, a rich, lighthearted sound that never failed to make Sara smile. "I love watching those guys straighten to attention when you walk in. They hold you in awe."

"I doubt awe is the correct term. But they pay attention when I'm there—that's for sure." She sighed. "You're going to make a terrific dive instructor."

"I hope so. I feel pretty confident this course will teach me what I need to know."

She disengaged and stepped back. "All right. Let's get you packed. We've got a new adventure to start."

Chapter Fourteen

CARS MOTORED by on the street below as Jack walked along a second-floor exterior hallway. Being back in St. Thomas again was surreal—how different his life was this time. Seascapes Diving was located in Charlotte Amalie, by far the busiest town on the island. Several cruise ships were in port, and there was a cacophony of noise surrounding him.

Hopefully I can get some sleep in this place.

He had checked in at the Diving School office and met Scott Davis, his instructor, who had given him a key and directions to his shared efficiency apartment in the complex. Scott also gave Jack instructions to take it easy because their orientation would follow over the next two days.

At the end of the walkway, Jack unlocked the door to Room 8 and entered a large open room with two twin beds, one on each end. Matching dressers and desks sat on the opposite side, making for two mirror images. The room had a slight musty smell but was clean.

To Jack's right, a twenty-something man with shaggy light-brown hair and gray eyes turned around and nodded at Jack.

"Hi. You must be my new roomie." The man was about Jack's height as they shook hands. "Blake Stevens."

"Jack Powell."

"I just set my stuff down on this side," Blake said. "But if you'd rather have it, that's no problem."

"It's all the same to me. I'm just glad we don't have bunk beds."

Blake laughed. "The place isn't too bad."

Jack tossed his duffel of dive gear on the bed and set his rolling bag next to the bed. A quick peek at a short hallway revealed a small bathroom and a kitchenette.

He returned to the main room, relieved to find everything he would need for the next month. Except Sara, of course. "This will do. Where are you from?"

"Denver, originally," Blake said. "But I like the beach instead of the mountains. I've been here for a few months. How about you?"

"I've lived in St. Croix for about a year and a half. I'm a divemaster at a resort there."

Blake straightened. "Oh yeah? Did you manage to get them to pay for your course?"

"Yeah, it's kind of a family operation."

"I'm jealous. I'm shelling out cold hard cash, but that keeps me a free agent too. I'd love to get a job somewhere in the Florida Keys when I'm done."

Blake left to place his dive gear in his locker. Jack had just finished placing his things in the bathroom when Will texted him.

Will: Dude, are you here yet?

Jack: Yeah, just got unpacked. You want to meet for dinner?

Will gave him directions to Amalie Grill, a nearby bar and grill, and Jack had a momentary twinge of guilt as he thought about Blake. *Should I invite him too?* But Jack hadn't seen Will since Christmas, and his new roommate wasn't around at the moment, anyway. He settled for leaving a note about meeting up with his brother.

The restaurant was within walking distance, which was good since Jack hadn't rented a car. A rope fence surrounded a large outdoor patio, with tiki torches flickering against the red brick building behind the patio. Jack swept his gaze around the area and spotted his brother at a table off to one side.

Will's long face broke into a big smile as he saw Jack and the two embraced. When their Leatherbacks arrived, they toasted, and Jack laughed. "I still can't believe you moved here."

"I like it. The tour guide job is ok, but I really enjoyed my rescue diver class. I'll be working for the dive shop after I get my divemaster license, and I can't wait."

Jack still thought Will was rushing through his training, but kept his peace. *I'll find out how good he is when we dive together.*

"What about you?" Will asked. "You looking forward to being an instructor?"

Jack took a drink, collecting his thoughts. "Yes, but I'm a little nervous about this course. It's intense."

"I guess. My divemaster is ten days, but you're going to be here a month."

Jack's divemaster course had been a week longer, but Will was aware of Jack's feelings on the matter. He continued, "We have two days of introduction and then we take the Oxygen Provider/First Aid Instructor course the following day."

"Oh yeah," Will said. "I had to take that for rescue. It wasn't a whole day though—that seems like overkill."

Jack couldn't suppress a sigh. "Instructor, not student,

Will. I'll be able to teach both those. By the end of the second week, I should officially be an open water instructor. After that, I'll take the Specialty Instructor Courses, then I'm staying on an extra week to help teach students. When I go back home, I'll be able to teach any scuba course except other instructors."

Will laughed. "Good. You can help me brush up on my skills when I need them. How's Sara?"

Warmth spread through Jack's chest, but that was replaced by a flash of anger when he remembered his final day. But Diane was fully in the past now, with no way to contact him anymore. And he didn't want to waste another moment thinking about her. "It's going to be a long month."

Will arched a brow. "You two getting serious?"

"We're living together, Will."

"But just living together? No talk of a... more permanent arrangement?"

Jack twitched the corner of his mouth. "We've talked about marriage a bit. Sara's a bit more gun-shy about the subject than me. Just moving in together was a big step for her. We'll see where this goes. I can be patient."

Will stared at him, his face even. "Sounds like you'd go ring shopping right now."

Jack drained the rest of his beer and shrugged. "She's an incredible mixture of feistiness mixed with a softer side. I love her a lot." Then he frowned. "Why are you so interested in my love life? Get one of your own."

Will rested his head in one hand. "I'm trying. I dated a woman a few times, but it didn't go anywhere. I seem to be the one Powell who can't find love."

"You might try staying in one place for a while."

Will's gaze drifted across the patio to the trace of pink light remaining on the horizon. "I know. Maybe this is it."

As Jack strolled back to his room, he dialed Sara. "Good evening, beautiful."

Her long sigh came through the phone. "I miss you already. A phone call just isn't the same. Did you get settled in? What's it like?"

He described the apartment and his new roommate. "I just finished dinner with Will, and now I'm headed back. I'll have plenty of time to get to know Blake. How are things at Aqua?"

"Going pretty well, actually. The salon is coming together well, and they delivered the stacked stone at the end of the day."

Jack closed one eye, trying not to wince. "Is the stone ok?"

He relaxed at Sara's laughter. "Yes, believe it or not! It looks beautiful. They can't install it for a while though, so I'm still waiting."

"Sounds like things are moving in the right direction."

"I sure hope so. George said we might be looking at a late-March opening."

"That's only six weeks from now."

"I'm trying not to get my hopes up."

Jack climbed the stairs of the apartment building. "I'm about there, so I'd better go. Sleeping without you is going to be rough."

She paused. "For me too. Hope is staying with me tomorrow night. She's insisting on bringing Cruz for some reason, probably Alex."

Jack grinned. "Don't want two beautiful women staying all alone without protection, you know. I love you, Sara."

After they ended the call, Jack took one final look at the western horizon, which was nearly dark now, only a faint crimson line streaking across the sky Then he turned to face his future.

Chapter Fifteen

MARCH…

The mid-morning sun warmed Sara's face as she gathered her bright-red skirt, hurrying down the steps of the pier onto the sand. She had an hour between clients and couldn't resist a peek at Aqua to check out the long delayed stacked-stone installation, which had begun that morning. Jack had been gone two weeks, and Hope and Heather tried to keep her busy in the evenings. Hope had stayed over two nights, but Sara felt perfectly safe at the Love Shack, and finally told her sister to spend the nights with her husband.

Sara was safe, but her bed was cold and empty.

She cast a professional eye over the building as she approached. From the outside, Aqua looked finished. Even the landscaping was completed. Potted palms were evenly placed along a river-rock-lined bed running the length of the building. Several fountains were spaced between the plants, the sound of their trickling water competing with the waves lapping the beach.

The one-way glass walls of the treatment rooms and the beach entrance were the same color surrounding Ember, giving the large building a cohesive look. Sara stepped onto the brick-paved patio where tables and chairs would eventually be placed. Increasing her pace as she neared her goal, a smile rose to her face at her thrumming heartbeat.

She pushed through the glass door and stepped into the bright interior. Once the central river had been confirmed waterproof, it had been drained to conserve water. The enormous feature wall on the other side of the room was an integral part of the building concept, and the feature Sara was most eager to see finished. As she neared a bridge spanning the channel, her eyes lifted eagerly to the gray cement wall to check the progress of the stacked stone installation.

She stopped cold in the center of the room.

At first, she was confused. Two men, including Harry who had caught the canal leak in the salon, were troweling mortar and placing the thin stones on the wall as a boom box in the corner played classic rock. But instead of an orderly progression of stone rising from the bottom of the wall upwards, the leftmost three feet of wall was covered from ceiling to the now-drained pool as the men worked from left to right. Each piece of stone was placed vertically rather than horizontally.

Then, like an out-of-focus camera being adjusted, the image before her made sense and Sara's heart nearly stopped. Heat raced through her body and her hands balled into fists at her sides. She stormed across the bridge toward the wall, her foot-falls echoing in the cavernous room.

"Harry! What the *hell* are you doing?" Sara usually made an effort not to swear at the workers but was beyond such niceties now.

The large man turned around, his dark brown eyes

perplexed as he held a rectangular gray stone in one hand. "What do you mean, Miss Sara? We're layin' the stone."

Sara was half Harry's size, but that didn't stop her from stomping up and stopping right in front of him. Her face must have been fierce, because his confusion turned to alarm, and he took a large step backwards. She clenched her jaw and spoke through her bared teeth. "You're stacking the stone in a vertical orientation instead of horizontally! Who told you to do that?"

Harry's dark face turned back to confusion as he stared at the wall. "Nobody. We just thought with how the wall's gonna be used, vertical made more sense."

"What? Have you *ever* seen stacked stone installed vertically?"

"Well, no. I guess not."

Sara darted a furious glare around, noting the two men were alone. "Where is George, anyway? He ok'd this?"

Rick, the other worker, apparently thought it was his turn to get yelled at. His face was turning redder and redder, matching his hair. "No, he had a meeting this morning, so we started alone."

Sara flung out an arm, pointing a pink-tipped finger at the offending stone. "Well, start tearing it down! Now."

Harry lifted his baseball cap to scratch his head. "You... want us to start over?"

"*YES!*" Sara shouted this nearly at the top of her lungs, and both men stepped away, wearing matching wide-eyed expressions.

The main glass entry door from the parking lot on the jungle side opened and George walked in, scowling. "What is going on in here? I could hear you in the parking lot—" He caught sight of Sara's expression, and his face instantly mirrored his workers'.

Sara ground her teeth, both hands clenched again as she heaved rapid breaths, glowering at the supervisor.

Almost in slow motion, like he was afraid to look, George swiveled his head and surveyed the wall. "Oh, *goddammit.*"

"George," Sara said tightly. "I'm glad we're swearing today, because I am trying very hard not to completely lose my shit here."

George wiped a hand over his forehead as he turned back to Sara, rearranging his face into a placating expression. "I understand. Don't worry, we'll tear that down and start over."

Sara couldn't help but feel a small sense of satisfaction at the beads of sweat breaking out on his forehead.

Maybe you shouldn't leave the kindergartners unsupervised, George...

But she didn't say that out loud. As angry as she was, she actually liked Harry. She took a deep breath and spoke evenly, making eye contact with all three men. "I need to make myself very clear here, gentlemen. I do not want you using *any* damaged product on that wall. If a stone comes off with so much as a tiny chip in it, you need to discard it." She sent another furious glare at the project manager. "Are we going to have to order more stone because of this?"

Swallowing hard, George turned back to the wall, while Harry and Rick stared at the floor. After a quick survey, the supervisor turned back. "We should be fine. They haven't gotten that far yet. I promise we won't reuse any stone. I ordered extra, so we should have enough. I know you're angry, and I'm none too pleased with these two myself, but this won't set us back more than a day or so."

Harry and Rick ducked their heads even more, resembling turtles now.

Sara still wanted to explode, but realized it would serve no purpose. "Well, get back to work then. Let's not delay things any further."

Harry's large eyes turned imploring. "I'm very sorry, Miss Sara. We just thought it would be more modern to place them the other way."

At his wrinkled brow, Sara's fury disappeared. Tears pricked at the corner of her eyes, frustration threatening to overcome her, but she bit them back. "Thank you, but I most definitely want that stone stacked horizontally. *And* with the two colors interspersed randomly, too."

Rick brightened, nodding. "Oh, no problem there. We were already doing that."

"Amazing," she muttered.

As Sara turned and headed across the floor, which was still uncovered cement, she surveyed the salon to her right. Two workers installing large white tiles gaped at her, but quickly returned to work when she glared at them. The salon was nearly finished, with its row of hair stations and sinks along one wall and mani-pedi stations along the other. She had decided against the fish pedicure station, determining that trend had run its course.

As the door closed behind her, George laid into Harry and Rick, but his raised voice gave Sara no satisfaction.

What if my dream just isn't meant to be? Maybe the universe is telling me something here.

She stopped at the edge of the brick patio, letting her gaze drift slowly over the gentle ocean before her. Tension drained from her shoulders, bringing the threat of tears again. "No—not today. I can't go back to work all weepy and red-eyed."

Swallowing thickly, she headed toward the glass-encased end of the building. Red and orange streaks were painted on the exterior and large red letters read *Ember* over the door. Fiery painted streaks ran through the smoked-glass door. Sara entered the art gallery, immediately surrounded by the soothing sounds of smooth jazz. The glass here wasn't one-way, instead remaining dark on the inside, and the interior was brightly lit by cleverly placed LED lights.

Heather stood behind a desk constructed of orange glass and looked up. "Hello there, Sara! This is a nice surprise." Dressed in a long-sleeved white blouse and black pencil skirt, she walked across the room. Her smile fell. "What's wrong?"

Sara gave her a small smile, trying to brush off her funk. "More problems at Aqua. I have some time before my next client, so I thought I'd remind myself projects actually get finished."

Heather held out her arms and embraced her. Though she was much taller and thinner than Sara, the contact was still comforting. "I'm sorry."

"I really miss Jack. He is so good at keeping me on an even keel."

Heather pulled away and patted her shoulders. "You'll just have to call him tonight."

"If he's not already asleep. At least one of us is happy—he's loving his class even though it's challenging."

"Is there a problem with the stacked stone? I know you've really been looking forward to seeing that finished."

"Yes, they screwed up the installation, but George assured me it won't actually set us back much. I'm just so over all the problems!"

Heather put an arm over Sara's shoulders and steered her to the side of the gallery where her watercolors were displayed. "Maybe this will cheer you up. I've sold three of your paintings! Do you have any more to bring in?"

The empty places on the wall made Sara smile, and her frustration finally slipped away. "One, and I'm painting another now. With Jack gone, I've been painting more to occupy my time. Wow—I'm an official artist now! At least one dream is becoming a reality."

She examined the paintings and photographs spaced throughout the gallery. "Robert still has a lot of pictures here, huh?"

"Yes. As well as they've been selling, I'll take however many he wants to give me." Heather pointed to the other side of the space, where several watercolor paintings of St. Croix were displayed. "And Hope gave me the contact info for a local watercolor artist. His work has been doing well too. Ember is a success!"

"I had no doubt, with you and Hope behind it. Things are going well with Robert?"

"Very. We went to a baseball game with his parents last night, and we still help at the pet shelter too."

"Sounds like you have a nice life carved out for yourselves."

Heather smiled and tilted her head. "That's a good way of putting it. It does feel like we had to carve it out. But now that we have, neither of us could imagine life any other way."

Sara checked her watch and sighed. "I'd better head back to Hibiscus. I'll give Aqua a wide berth, so I'm not tempted to attack anyone. I'm surprised you couldn't hear me yelling in here."

Heather grinned. "Not a word. Maybe they put extra insulation between the two units. You definitely have those guys jumping whenever you show up."

Sara closed her eyes and laughed. "Believe me, today didn't change that."

***

By the end of the day, Sara's furnace of anger had fizzled to a dull despondency, coupled with regret at how she'd blown up at the two workers. She smiled warmly at her final client as she left, but breathed a big sigh when the door closed. Selena was with a client and Evie, their part-time helper, had left for the day. After making sure there wasn't anything for Selena to clean up, Sara trudged down the steps, picturing her hollow cottage.

As she came around the corner, Alex and Hope stood before the deserted dive shop wall. They acted professionally when guests were present, but when they were unobserved, it was a different story. Hope was pressed against the wall as Alex leaned in, one arm pushed against the wood. They wore identical smiles as she slid her nose across his, then swept a soft kiss over his lips.

"Oh, sure," Sara said grumpily. "Like I'm not lonely enough. Now I have to watch you two make out every time I turn around."

Alex straightened and turned his head toward her, irritation flashing in his eyes before he quickly covered it. Knowing she'd struck a nerve with her comment made Sara feel a little better. She enjoyed getting under her brother-in-law's skin, and since he was the cause of her present misery, she wasn't about to let him off the hook. Now his face was blandly pleasant, a sure sign he was hiding his emotions. "Nice to see you too, Sara."

The chagrin on Hope's face was more genuine. "I'm sorry. It's rare we find ourselves alone. All done for the day?"

Sara nodded. "Done and looking forward to returning to my empty house."

Alex's jaw tightened, but this time Sara didn't take any pleasure in the sight as a twisting pain settled through her gut. *My Jack-less house...*

"I need to process some certifications," Alex said. "See you guys later." He brushed Hope's hand with his as he turned away.

Hope watched his progress for a moment before turning to

her sister. Her brow was lined, worry clear in her eyes, making Sara feel even more guilty at taking out her ire on them. She stepped forward and rested her hand on Sara's shoulder. "I heard you had a rough day. Want to talk about it?"

And with that, Sara burst into tears.

"Oh, sweetie," Hope said, gathering her into her arms.

Sara wept on her shoulder for several minutes before her tears abated to occasional sniffles. "I can't believe I'm such a wreck when he's only been gone two weeks."

Hope pulled away to smile at her. "Because you've never been this deep in love before. You need to go to St. Thomas for a visit. When is Jack's next day off?"

"I'm not sure, but it better be soon. I plan on calling him as soon as I get home."

"Make it happen. We can reschedule your clients if we need to. And the stacked-stone debacle won't set things back much. Chin up, sis. You're a survivor."

Feeling better, Sara strode up the pier and to her car. Passing by the pool bar, she waved off an offer for a free drink from bartender Clark and headed straight for her car. There was only one person she wanted to talk to tonight, and she couldn't wait to get home.

Chapter Sixteen

A GORGEOUS TROPICAL scene lay before Jack as he loosely held a Coke in one hand. He stood on the powdery white sand of Magens Bay, the signature beach on the north side of St. Thomas. A long crescent of white sand stretched across the base of the expansive horseshoe, the two open ends tapering to dense, hilly jungle. The bay itself was dotted with moored boats, and a cooling breeze gave relief from the hot sun. After class, Scott had brought his group of instructor students to the busy beach as a combination pressure relief and team-building exercise.

Blake joined Jack's side. "At least this course isn't balls to the walls all the time."

Jack laughed. "Yeah, a break was definitely needed."

As promised, their IDC had been a whirlwind. He and Blake got along well. Jack was the more experienced diver, and Blake had been a bit insecure and nervous to start. How far he had come was a testament to Scott's skills as an instructor.

Blake surveyed the sandy area around them and the people spread along its length. "This is a beautiful beach. Busy though."

Jack took a swig and nodded. "It's pretty much a mandatory

stop for every tourist. But there are some secrets." He pointed to their right at a heavily wooded hillside arcing toward the open ocean. "When I lived here before, some divemasters and I used to hike down to a secret beach over there. It's not easy to get to, but that's the whole point. It's usually deserted. Not sure I'll have time to get over there this trip though. It'll probably be a late night tonight."

Blake stared at him. "Are you seriously going to study more tonight?"

"I'd like to try. We have another full day in the water tomorrow before the last open water session on Friday."

"Not me, man. I'm probably going to dream about atmospheric pressure." He laughed, taking a drink of his soft drink as he glanced at their instructor. "I imagine you won't have any trouble explaining why it's so dangerous to hold your breath on ascents."

Jack closed his eyes and exhaled. "Oh God. I don't even want to think about that."

Scott had given each of the ten IDC candidates a subject to study and give a presentation on, which they had performed that morning. Then the instructor had pretended to be clueless about their explanations, making them explain the issue until they could do so in multiple ways. He had grilled Jack, requiring three explanations of why a diver's lungs expand the most in shallow water, and why the consequences of a diver holding their breath could be fatal.

Blake pulled his phone out of his pocket and frowned. "I've got a voice mail. Must not have heard it." As he played the message, his eyes became rounder as his smile grew. "Yes!" he said, shoving the phone back in. "That dive shop in Key Largo can interview me this weekend." Seascapes Dive School maintained a list of dive shops looking for instructors, and Blake was hoping to find work within the continental US.

"Good luck. Scott said this shop usually hires his graduates, so you should be a shoo-in."

Furthermore, Blake's absence for the weekend started all kinds of thoughts spinning in Jack's head. A smile grew on his face.

Perfect time for Sara to visit.

LATER THAT EVENING, Jack sat at his desk, highlighting passages about dive emergencies in his textbook. Blake decided to forego studying and lay on his bed, scrolling on his phone. Jack set the yellow highlighter down and rubbed his face with both hands, ready to call it a night.

Another night in my tiny bed. Without Sara. An image of Sara's lush curves appeared in his head, which didn't help his loneliness.

As if the thought summoned the act, his phone rang, Sara's warm smile lighting up his screen. Grinning, he picked up the phone. "I was just thinking about you."

"You should be glad to be far away from me today."

Her voice was soft, and she snuffled loudly. Jack's smile fell quickly as he got up from the desk. He held his hand over the phone as he whispered to Blake, "It's Sara." Blake nodded and Jack exited the apartment, trotting down the stairs. "You don't sound real happy. What's the matter, darlin'?"

"They installed the stacked stone wrong, and I unloaded on the two guys doing it." She sighed heavily. "I need to apologize to Harry. He's very sweet."

Frowning, Jack crossed the parking lot to a green area with picnic tables by the dive shop. He sat down. "Oh, Sara. I'm sorry —I know how much you were looking forward to seeing that wall."

"I really need to see you. When's your next day off?"

Jack's smile returned. "We have this entire weekend off, since it's the end of the main course, and we have our exam over two days next week."

"That's music to my ears." Now there was a smile in her voice that made him relax a little. "I'll be on a plane Friday afternoon."

"Blake is taking off for the weekend too, but why don't you get a hotel room? My bed is tiny. I think we'll need the room." His smile turned into a grin.

She laughed, and the sound warmed his heart. "You're amazing. I absolutely can't stay upset around you. How do you do that?"

"Experience. We've been together a while now, you know."

"Believe me, I do. You don't have any major plans for the weekend?"

That reminded him of something. "Yesterday, Will called and asked about dinner Friday night and a dive Saturday morning. You ok with that?"

"I'd love to see him again! We'll get plenty of alone time. If the three of us go diving, you can practice all your new skills on us."

Jack groaned. "Don't say that! When I dive with you two, I just want to relax and enjoy myself. I was thinking of practicing other skills on you."

"Oh, I'll make sure of that."

They both laughed, and Jack looked out at the moonlit bay, wishing she was already at his side.

"So you survived your presentation?" she asked.

"I did well, I think. Tomorrow, we have our final session teaching open water skills. I'm sure Scott will have more surprises in store for us."

"And I have no doubt you'll do fantastic."

Jack stretched his legs out, crossing them at the ankles. "I hope so, but now I can face it with confidence, knowing what's waiting for me on Friday. You."

"I'm not the best at waiting, but for you I'll make an exception. I love you, Jack."

"I love you too. Try not to kill anyone in the next couple days, ok?"

<hr>

JACK FLOATED several feet off the sandy bottom of the bay in front of Seascapes, stretched out horizontally in twenty feet of water. Blake kneeled in front of him, staring at him blankly as Jack demonstrated how to remove his mask. The salty water became blurry as he removed it, then returned it to his face and blew a steady stream of air bubbles through his nose into the mask to clear the water out of it. It was a maneuver he had performed hundreds, maybe thousands, of times.

But today was different.

He had never had to do the skill while hovering motionless and being expected to maintain perfect neutral buoyancy. He drifted up a little, but much less than his earlier attempts. *I'm getting there... just keep working on it.*

The previous month, Jack had assisted Alex when he'd certified a group of six divers. The former SEAL had performed this exact skill while remaining completely motionless in the water except for his head and arms. Jack had a newfound respect for him.

Yeah, well, I'm not a SEAL, am I?

Jack pointed to his mask, then to Blake, instructing him to remove his own. Instead, Blake just stared at him, like he had no idea what Jack wanted. Even though Jack had seen him remove his mask at least ten times during the course so far.

Hello! Anybody home?

This must be Scott's challenge for me.

Jack fluttered his hand in front of Blake's face, but he just tilted his head and shrugged. Jack pointed at Blake's eyes, then his, and repeated the skill, greatly exaggerating his motions. When he cleared his mask and could see again, Blake was nodding at him and gave him an ok signal. He stripped his mask off and exhaled a furious explosion of bubbles out of his regulator, windmilling his arms for good measure.

Jack kept a straight face as he calmly placed a reassuring hand on Blake's arm and guided the mask back to the man's face. His eyes were screwed shut, so Jack placed his hand over Blake's and pressed the mask against his face. Jack tapped the diver's regulator, knowing he could feel it even though his eyes were closed. This time, Blake calmly blew through his nose and cleared the mask, grinning cheekily around his regulator as he opened his eyes.

Success!

Out of the corner of his eye, Jack saw Meg, another student, swim away.

What the hell?

Kicking quickly, Jack reached out and tugged on her fin. She half-turned and glared at him, shaking her head. Jack beckoned, trying to bring her back to the group. Instead, she glowered at him and swam for the surface.

Fighting back irritation, Jack was at least pleased she exhaled a steady stream of bubbles all the way up. *Hey, she listened to my presentation!*

Jack glanced at his group, with Scott half-kneeling to one side. They all watched him, paying close attention, and he held out both hands to them in the universal *wait there* signal. He quickly surfaced in front of his errant "student".

"What are you doing up here? The party's down there."

Meg shrugged. "Changed my mind. I don't want to get certified anymore. I'm going back to shore."

Ok, challenge number two...

He softened his expression. "Sure you do, and you've done great so far. I can't leave students by themselves, so I really need you to accompany me back down there. Will you do that for me?"

She frowned, glancing down. "This is scarier than I thought it would be. The wetsuit is tight around my neck."

"You just need to get used to it, and it will loosen up once you're underwater a little longer. Come on back down. You'll do fine—piece of cake."

Meg stuck out her bottom lip. "I can't believe I wanted to do this. Who wants to breathe underwater anyway?"

"Aquaman does. Who knows, maybe you'll see Jason Momoa down there."

She grinned. "Ok, that changes everything. Good job, Jack—I would have slugged me."

When they submerged and returned to the group, Scott hovered in the middle. He looked at Jack and applauded him, then pointed to the end of the line, where Jack kneeled down, breathing a relieved sigh of bubbles.

Ok, looks like I passed that test...

SEVERAL HOURS LATER, Jack basked in the late-afternoon sunshine near the dive shop, warming up after several hours in the ocean. He was pleased with his performance. After returning to the circle, Scott had given Jack a slate with his instructions to cause problems for the next student. It had been fun—when he wasn't the one on the hot seat. His phone rang, and he fished it out of his pocket.

"We still on for dinner tomorrow?" Will asked without preamble.

"We are. Sara texted that her flight lands at 4 p.m. We could meet you at Amalie Grill at 5."

"Works for me, *hermano*. I'm looking forward to seeing her again. Just hope you two don't ditch poor old Will."

"We might. I've been lonely."

"It's only been two weeks, for God's sake. Besides, I've been good company."

"She's much better looking than you are."

"I'm not denying that. Oh, I might have a little surprise for you tomorrow. I'm looking into a new business opportunity and should know whether it's a go by then."

Jack rubbed his eyes. "Do I need to be concerned if this is legal?"

A loud mock-gasp sounded through the phone. "How dare you! Nah, I'm pretty excited. This gig might be just what I've been looking for. But my lips are sealed until I see everything in person."

Jack drew his brows together. "Fine. Be all mysterious. See you tomorrow." Then he grinned. "We'll try to be on time. But if we're late, I'm sure you can figure out why."

Chapter Seventeen

THE SMALL PLANE thumped onto the St. Thomas runway with a resounding return to terra firma, and Sara unclenched her hands from the armrests. She frowned at her watch—it was nearly 5 p.m. A fast-moving thunderstorm had delayed their departure from St. Croix and resulted in a longer than usual flight path.

Not that it had been smooth flying.

Sara had never flown in such a small plane. There were only eight seats, one on each side of the narrow aisle. The plane bounced and jolted its way to St. Thomas, making Sara's stomach rise into her throat. But surreptitious glances at her neighbors showed relaxed passengers watching videos on their phones and reading magazines. One lucky man was even fast asleep with his head against the window. These signs of normalcy slightly reassured Sara they weren't going to plunge into the ocean at any moment.

But the delay meant she and Jack wouldn't be able to meet Will on time. Since Jack hadn't rented a car, he was going to meet her at the hotel she had reserved, a modest but tropical building not far from Seascapes Diving. And with taxis in ready supply, she hadn't seen any reason for a rental either.

And we'll probably spend more time in the hotel than sightseeing anyway, Sara thought with a smile.

Heat shimmered over the black tarmac as the plane rolled to a stop. The passengers quickly deplaned, traveling in a loose line toward the terminal. Sara fanned out the skirt of her yellow tie-dyed dress, making sure the wrinkles weren't too bad, and entered through double glass doors into the slightly cooler arrivals area, an open room packed with expectant faces lined up on both sides, looking for arriving loved ones.

Not for me quite yet...

She spotted the *Taxi* sign and stepped up her pace, more eager than ever to get to the Seabreeze Inn.

And Jack.

She was almost at the end of the line of waiting people when she heard the voice.

"Sara."

Am I hearing things? She stopped in her tracks and slowly turned to the right.

And there he was.

Jack stood in the front row of waiting people, wearing tan cargo shorts and a button-down blue shirt. He was also holding an enormous bouquet of tropical flowers. She had no control over the gigantic smile that rose on her face.

She ran to Jack, throwing her arms around his neck and pressing tight as he laughed.

"I can't believe you're here!" He was warm and solid as a rock as he wrapped one arm around her waist.

"Careful. Don't squish the flowers."

She moved her torso away but clasped his face in both hands and gave him a long kiss. His lips were soft and yielding under hers, his beard longer than usual under her fingers. "I am so glad to see you!"

"Me too." He held out the flowers to her. "You can take these. I feel like I'm in some romance movie or something."

She took a deep inhalation of the heady scent before smiling at him. "I thought we were meeting at the hotel."

Jack took the handle of her carry-on, and they began walking. "And miss thirty precious minutes together? We've already gotten robbed of almost an hour because of the delay. Let's get out of here."

As they took a taxi to the hotel, Sara caught him up on the progress at Aqua. "My meltdown seems to have lit a fire under everyone. They got all the vertical stone torn down and this morning the new stone was going up—correctly placed this time. And the floor crews are laying the floor tile. The glass check-in desk has arrived, and they'll install it as soon as the wall is done and the floor's in."

He took her hand and squeezed. "Sounds like it's coming together."

"I'm almost afraid to say that. We still have to pass the final inspections to get our business permit. But that shouldn't be an issue." She resisted the urge to kiss Jack in the taxi, settling for brushing the fingers of her free hand over the back of his. "And how are things with your IDC?"

"I'm unofficially an instructor now. Class is over!" The relief on his face was palpable, but it was quickly replaced by a wince. "Of course, there's also the minor detail of two solid days of examinations next week."

"You'll pass with flying colors."

Jack smiled. "I feel good about it, actually. Assuming I pass the exam, I start classes for the specialty instructor certifications right away."

"Then you come home?"

Her face must have looked as hopeful as she felt, because Jack's smile dimmed a bit. "Not quite. I'm staying an additional week to teach as many students as I can. Alex worked it out with Scott so I would get experience in teaching different classes."

Sara scowled. "Damn Alex. Next time he comes in for a haircut, my clippers might accidentally slip."

Jack laughed. "Don't do that! It took you long enough to finally convince him you wouldn't shave him bald or something."

"It would be worth it." She arched a brow at his beard and longer hair. "You already need a trim."

He shrugged. "That's been the last thing on my mind. Why, did you bring scissors with you?"

Sara laughed. "No, we definitely have more important things to concentrate on than haircuts."

Jack's eyes took on a speculative gleam as the taxi pulled to a stop in front of a four-story light-green hotel. It was over a hundred years old, but the paint was fresh and the grounds in front were immaculate.

Their room was on the top floor, a large traditional Caribbean room with a spinning ceiling fan and solid mahogany furniture. Sara set the flowers on the dresser next to the glass vase the front-desk agent had lent her. The air conditioner hummed steadily as she crossed to sweep back the drapes covering a sliding glass door. A balcony lay on the other side with a wide view of Charlotte Amalie harbor.

With a happy smile, Sara turned around. Jack strode straight to her, his eyes on fire. He placed both hands behind her head and kissed her deeply, plunging his tongue into her mouth. A jolt went through her as she returned his kiss, rubbing her breasts against his chest.

He kissed across her cheek to whisper in her ear, "I've missed you so much."

"Me too. I hate sleeping in that house without you." She stroked his back with both hands, enjoying the muscular planes beneath his shirt. And most importantly, that he was in her arms. But reluctantly, she pulled back and glanced at the clock on the nightstand. It was 5:30. "Does Will know I was delayed?"

Jack shook his head and pulled out his phone. "I'll text him that we're on our way." Without moving his head, he moved his eyes to hers. "We'll just have to finish what we started later."

A corner of Sara's mouth twitched as he started typing. "Anticipation is a kind of foreplay, you know."

Sara stepped through the opening in the cordoned-off patio of Amalie Grill, already liking the casual vibe as classic rock emanated from hidden speakers. Jack immediately headed toward the side of the patio, and Sara peeked around him as Will rose from a table. She broke into a grin at seeing his long, lovable face again.

He still looks like a dark-haired Owen Wilson!

They embraced, Will saying, "Long time, no see."

"Good to see you too, Will. Know your way around St. Thomas yet?"

"At least he knows what island he's on now," Jack broke in with a laugh.

Will frowned at him. "Anyone could have made that mistake. Every damn island down here is called Saint Something-or-other. Anyway, I need to confirm something Jack told me a couple of days ago," he said, staring at Sara as they sat down.

"What's that?"

Will bit his bottom lip, trying not to laugh. "Is it true he dumped a bucket of water all over you?"

Jack groaned as Sara couldn't help smiling. "That's actually how we met."

Will slapped the table and burst out laughing. "Knew it! That's Jack Powell for you—Mr. Smooth Operator."

A bright red flush spread across Jack's face. "Great. Does the whole family know now?"

"Not yet, but my silence can be bought. Beer should do it."

"You're on." Jack wrapped his arm around Sara's shoulder and kissed her temple. "Sara and I didn't exactly hit it off right away."

Will nodded at her. "I understand. Jack makes a terrible first impression, then grows on you. He's kind of like fungus that way."

They ordered a bucket of beers and Sara got Will caught up on the goings-on with Aqua and her harrowing journey to the island. As soon as they sat down, Jack had placed a hand on her leg above her knee. His hand was moving slowly but steadily higher. "Do you like being a tour guide?" she asked.

Will lifted a shoulder, but a sly smile accompanied it. "Now that I've got my schtick down, I get pretty good tips, so it's paying the bills. But being a tour guide isn't in my long-range plans."

Sara suppressed a smile that he even had long-range plans. "Jack mentioned you were trying out some youth ministries but hadn't found a good match."

"No, I'm turning in another direction now, away from kids."

"Oh? Something specific?"

Jack had been taking a drink and set his bottle down. "Does this have anything to do with the mysterious news you were talking about yesterday?"

Will burst into a blinding smile, and Sara couldn't help

laughing in response. A backpack hung over Will's chair and he reached into it, wrangling something out before setting it on the table with a flourish. "Ta-da!"

Sara stared at the object. It looked like a large scuba mask, only with a built-in regulator's second stage.

Jack picked it up, drawing his brows together as he turned the object around in his hands. "A full-face mask? What's this for?"

Will, still wearing the gigantic smile, leaned forward with his arms folded on the table. "Diving!"

Jack stared at him, narrowing his eyes. "I already figured that out. Why, exactly?"

"I bought five of them. So a group can communicate underwater."

Sara was still grinning at his enthusiasm, but Jack scowled and dumped the mask back on the table. He replaced his hand on her thigh, higher than before. "Thanks a lot, Captain Obvious. I should have just skipped the IDC and listened to you."

She burst into laughter, bringing a hand to her mouth, but Will just grinned back at Jack. "This is the business opportunity I was talking about. Since I'm becoming a divemaster, it all makes perfect sense."

"*What* makes sense?" Jack stared at him, but Sara could tell he wasn't really upset. This banter was evidently par for the course between them.

Will drummed both hands on the table. "I'm going to perform underwater weddings!"

"Really?" Sara asked. That was the last thing she'd been expecting.

"Oh yeah. I can work as a divemaster and make additional cash on the side performing weddings."

Jack arched a brow at Will while sliding his hand further up Sara's leg. "That's actually not a bad idea. Dive weddings are popular, and this would definitely give you an advantage when applying for jobs."

Will held both arms up in a touchdown gesture. "How about that? Big brother actually has some praise for me!"

Jack laughed. "Did you only get the masks?"

"No, a guy was retiring so I bought his entire catalog. Masks, regulators, sermons and vows, some wetsuits and fins. All kinds of stuff. I'm super excited."

"I can see that!" Sara said with a laugh. "You're in your divemaster class right now, aren't you?" Jack had confided he wasn't very confident in the dive shop Will had chosen.

"Yep, I finish next week and take the test on Thursday. The dive shop said they might be interested in hiring me."

"I'm sure they'd be lucky to have you," she said.

Then the server brought their entrees, and their conversation—not to mention the journey of Jack's hand on her thigh—was interrupted.

After they ate, their thoughts returned to plans for the following morning. "I reserved us spots on the morning trip at Seascapes," Jack said. "The three of us will dive by ourselves and not follow the group."

Sara looked back and forth between the two men. "I'll certainly be well looked after. A private dive with two professionals. What more could a girl ask for?"

Jack rolled his head to her, and a slow smile broke over his face. "Oh, darlin'. You can ask for a whole lot more than that tonight."

She stared into his beautiful brown eyes. "Keep talking, handsome."

Will tossed his napkin on the table. "Ok, that's my cue to split. I'll meet you guys at Seascapes tomorrow morning."

After leaving the restaurant, the couple strolled hand in hand down the street. Sara enjoyed the busyness of Charlotte

Amalie. Christiansted was the closest to a big town St. Croix contained, but it was much smaller. As they passed a dim lane between buildings, Jack veered into it and pulled Sara with him, pressing her against the wall as he kissed her.

"I've been wanting to do that all evening," he said.

She hummed appreciatively before saying, "Then why are we stopping? Let's get to the hotel." She started to slide around him when Jack pressed his hands against her shoulders.

He glanced further down the lane. "What about here?"

Sara's mouth dropped open. "Are you kidding? No way!" Jack had helped her with her body consciousness immensely, but she wasn't quite ready for this.

He nibbled on her jawline, making her moan, before moving to her ear. "It would be a new experience for a new place."

"So would making love in our nice, big hotel bed. People don't actually have sex in dark alleys, you know. It's an urban myth."

Jack grinned at her. "Is that right? You sound like quite the expert."

"N-no," she stammered, heat flaming across her face. "But I want to feel safe and comfortable tonight."

His face relaxed immediately, and he kissed her nose. "Then why are we stopping? Let's get back to the hotel."

They both broke into laughter and re-clasped hands, continuing their walk.

Sara kissed Jack's shoulder, still damp with sweat. They'd left the drape open, and a dim glow lit the hotel room from the streetlights outside. They lay on the mattress, and she half sat up to pull up the rumpled covers from the foot of the bed, settling the sheet around them. The air around them was filled with the floral scent of her bouquet, still sitting in its paper wrapper on the dresser. "I feel guilty not putting those flowers in water."

Jack stretched like a cat, pressing a kiss to her temple. "You've got nothing to feel guilty about. The flowers can wait. We'll just have to leave them here anyway. Blake might look at me strange if I bring a flower bouquet back to our room."

Sara laughed softly, settling against him. "Just stay out of alleys. I can't wait to have you home again."

"Why, has the house fallen down around your ears?"

She elbowed him in the ribs, and he laughed.

"No!" she said. "The house is holding up well, except for a broken floorboard on the porch. But it's not the same without you. At all."

Jack tightened his arms around her. "I know. It's been hard for me too. But we're more than halfway through." He paused for a moment, drumming his fingers on her upper back. "This has been a good move for me—I can feel it. Thanks for supporting me. I have this feeling coming to St. Thomas could be a real game changer."

"Of course I support you. Even Aqua looks like it might be entering the home stretch." She reached up and rapped her knuckles against the wooden headboard. "If being apart has taught me anything, it's that I'm not Carefree Sara anymore. I need my man around." She lifted the corner of her mouth. "We've only been apart for a couple of weeks, yet I feel like the best part of me has been missing. Because you have."

Sara brushed a soft kiss across Jack's lips, then settled her head against his neck, tossing a leg over his. With a long sigh, she closed her eyes and fell asleep immediately.

Chapter Eighteen

JACK TRAILED SARA, holding her tank valve with a steadying hand as she walked to the stern of the boat. After placing her hand over her mask and regulator, she stepped off the platform and into the ocean with a gigantic splash. Within seconds, she reappeared, bobbing on the surface next to Will. Jack put his mask on and nodded to the boat driver, who gave him a wave. He made sure his form was as perfect as possible as he made his giant stride, something he'd never even thought about as a divemaster.

As they descended, he studied Sara and Will, assessing their comfort and ease in the water. He had always done this when leading dives and could tell within seconds what divers might have problems. But now he was able to pick out finer nuances and quickly problem solve like never before.

Sara and Will were both descending in a relaxed manner, watching the approaching reef below them. Jack took a moment to admire Sara, who had made enormous progress and was now an accomplished and confident diver.

That's my girl!

Will still used a lot of unnecessary movement, twisting this way and that as he inspected the reef. Jack smiled around his regulator. His brother would learn how much extra air that style of diving would use. Then he frowned.

Will is almost a divemaster—he hasn't figured that out yet?

As the trio settled at fifty feet, swimming slowly across the reef spread out below them, both Sara and Will looked at Jack, expecting him to lead. A warm flush went through him as he beckoned, then set a course on his compass so they could return. He'd led many dives with Seascapes over the previous weeks, but this was a new site. The coral and fish life weren't quite as plentiful as on St. Croix, a result of more people—and pollution —in the water.

But the reef was still colorful, with many fish flitting about, and the water was clear and warm. They passed a brownish sea fan with a pair of butterfly fish hovering at the base, using the fan as protection from predators. Jack got Sara's attention and turned on the flashlight he always carried.

Instantly the drab sea fan became a brilliant crimson, and the two fish a vibrant white and yellow. Sara exclaimed through her regulator at the difference. This was one of Jack's favorite tricks while leading dives. As depth increased, colors filtered out except for blue, making the reef look monochromatic. But shining a flashlight immediately brought the fantastic colors to life. Will gave an ok signal, and they swam on.

Nearly thirty minutes into the dive, Jack made a lucky find. As he stared at the fish, he was surprised he'd seen it. The large scorpion fish was nearly two feet long and potentially danger-ous, especially to careless humans. A master of camouflage, the tan and white fish sat motionless on a broad piece of coral, closely matching its color while waiting for unwary fish to swim by so it could ambush them.

He turned to Sara and pointed, but her lined brow indicated she didn't see the fish. Jack got closer and drew an imaginary circle around the creature with his finger, taking care not to touch it. The fish didn't move except for its protruding eyes, which followed the progress of Jack's finger. He saw the exact moment both Sara and Will saw the nearly invisible fish and laughed.

He moved to the side, and Sara came in for a closer look. She was also familiar with scorpion fish and made sure not to come in contact with it. Inhaling a lungful of air, she rose several feet to get out of the way so Will could get his turn.

Jack's brother closed in, twisting his head back and forth. Then he waved a hand at the fish, laughing when it remained still. When Will reached his open hand down toward the fish's back, Jack darted his arm out fast as a snake. Shocked, he grabbed Will's wrist, yanking his hand back as the fish bolted away, going from motionless to full speed in an instant. It settled again six feet away.

Will turned an irritated glare to Jack and held out his other arm. *What's the problem?*

Jack just stared at him, disbelieving. He carried a dive slate clipped to his BCD, something Alex required of his dive leaders, and Will reached over to detach it. He turned it around after writing on it.

I wasn't going to hassle it. I just wanted to stroke its back and see if it moved.

Jack rolled his eyes and grabbed the slate back, writing:

They're POISONOUS, you dumbass!

Will's round eyes betrayed his confusion. He obviously had no idea, even though the poisonous barbs which covered the fish's back and lateral fins were well known to divers, earning the fish a healthy respect.

Will gave the scorpion fish a long look, then shrugged at Jack and moved off to look into a crevice. Jack turned his frown to Sara, who gave him a smile and squeezed his upper arm.

How the hell could he have gotten all the way to divemaster without knowing that?

Then Jack relaxed, the answer obvious. *Because he's Will.*

Jack gave Sara's hand a quick squeeze before swimming on. He watched Will as they continued, a sinking feeling developing at his brother's erratic movements and lackluster buoyancy control. Sara was a much better diver.

Soon they were in a large sandy patch, and an air check revealed it was time to head back toward the boat. Jack was about to check his compass, then thought of a better idea. He pulled out his slate again.

Divemaster Will. Why don't you lead us back?

Will reared back, his eyes once again becoming round. Jack raised a brow and nodded.

If you're going to be a divemaster, you're gonna need to lead.

Will's face turned sheepish as he took the slate and wrote:

I don't have a compass with me.

Jack stared narrowly at him, but gave Will his, making a broad *after you* motion with his arms. Will swallowed visibly, but bravely took the lead, guiding them back. Jack had memorized coral structures on the way out and could see Will was slightly off course. But after a couple of corrections, the trio was soon under the boat again as the main dive group milled about, performing their safety stop.

Jack turned to Will and held motionless, fixing an expectant look on his face. Will stared back, then Jack could almost *see* the lightbulb go off. He gave Jack and Sara the safety stop signal, and they ascended to fifteen feet a short distance from the other group. Jack couldn't help but laugh, even though it was pretty obvious Will wasn't ready to lead dives.

And that concerned him a lot.

Two minutes into their three-minute safety stop, Jack caught movement in the blue water. He grabbed Sara's arm and pointed frantically as two Caribbean reef sharks swam slowly by fifteen feet away. Unconcerned with the divers, the sharks hardly gave them a look as they drifted by and out of sight. Jack craned his head in the opposite direction, but the other group was on the surface and re-boarding the boat.

This special treat had been only for the three of them.

They surfaced, and Will gave a loud whoop. "Awesome dive! That weird fish was poisonous, huh?"

Jack refrained from thumping him on the head. "Yes! Their spines won't kill you, but if you touch one, you'll have a really bad week."

"Cool. Now I know. How about those sharks?" Will's laughter was contagious, and Jack couldn't be mad at him.

And I'm not the scuba police anyway. He'll learn one way or the other.

After they got their tanks off, Jack pulled Sara in for a short kiss. "It's great to be back in the water with you."

"I've missed it too. We'll have to dive our reef when you get back. I need to see how my baby fish are doing."

Will's mouth dropped open. "You guys have your own reef?"

"Yeah," Jack said. "It's just off our beach."

"Damn. Get ready for some visits."

AFTER THE DIVE, they changed into dry clothing and headed to Amalie Grill for lunch. Will was on fire with excitement, but Jack was trying out ideas of how to ditch his brother. As much as he loved him, this weekend was about Sara. She ran her hand across his thigh as they sat across from Will, letting Jack know her thoughts were similar.

Will must have seen them making eyes at each other,

because he set down his cheeseburger. "Don't worry, I'll split after lunch, so you two have plenty of alone time. But I do have one request."

Sara smiled and draped an arm across Jack's shoulders. "And what would that be?"

"I'd really like to dive again tomorrow. Pretty please?"

Sara shrugged and turned to Jack. "It's ok with me."

A war was going on inside Jack. He'd missed Sara terribly, and seeing her again had only driven home how much he loved her. But Will was playing up his sad eyes, making him very hard to resist. "I'd love to dive with you again, but why don't we do it in a few days?"

Will grinned. "Can't. I need both of you."

"Both of us? Why?" Sara asked.

Will held both arms out from his sides. "I just bought all this wedding gear, and I need to make sure it all works. So let me test it on you two!"

Jack's heart dropped into his stomach, and he darted a glance at Sara, who was wearing what had to be a similar expression to his—wide-eyed astonishment.

Will burst out laughing. "Not a real wedding ceremony, you guys! Just a practice one so I can figure out how everything works. No pressure."

Jack laughed, trying to cover his shock. "Ok, you had us pretty floored there."

"Come on! This is the perfect opportunity!" Will said. "You two just need to wear the masks, and I'll wear the third one. We can tell jokes or something. Jack, you told me Seascapes has a good open-water training area just off their dock. We can use that."

"How long have you been thinking about this?" Jack asked.

"A few minutes."

Sara burst into laughter. "Figures."

Will's smile got even sunnier. "I'm a make-it-up-as-I-go kind of guy." He leaned forward, clasping his hands on the table. "Tell you what. If you do this for me tomorrow morning, I promise to leave you completely alone for the rest of the weekend."

"Now *that's* music to my ears!" Jack said, running a hand through his hair.

"You'll bring the jokes?" Sara asked Will.

"I'll spend this afternoon combing the internet. Only the best for you two."

Jack couldn't help laughing, and Sara gave him a nod.

"Ok," Jack said. "We'll do this just for you. But you owe me big time, little brother."

Chapter Nineteen

SARA PLAITED her hair into a long braid, then tossed it over her shoulder. In the hotel bathroom mirror, she glanced over her pink tank top and black shorts, making sure she was presentable.

You're stalling, Collins.

Jack had showered while Sara finally arranged her beautiful flowers in the vase, her fingers trembling at the thoughts colliding in her head. When it was her turn to wash off the saltwater, she had taken longer than her usual amount of time, reluctant to go back into the bedroom. Reluctant to face up and admit what she was feeling.

And thinking about.

Terrified, really.

She met her eyes in the mirror. "Do you really mean this?" Her brown eyes stared back, but there was no flightiness in them. She was sure. "But what about Jack?"

That was the thought causing the terror.

Well, I can't hide in the bathroom all afternoon, now can I?

Squaring her shoulders, Sara turned around and walked into the bedroom.

Dressed in a T-shirt and shorts, Jack lay on the bed, leafing through a St. Thomas tourist magazine. He glanced up at her entry, his features softening into a smile. "How do you do that? Wet hair, tank top and shorts, yet you're the most beautiful thing I've ever seen."

Tears sprang to her eyes as she crossed the room and sat on the edge of the bed. She leaned over and gave him a soft kiss. "You're much too good to me."

"No, I'm not." He tossed the magazine aside. "I had fun this morning."

She drew up one leg, sliding an ankle under her other thigh, and took a deep, calming breath. "It was. I can't believe Will didn't know that scorpion fish was poisonous!"

Jack laughed. "Will has a way to go yet. But I imagine he'll get there."

Sara looked down, brushing at her shorts.

Jack reached out and placed his hand on her knee. "You've been quiet since lunch. You ok?"

"I'm fine. I'm with you, aren't I?"

He smiled, but his eyes were grave. "Is it because of Will's grand scheme tomorrow? If you're uncomfortable with it, just say so, and we'll call it off."

"No, I don't want to let Will down. It's fine."

"If you say so. Just remember, it's only a pretend wedding."

Sara's heart leapt into her throat, crashing in her ears. She opened her mouth, then closed it again.

Jack squeezed her knee. "Talk to me. Whatever's bothering you, we'll work it out."

"Communication, right?"

"One hundred percent."

Sara couldn't look away from him, her heart still hammering. She took a deep breath and jumped into the unknown. "What... what if it wasn't a pretend wedding?"

At first, Jack just stared at her. Then his brow cleared, his eyes growing bright. "What are you saying?"

She laughed, but it came out shrill. "We're pretty serious about each other, right?"

"I've never been more serious."

"Neither have I. Ever." Sara's voice was soft, just above a whisper, and she cleared her throat, speaking more loudly. "I haven't been able to stop thinking about what Will said. More specifically, how I reacted before he said it was a practice ceremony. A soft light traveled through my whole body, Jack. I was disappointed when he backtracked, but I was too stunned to put it into words."

Jack sat up, leaning toward her, and a smile crept across his face. "Sara Collins, are you asking me to marry you?"

Sara laughed and covered her face with her hands. "Oh, God! That's not right. I'm as far from traditional as you can get, but I am *not* asking you to marry me." She pulled her hands away and arched a brow, sending him the signal as clearly as she could. But before Jack could respond, her hesitancy roared back. "But I don't know how you feel."

His eyes softened. "I've never been as happy in my life as I have since we've moved in together. You have a way of making me feel needed, while still letting me chase my own dreams." He moved his hand from her knee and took her hand. "I can see now that my marriage to Diane was doomed from the start. Because I didn't have enough confidence in myself, enough courage. I always thought everything was my fault, and she let me think that."

"Your marriage was doomed because Diane is an uptight, malicious bitch."

"That too. The point is, you're the exact opposite. You can be a pistol, but I never doubt your love for me. And your fire is one of the best things about you."

"Thank you. But *you're* the best thing about me."

He shook his head. "Not even close. But maybe that's why we're so good together—we both think the other is the best thing that's ever happened to us."

"Does that mean you want to get married tomorrow?"

Instead of answering, Jack rose from the bed and crossed to the dresser. He picked through the flowers in her bouquet. Eventually, he drew out a single white rose. He returned to her and held out a hand, pulling her to her feet before letting go again.

Then he lowered to one knee, holding the rose out to her. Sara's eyes filled with tears as they locked gazes. There was no uncertainty in his, only anticipation. "Will you marry me?"

Sara's tears spilled over, and she laughed. "Yes! Absolutely, yes." She accepted the rose, lifting it to inhale the heavenly scent.

Jack grinned as he stood. Pressing a hand against her cheek, he softly whisked his lips over hers. He pulled back and winked at her. "Then let's get married tomorrow, darlin'."

THEY ORDERED a bottle of champagne from room service and toasted their engagement. Jack studied her, serious now. "Are you sure you're alright with this? We're talking about a pretty spur-of-the-moment wedding here. And for a woman who loves getting dressed up, an underwater ceremony is about as unglamorous as you can get."

Sara laughed. "I love the idea! I've never had any interest in a big, fancy wedding. I prefer doing something different. But can we really get everything ready by tomorrow?"

"If Vegas can do it in minutes, I'm sure St. Thomas can do it in a day."

"Where do we start?"

Jack bit his lip, the gears in his head almost visible. "With Will. He's the one who makes it legal." He looked sharply at Sara. "Or we could do a ceremonial wedding and have the official one at home."

Sara shook her head emphatically. "Nope, you're not getting off that easily. We're getting married tomorrow. Legally."

Picking up his phone, Jack grinned and rose from the small, round table where they were enjoying their champagne. "Guess I'd better get hold of Will."

After Jack told him the news, there was a long pause. Jack's brow grew steadily more lined as he held the phone against his ear. "Hello? Are you still there?" Then Jack laughed. "Yes! We're completely serious, you idiot. Can you legally perform a wedding here?"

As Will explained, Jack nodded at Sara and gave her a thumbs up. "Ok. We'll let you know the exact time tomorrow, but it might be later than we originally thought." There was another long pause as Jack listened to Will, pacing across the carpet as he sobered again. "Yeah, good point. We'd better get moving on that. I'll keep you posted. Thanks, Will."

Jack returned to his chair and leveled his gaze at Sara. "Since St. Thomas is a US territory, Will is ordained here too. So that's no problem. But we have to get the marriage license and arrange for two witnesses."

Sara sat back and looked at her watch. "Oh, wow. It's almost three. We better head to the courthouse. Is that where you get a marriage license?"

Jack shook his head. "Will said it was the county clerk's office."

Sara did a Google search and discovered the office was in Charlotte Amalie. "It's on the other side of town. Let's get a cab."

. . .

THE COUNTY CLERK's office was in a light-yellow cottage-style building with a line of palm trees out front. Sara and Jack entered and walked over a scuffed wooden floor, then through a single-panel door with loud, squeaky hinges.

A large woman with a halo of black hair and gleaming dark skin sat behind a wooden desk. She gave them a brilliant smile. "How can I help you two?"

"We'd like to get a marriage license," Jack said, and a dizzy thrill rolled through Sara's abdomen at the words.

The woman's smile became even more blinding. "Oh, congratulations! I'm Lenore and I'll get you set up. Don't worry about a thing." She gestured for them to sit in two uncomfortable metal chairs in front of her desk. Then she rummaged through a file drawer, handing Jack several pieces of paper. "Here's the application, and there's a fee, of course. And it has to be typed—no handwritin'! The application is also online, if that's easier for you. Once I receive it back, I certify the application and we mail the license out. The whole process only takes a week!"

Sara's face crumpled. "We're getting married tomorrow!"

Lenore's smile dimmed a bit. "Tomorrow? But it's almost four now!"

Jack placed a supportive arm around Sara's shoulders. "We just decided on the spur of the moment, and Sara has to return to St. Croix on Monday morning. So it has to be tomorrow. Can we rush the license?"

"Please?" Sara asked, a fine sheen of sweat breaking out on her forehead that wasn't from the warm room.

Lenore tilted her head and the smile returned. "Of course. There's an additional fee to expedite the matter. But because you two are such a lovely couple, I'll type out the application right now and process it tonight. You can pick up the finalized license tomorrow morning between 9:30 and 10:30. Will that work?"

Sara wasn't about to argue with her. "That sounds fantastic. Thank you."

Lenore cackled, waving a finger at them. "You two are just lucky Cicely isn't workin' today. She's a real stickler for rules. You'd have gotten nowhere with her, let me tell you!"

Jack grinned. "This has been our lucky day for sure."

Lenore beamed at them. "Let me see your IDs and we'll get this thing filled out in no time!"

They walked out of the building just after 5 p.m., and Sara's head spun. "That was a bit of a whirlwind, but we got it done. Though we still have to find the witnesses."

Jack flagged down a taxi. "I'm sure a couple of staff members at Seascapes could do it."

"Let's head there now."

They sat in the taxi, and Jack winced. "Oh shit. Seascapes closes at five. No one's there." Then his frown deepened. "Plus, they have an open water class and two big dive groups tomorrow. We were lucky to get on the boat today. Blake's out of town too."

"Crap." Sara thought for a moment. "We'll talk to the hotel! I'm sure they have staff available. They must do weddings there."

"Good idea." Jack gave the driver the hotel's address, and they were off.

When they crossed the homey hotel lobby over yet another creaking wooden floor, Sara was pleased that the shift supervisor was behind the desk. "Hi, we're in room 416. We need to ask a big favor for tomorrow."

"Of course. It will be my pleasure." The young man, whose

nametag read Tad, had a polished manner and his blond hair was short and neat.

"We need two witnesses for our wedding," Jack said. "We're having it tomorrow."

Tad broke into a smile. "Congratulations! That shouldn't be a problem. There will be a charge, but I'm sure we can spare a couple of people. Where is it? Not here at the hotel, I know."

Sara was getting ready to answer when Jack groaned. "It's underwater," he said, screwing one eye shut. "I don't suppose you have two people on staff who are certified to dive?"

Tad's brows rose halfway up his head. "We do, but they're in key positions and can't leave the hotel. This is a tall order. Can the dive shop provide someone?"

Jack sighed. "We already thought of that. They're all busy." He turned to Sara. "Let's head upstairs and think about this some more."

"I'll let you know if I come up with anything," Tad said as they walked to the elevator.

After they entered the room, Jack tossed his wallet on the dresser and poured out the rest of the champagne, still cold in its ice bucket. Once again, they sat at the round table, though more somber than the last time.

"I still think that front desk guy could have helped a little more," Jack said.

"Yeah." Sara rested her chin on her palm. "This is where Hope really comes in handy, being a former front desk manager herself. Too bad she doesn't know St. Thomas."

Jack took a long drink, then sighed. "Well, we've got all morning to come up with something. But Tad was right. Finding two witnesses who can both scuba dive isn't going to be easy."

The answer came to Sara. It was so clear. She leaned over her lap, laughing. "Oh my God. How perfect! Why didn't I think of this to start?" She straightened up and Jack stared at her, brows drawn.

"Care to enlighten me?"

Sara picked up her phone. "I know *exactly* who our witnesses will be."

Chapter Twenty

SARA COULD BARELY CONTAIN her excitement as she placed the call, grinning at Jack. It was answered immediately.

"Ok, I'm a little worried that you're calling me on your romantic weekend away," Hope said. "Is something wrong?"

"Not at all. Maybe I just miss my beautiful big sister."

"Uh-huh. I'm getting suspicious, Sara."

"Really! And maybe I'm missing my very handsome brother-in-law too."

Hope's sigh was loud over the phone. "When you start complimenting Alex, I know something's up. Are you two in jail or something?"

Sara giggled. Hope was always fun to mess with. "It's just that Jack and I are having so much fun. I feel guilty that you and Alex are over there in St. Croix working yourselves to death. Why don't you two fly over here tomorrow and spend the day with us?"

Jack's eyes lit up. He gasped, then slapped a hand over his mouth to cover it.

Hope paused for a long moment. "Sara, get serious! Are you

sure nothing's wrong between you and Jack? Alex and I can't just drop everything and fly off with no notice! We're both working tomorrow."

Sara's grin fell off her face. *Shit! This might be harder than I thought.*

Jack stared at her and removed the hand from his mouth to make a twirling, *get on with it*, motion.

Sara nodded back and got to the point. "I need a favor and it's a big one, Hope."

"What's going on? Please tell me!"

Sara rushed through the words, her heart in her mouth. "Jack and I are getting married tomorrow. We need you and Alex to be our witnesses."

There was no response except for the sound of Hope's breathing coming over the phone speaker, faster than before.

"Uh, Hope?"

"I'm going to need you to repeat that last sentence. It *sounded* like English, but there's no way my sister would have uttered those words."

Sara laughed, and her stomach settled again where it belonged. "You heard me right. Jack and I are having an underwater wedding tomorrow and need witnesses who can dive. You and Alex are the obvious choices. Will you come?"

Hope inhaled a huge, gasping breath, then let it out in a squeal. "I can't believe this! You're getting married? Really?"

"Don't sound so shocked," Sara said dryly.

"I knew you two were serious, but I wasn't expecting marriage. Tomorrow?"

"Yeah, I know it's short notice, but we just decided. Jack's brother is a pastor who's starting to perform underwater weddings. We decided the universe was sending us a big, fat signal."

Hope burst into laughter. "Underwater! Oh my God, we'll

be there if only to be a part of that. But I am so excited for you, Sara! I'll have Alex get to work getting his shift covered. I don't have anything I can't reschedule."

"Swinging in your hammock will have to wait for another day."

"Oh, shut up. What time is the wedding? Do we need to get there tonight?"

"No—tomorrow morning should be fine. We don't have a set time for the ceremony and the marriage license won't be ready until 9:30 anyway."

"Fantastic. That gives us a little more time to get things settled."

"You think Alex can get his shift covered? Robert's working a lot of photo gigs these days."

"We'll figure it out. Alex is coming even if I have to threaten him with bodily harm. I'll text you when we get our flight booked. I can't wait!" Sara held the phone away from her ear, flinching as Hope screamed again. Jack grinned on the other side of the table and downed the rest of his bubbly.

After ending the call, Sara rubbed her ear. "I think I'm deaf now."

Jack shook his head, smiling broadly. "You're right. Alex and Hope are the perfect witnesses. I guess they can double as best man and maid of honor too."

"Matron of honor," she said absently, picking up the bottle to discover it was empty. She let it slip back into the ice bucket.

"What's the difference?"

"Maids are single, and matrons are married."

His smile faded. "Are you sure about this? We can do the official ceremony later, so you have more time to plan it out. I don't want you to rush through this. Weddings are a big deal to women."

She took his hand and held it in both of hers. "Not this

woman. I want to marry you tomorrow. It doesn't matter whether I'm wearing a wetsuit or a white dress." She cocked her head. "But would you rather have something more... traditional?"

Jack grinned and shook his head. "I think the underwater wedding is perfect! Not too many couples can say they got married on scuba. I can't wait."

THE FOLLOWING MORNING, Jack and Sara made the round table part of their war room. Over a room-service breakfast, they planned their theater of operations. Their breakfast was a modest affair, which was good because Jack was unusually fluttery in the stomach.

"Ok," Sara said. "Hope and Alex land soon, at 9 a.m., but we have to pick up the license at 9:30. I wanted to meet them at the airport, but we don't have time. Should we just tell them to take a cab here to the hotel while we're at the clerk's office?"

Jack swallowed his danish. "Why don't we divide and conquer? You meet them at the airport, and I'll pick up the license. Then we'll all meet here."

"Good idea."

He nodded, giddy relief washing over him. There was one important item Sara hadn't mentioned, and he suspected it had slipped her mind. Splitting their tasks would give him the opportunity to surprise her.

They finished eating and were soon entering their separate taxis. When Jack opened the door of the county clerk's office at precisely 9:30, Lenore gave him a wide smile. She held up a white piece of paper with a green border, fluttering it. "Here it is! And you're right on time too. After you get the necessary signatures at the ceremony, just mail it back to us and we'll get you the marriage certificate within a month. But this is all you need for a legal ceremony."

Jack looked over the document, noting the places for the officiant and two witnesses to sign. "That should work. Thanks for your help, Lenore. We'd be sunk without you." Then he laughed at his turn of phrase.

The clerk didn't know anything about the underwater part of their ceremony, and just took his statement at face value. "I'm so glad to help! You two have a wonderful weddin' and a beautiful life, you hear?"

Jack left the building and stood on the sidewalk. The morning was sunny and still, but fairly cool. By the time the afternoon heat took over, they might all be grateful for the underwater ceremony. A busy commercial street of Charlotte Amalie was two streets over, and he headed toward it with a spring in his step.

One thing I learned from six months of living here is that I should have plenty of choices for this little errand.

The avenue was still mostly empty and sleepy, with no hint of the throng of tourists to come. Colorful hanging baskets hung from lampposts, still dripping water from their morning soaking. Jack looked up and down the street, confirming several jewelry stores on this block alone. Selecting a nearby local shop, Jack opened the door and entered. A middle-aged woman with short, dark-blonde hair greeted him.

"I need to buy a wedding ring set. His and hers."

"You're in the right place then! Congratulations, my name's Yvette. Just you shopping?"

"Yeah. My fiancée," a small thrill ran through Jack at saying the word, "is handling another part of the wedding at the moment. We're getting married this afternoon."

Yvette's eyes became round. "Well, we'd better get to work then! What are you looking for?"

Jack didn't have the budget for a big diamond ring, and Sara wasn't the type to be overly impressed by that anyway. "White-gold bands for both, maybe a half-carat or so for the woman's ring."

Yvette led him across the room and unlocked a glass cabinet, bringing out a black velvet case that held a plethora of wedding sets. "I really like this display. These are all coordinating sets of men's and women's rings. They're similar, except the woman's is more ornate, of course."

Jack liked several sets. After a period of inspecting and then doubting himself, Yvette helped him make his choice. Both wedding rings were similar brushed white gold. A simple classic band for himself and a similar but thinner one for Sara, accented by an embedded row of small diamonds. Her set also contained a half-carat diamond solitaire ring with a cluster of tiny diamonds surrounding it. The entire set was simple yet classic, and he was confident Sara would like it too.

"This is a lovely choice," Yvette said. "I'm sure your bride will love it. Do you know what size she'll need?"

This was the question Jack had been worried about. But as he studied Yvette, he had his answer. The jewelry-store employee was plump, but her fingers were shapely and elegant. "Sara's actually pretty similar in size to you."

After checking her stock, Yvette recommended a band that was slightly bigger than her finger. "That way you can be confident it will fit for the ceremony. You can easily have it resized later."

"I think we're in business then." Jack pulled out his credit card, only wincing slightly at the total. Then he twitched a corner of his mouth.

At least the set costs less than at those touristy jewelry stores. And Sara is absolutely worth it.

His text tone went off during the cab ride back to the hotel.

Sara: Hope and Alex are here. We're nearly back to the hotel.

Jack: I'm on my way too. See you soon.

HE ENTERED the hotel and panned his gaze around, but the lobby was empty. Jack headed for the elevator, patting his back pocket to ensure both velvet boxes were secure. When he opened the door, Hope and Alex stood in the middle of the room, both wearing dressy tropical shorts and shirts. They broke off their conversation with Sara and turned to him. Hope saw Jack and screamed, running over to wrap him in a hug that drove him backward several steps.

"I'm so happy for you!"

Jack burst into laughter, returning the embrace. "Thanks. We're pretty happy too."

Flinching, Alex removed both index fingers from his ears before breaking into a wide smile. He moved forward to shake Jack's hand. "Congratulations."

"Thanks. Did you get Robert to cover for you?"

Hope squealed again, jumping up and down, while Alex closed his eyes and exhaled. Jack's confusion lasted until the bathroom door opened and the photographer himself stepped out. A smile lit up his face as he walked across the room to join them. "I wasn't about to miss this little party."

"Surprise!" Hope said to Jack, still aflame with excitement. "You need a wedding photographer, and you have rather specific requirements, you know. So here he is!"

Jack laughed, looking at Sara, who shrugged. "I didn't know either until the three of them arrived."

Jack turned back to Robert, matching his smile. "Photography is one item that never even crossed my mind. Thanks, man. This means a lot to us."

"Don't mention it. I've never even seen an underwater weddin', never mind shot one! This'll be great for my portfolio."

"We all put our heads together last night," Alex said, still grinning. "April said she could never refuse Sara, so she rearranged her day to cover for me." Then he frowned at the suitcase next to the door. "Though Hope brought enough clothes for us to spend a week."

"I didn't know what to pack!" Hope turned to her sister. "What kind of dress are you wearing?"

Sara burst into laughter. "It's an underwater wedding, Hope! I'll be wearing a wetsuit with a swimsuit underneath—like everyone else."

Hope's face fell. "What? You have to wear a dress, Sara, even if it's a simple one. Ditch the wetsuit."

"A dress will get *wet*," Alex said, arching a brow.

"So what? And what are you wearing, Jack?" Hope turned her hazel eyes to him, eyeing him steadily. She had a heart of gold, but when she was determined, nothing stood in her way.

"Um... I was planning on a wetsuit too."

Hope propped both hands on her hips. "Come on, people! This is a wedding we're talking about. I can't imagine the ceremony will be that long, since it's underwater?"

Sara looked at Jack, who shrugged. "I haven't talked about the specifics with Will yet, but probably not."

"Then we don't need the insulation wetsuits provide! Tropical casual it is. Don't you guys argue with me."

"Hope," Alex said. "It's their wedding. Maybe *they* should decide what they want to wear."

Robert raised a finger. "Speakin' as the photographer, normal clothes will look a lot better underwater."

Hope nodded. "Especially dresses, as Robert has shown us all."

"Dresses will look fantastic," Alex said with an exaggerated nod. "While you're kneeling in the sand and fish are chewing on the fabric."

Hope whipped her head toward Alex, narrowing her eyes, and the former SEAL actually ducked his head. Jack bit the inside of his cheek to keep from laughing. Hope turned to Sara. "Do you have any dresses here?"

Sara looked at her sister like she wasn't sure whether to hug or throttle her. "Yes, I have a light-pink one."

"That's perfect!" Hope said, then turned to Jack, eyeing him up and down. "You look fine just the way you are."

Jack looked down at his blue-striped polo shirt and khaki cargo shorts, then shrugged.

"Excellent!" Hope said, clapping her hands. "It's settled. What's next on the agenda?"

Four pairs of eyes stared at her, no one speaking.

"*Hope,*" Alex said, almost hissing as he held out a placating hand to her. "Stop it. Please?"

Her shoulders slumped. "Oh dear. Am I being bossy again?"

Jack gave up trying not to laugh as Sara crossed the room and embraced her sister. "You can't help it—it's part of your DNA. But we forgive you."

Hope hugged Sara tightly. "I'm just so excited for you."

"I know." Sara disengaged and moved to Jack's side, sliding an arm around him as he returned the gesture. "But you're right. We need to make sure we've got everything ready." She looked at Jack. "Maybe you should call Will and get some details?"

"I can do that."

"Speaking of details," Alex said. "Do you want me or your brother to carry the rings?"

Sara's face slackened. "Rings! That's never even crossed our minds." She turned to Jack, panic etched on her face. "Do we even have time to get rings?"

With anticipation building, a slow smile crept across Jack's face. "Well, actually..."

Chapter Twenty-One

JACK WORE THE STRANGEST EXPRESSION. Sara studied him closely as he turned toward her. His face was nearly shining, as if he were about to burst. Her alarm dissipated, turning to curiosity. He reached into his back pocket, and she gasped when he withdrew a small, gray, crushed-velvet box.

"I made a stop after the county clerk," Jack said, a smile growing on his face as he hinged open the box. "I know we might be in the running for the world's shortest engagement, but I wanted you to have a ring."

Inside the box was a white gold band and a second, white solitaire ring, which Jack pulled out. Closing the box, he absently handed it to Alex before grasping Sara's left hand and sliding the ring onto her third finger. Sara's heart nearly exploded as she gazed upon the ring with its glittering diamonds.

She met Jack's eyes. "I love it!"

Then she threw her arms around his neck and smashed her mouth to his. Hope, Alex, and Robert all applauded. Tears rolled down Hope's face and Alex wrapped an arm around her, pulling her tightly against him.

"I can't believe you bought a ring!" Sara said.

Jack laughed. "I was a little nervous picking out something without you, but wasn't sure we'd have enough time. If you don't like the wedding band, I'm sure we can go back and look at something else." He took the box back from Alex and showed her the white gold band with its inlaid diamonds.

"I can't imagine anything more perfect."

He twisted the solitaire ring on her trembling finger. "It's a tiny bit loose, but we can get it resized after returning to St. Croix." He pulled another gray box from his pocket and opened it, revealing a similar ring without the inlaid diamonds. "Mine is from the same set."

Hope held both hands against her chest. "Oh, Jack! That's incredible."

Sara couldn't take her eyes off him. "I love you so much."

"Love you too." He was turning a distinct shade of red now as he handed both boxes to Alex, so it was time for a subject change. "You want to call Will and get started?"

LESS THAN AN HOUR LATER, Will joined them in the hotel room, carrying a large nylon bag. He set it in the middle of the carpeted floor with a thump before unzipping it and pulling out a full-face mask with its attached regulator. "The rest of the gear is in my car. We should just need tanks and weights. Can you get those from Seascapes?" he asked Jack.

"Yeah, that shouldn't be any problem."

"Good, because it might be a bit of a process to figure out how all this works. I called this a practice session for a reason, you know. Now I'm all nervous!"

Sara laughed. "Well, you can join the club then." Her eyes softened. "We'll figure it out together, Will. Don't worry about it."

Alex bent down to the bag and pulled out a mask, turning it over in his hands as he inspected it. "This is a fairly standard-issue full-face mask with comms. I can hook it up no problem."

Will turned to him. "Oh, cool. You've used these things before?"

Jack rolled his eyes. "Jeez, Will. I already told you he was a SEAL."

Will shrugged at Jack. "Doesn't mean he's used one." Turning to Alex, he asked, "But I take it you have?"

Alex's face held the carefully bland expression that meant he was trying not to laugh. "A time or two. Communicating on ops is kind of important."

"Good deal," Will said, tossing the equipment back into the bag. Alex replaced his mask more carefully.

Hope swept her gaze around the small assemblage. "Is there anything else we need?"

Sara looked at Jack, who shook his head. "I don't think so."

"We'll have to dispense with the tradition of bride and groom getting ready separately, since there's only one room," Hope continued. "Sara and I can change in the bathroom, while you guys get ready out here."

"What exactly do you mean by 'get ready'?" Alex asked, brushing a hand down his shirt. "We're all pretty much ready right now. You already approved our wardrobe, remember?"

Hope inclined her heat to her sister. "I'll defer that decision to the bride."

Sara evaluated Jack, wanting to eat him up. "You look great to me, unless you want to change."

"Yeah, I think I do." Jack hurried over to the closet and pulled out a dark-red collared shirt. "I'd like to wear something a little dressier. Is this ok?"

"Perfect. We can snack on the rest of our room-service breakfast as we get ready."

"You guys gonna eat somewhere after?" Robert asked.

Sara and Jack shared a blank look, then Jack grinned. "How about lunch at Amalie?"

"An underwater wedding followed by lunch at my new favorite restaurant. I can't think of a more perfect afternoon."

HALF AN HOUR LATER, Sara and Hope stood inside the bathroom. Sara had changed into her pink floor-length dress, and Hope wore a more form-fitting soft-blue one. Sara braided her hair into a long tail as Hope gathered hers into a bun at the nape of her neck.

"Are you sure you're ok without the fancy hair and make-up?" Hope asked.

"Completely. I love that our wedding is different. I do hair and makeup all day long, so this is more fun."

Hope grasped her hand and squeezed. "You and Jack are a fantastic couple."

"Thank you. He's the best thing that's ever happened to me. We made this decision quickly, but it's been coming for a while now. I can't live without him, so we might as well make it official."

Her eyes filled with tears again, and Hope embraced her. "Isn't it incredible how completely our lives have changed because you entered me in that lottery?"

Sara gave a laugh that was part sob. When she pulled back, tears were in Hope's eyes too. "You were shut down and avoiding life. I was avoiding it too, by refusing to take anything seriously. Who knew what a game changer Half Moon Bay would turn out to be?"

"And it's still changing. Half Moon Aqua will be open soon."

Sara narrowed her eyes. "Stop that—we already settled this argument! The spa has to be separate from the resort."

"Fine. You can call it Aqua. But it will always be Half Moon Aqua to me."

Sara gave her a soft smile. "Regardless of the name on the building, I think there's room for both our versions. That's why we're such a good team."

"But it's not just us Collins girls versus the world anymore, is it?"

"No. We're surrounded by family now. Whether they share our blood or not."

Hope nodded and grasped Sara's upper arms. "Let's get you married, little sister."

JUST AFTER 2 P.M., they stood on the wooden dock of Seascapes, completed scuba kits in front of them. Except for Hope, who had made a last-minute restroom break.

Will wore a white polo shirt and pressed khaki pants, and Sara couldn't help but smile at the change in his manner. The casual jokester was gone. He was now somber and slightly nervous. "I've performed a few weddings, but they were traditional and by-the-book. Did you two have any specific vows or words you'd like me to say?"

Jack looked at Sara, who shook her head. "What you picked out is fine with us, Will."

He had shown her and Jack the vows he had chosen, asking for their approval. They were simple, yet unique and beautiful —she wasn't worried about Will. And after she read one particular sentence, Jack's surprise stop became even more perfect.

"Ok." Will looked around the group. "We'll descend and swim until we find a decent spot to settle."

"It's mostly sand here," Jack said. "I've taught quite a bit in this area, so we shouldn't need to go far."

Alex frowned at the cluster of buildings at the head of the dock. "If Hope doesn't get back soon, we might need to send you after her, Sara."

Sara grinned. "She didn't get a nervous stomach before her own wedding. I don't see why she'd have problems before mine."

"She's taking forever."

Just then, Hope turned the corner of the dive shop and trotted toward them, carrying something in her arms. Huffing, she stopped in front of them, and a wave of tropical scent wafted from her. "Sorry that took so long. I had trouble deciding." She unwrapped a covering of white paper to reveal two tropical-flower bouquets, handing Sara the larger one. "*Now* we're ready."

Sara got misty again. "You really thought of everything."

Alex smiled and kissed the top of Hope's head. "Just because this was planned quickly doesn't mean we can't do it right. And no one can get things done like my wife." He turned to Robert. "You ready?"

Unlike the other five, Robert was dressed in a shorty-style wetsuit. He nodded, pointing to a large camera encased in clear plastic. "Everyone just ignore me down there. I'll swim around tryin' to get the best angles. I plan to shoot both video and stills."

Alex patted the front pocket of his shorts. "I've got both rings here."

Will grinned, and his usual expression came back in a flash. "All right. Let's kit up and have a wedding then!"

Chapter Twenty-Two

THE SEAFLOOR WAS a series of ripples in the white sand, and the assemblage settled in twenty feet of water, the clear blue sky above providing an abundance of light. The full-face mask was a strange experience for Sara. It was cumbersome and covered her entire face. The mouthpiece contained both an intercom and an integrated second-stage regulator, making both breathing and speaking possible.

Jack grasped Sara's arm and helped her to her knees, settling to her right. She took a deep breath, easing the butterflies in her stomach.

"Doing ok?" His voice was clearer than she had expected.

Sara nodded at him, then remembered she could speak. "Yes. This is so strange! Too bad you're not recording voice, Robert."

"Who says I'm not?" Robert laughed as he swam in front of them wearing yellow fins and holding the large camera in front as he recorded.

"Really?" Hope asked.

"Yeah. I was able to wirelessly connect the audio to my camera. I'll just edit out all the chit-chat later."

They settled in a loose semicircle. Alex helped Hope to settle before quickly finning to Jack's right and easing to the sand with one knee down and one foot in front, flat on the sand. Hope fussed with Sara's dress, fanning it out around her knees before situating herself similarly. The flower bouquets were beautiful underwater. Sara had thought they'd be ruined, but they appeared completely unaffected by their submersion. Both bouquets were a mixture of colorful tropical flowers, with Sara's the larger of the two.

Last to descend, Will slowly drifted to the sand on his knees, then promptly tipped sideways, waving his arms. "Whoa, doggies!"

Sara burst into laughter, nerves escaping as a giggle.

Alex apparently didn't find it funny and frowned at him. "You've still got air in your BCD."

Will righted himself, sand rising in a dense cloud around him as he fumbled with his deflator button. "Oh, you're right. That will make things easier."

"Uh, guys," Robert said.

"What?" Jack asked, his voice tighter than usual.

"Will kicked up a bunch of sand. I can't see anyone, so you need to move."

A sigh sounded out of the speakers, immediately followed by Alex's voice. "He's right. Let's move six meters to the left. Over."

Hope giggled, breaking the tension. "Roger that, Commander. Sure it shouldn't be seven meters?"

Alex laughed. "Sorry. Been a while since I've worn one of these. Old habit."

"Let's try again," Will said. "Sorry about that."

Twenty feet away, the group resettled in the same formation, but the snafu had released Sara's nerves. Will took more care this time, Alex watching him carefully.

Will took a deep breath, and the ocean surface rippled twenty feet over his head. "Shall we begin?"

Jack and Sara nodded in unison, her heart filling with emotion.

Will's eyes sobered, and a new gravity emanated from him. "This group of dear friends and family is gathered to celebrate the joining of Sara and Jack. Since this is a somewhat... impromptu ceremony, you may repeat your vows after me. Please join hands."

Sara gave her bouquet to Hope, then faced Jack, joining both hands to his. They were warmer than the water surrounding them, immediately grounding her. Confidence filled her, absolute certainty over what they were about to do. She gazed into Jack's enormous brown eyes. Enclosed within the mask, he should have looked ridiculous, but the seriousness of the occasion pushed any such thoughts out of Sara's mind.

He was still her Jack.

"Can I have the rings?" Will asked.

Alex had been holding them in one hand and transferred them to the minister's palm. The two white-gold circles drifted slowly down in the water until Will closed his hand over them. Will handed her ring to Jack, who let go of Sara's right hand to slide the wedding band onto her left ring finger, snugging it against the engagement ring.

Their eyes never wavered as Jack said his vows to her. He swept a thumb over the back of her hand, and she gave him a squeeze back, her breast filling as he said his vows, emotion surging within her.

Then it was her turn.

She took Jack's ring from Will, and it fit his finger perfectly. "Jack, I give you all of my love from this day forward, and all the days ahead. I assure you that you will never walk alone.

"Your love is my anchor, and your trust is my strength. I

wish for my heart to be your shelter and the comfort of my arms to be your home.

"The ring I'm about to wear has no beginning or end, and neither does my love for you.

"Today I give you all that I am and all that I shall become."

Still holding hands, they turned their heads toward Will, whose eyes showed his smile. "By the power vested in me by the United States, I now pronounce you husband and wife." Then his eyes crinkled, the grin clear in them as the usual Will came roaring back. "These masks are pretty cumbersome. Why don't we all surface and get them off so Jack and Sara can seal this deal with a kiss?"

A round of laughter greeted this as all five people pushed off the bottom and rose, Robert swimming in rising circles around them as he filmed. Once on the surface, they all inflated their BCDs and tore off their masks.

Jack wore the same goofy, face-splitting smile that had to be on Sara's own face. At the same time, they swam toward each other, flinging their arms around the other's neck as their lips came together. Jack's mouth was warm and soft. Cheers and applause sounded around them as their kiss continued.

Finally, Sara laughed against Jack's mouth and felt his smile in return. They broke apart, both laughing hard when they saw Robert right next to them with the camera in front of his face. Hope floated next to Alex, both her hands clasped on his shoulder. Both wore broad smiles.

"Ladies and gentlemen!" Will called loudly, his voice echoing across the water. "May I present Sara and Jack Powell!"

Sara and Jack both beamed. Applause rippled over them from shore, where a group of curious people stood.

Will's grin was back. "Now let's get some beer!"

THE WEDDING PARTY filed into Amalie Grill, sitting around a large rectangular table on the patio. Triangular shades hung overhead, making the area cool and comfortable. Robert sat next to Jack on one side while Hope and Alex sat across. Will flopped down next to Alex. Everyone had changed into dry clothing, Sara wearing one of her favorites: a red, tie-dyed sundress. A server came to take their order, a young local woman with closely cropped black hair.

"Bring two pitchers of beer!" Will exclaimed. "We're celebrating a wedding here!"

Sara nodded demurely when the server asked who the happy couple was. Then she announced a regal, "You're welcome," to everyone when the woman announced their drinks would be on the house.

After they placed their food orders, Sara pointed a stern finger at her sister. "No speeches, promise?"

Hope shrugged. "You didn't exactly give me time to come up with anything, so I can live with that."

Alex raised his beer. "And I can definitely live with that. To the bride and groom!"

As far as Sara was concerned, the reception was perfect. Casual, just the people she loved most. Robert stayed on photographer duty, getting up several times to take pictures.

"How's the IDC going?" Alex asked Jack halfway through the meal.

"Good. You were right—there's a lot to it. But Scott makes sure everyone learns what they need to know."

"My man Jack will be at the head of the class, I'm sure." Will said, lifting his bottle. "And we have two diving certifications to celebrate. I'm going through a divemaster course now. Almost finished."

A mask came over Alex's face. "Really? Congrats—there's a lot to learn in that course too."

"It hasn't been so bad." Will shrugged, then a smile transformed his long face. "But I've heard Jack's had all kinds of surprises thrown at him."

Jack laughed, shaking his head. "And I'm sure more are coming during the examinations next week."

"Count on it," Alex said.

Jack stared at the former SEAL. "I imagine you went through a few unexpected situations during your training."

A tiny smile raised the corners of Alex's mouth. "A few."

Alex had an inherent reluctance to talk about his SEAL days, but Jack leaned forward, his expression rapt. "I'd really like to know."

"Me too," Will said.

Alex took a drink of beer. "Probably the most... instructive one was when I was almost done with BUD/S—that's the class you've probably heard about, SEAL selection. I was with a group of three other guys, and it was the last day of Hell Week. I was beat—we hadn't been allowed any sleep the previous night and had been in physical drills for almost twenty-four hours. The weather was brutal, with high winds and rain.

"We were in about sixty feet of water off Coronado Beach. I was team leader and the four of us had to do this super complex search and recovery pattern. The visibility was total crap. We were kneeling on the bottom—" Alex stopped to laugh. "—not so different from today, actually. Well, that part. Anyway, I was writing the pattern on my slate when the instructor snuck up behind me and used his knife to sever my air hose. Then he wrapped his arm around my neck and put me in a choke hold. He was behind me, so I couldn't get a hold on him."

All of them stared at him. Sara couldn't even imagine. "What did you do?"

Alex grinned, leaning back in his chair and crossing his arms. "Since he was choking me, I pretended to go unconscious.

Then, when he finally loosened his hold, I rammed my elbow into his throat, ripped off his mask, and punched him several times in the face."

"How did you breathe during this?" Hope asked, a deep line between her brows.

"I didn't. I couldn't. By the time I broke his nose and blood was running through the water, I needed to breathe. But there were other instructors in the water who were watching how I responded, and if I could handle the situation without help. So I made an emergency ascent to the surface, and that was the end of it. That was when I knew I was going to be a SEAL."

Jack, along with everyone else, gaped at him. Alex looked back at him and shrugged. "Don't worry. You won't have to face anything like that."

Sara straightened. "Good God. I certainly hope not!"

"I became friends with the instructor who jumped me, and I helped with BUD/S classes later in my career."

Hope had been staring at him, the line between her brows even deeper. Now she shook herself and took a long drink of beer.

"I can imagine your IDC was a piece of cake," Jack said, barking a laugh.

Alex looked back evenly. "No, it wasn't. Sure, I didn't have any issues with the diving, but people are very unpredictable. That's something recreational dive instructors have to deal with much more than the military. I knew my Teammates, inside and out. But each student is a mystery. You'll learn exactly what you need to, Jack."

Will stared at Alex like he'd never seen him before. Then he whipped his head back and forth. "Ok, then. I'm super glad I went to seminary school and not in the military."

Sara grinned and tossed an arm around Jack's shoulder, pulling him toward her. "So are we, Will."

A round of laughter went around the table, and Alex raised his bottle. "No speeches, but here's a toast to the new Mr. and Mrs. Powell!"

As SARA ATE, her gaze kept returning to her left hand and the sudden weight on it. Her rings hadn't been noticeable in the water.

But she felt them now.

Not weighing her down—grounding her to what was important.

She and Jack kept touching under the table, pressing knees together and stroking hands down thighs. By the time they finished their meals, Sara was shifting in her seat.

I'm ready for the party to end—time to be alone with my husband!

She froze as that final word ran through her head. And the new reality of it. She could hardly keep the smile off her face.

Hope pulled out her phone and started typing. "There's a flight back to St. Croix leaving at 5:00. That gives us enough time to get to the airport."

Robert nodded. "Works for me."

"You want me to give you guys a ride to the airport?" Will asked. "Your suitcase is already in my car."

"Perfect!" Hope said, a smile lighting up her face. When she turned to Sara, it faded. "Alex and I know how much you two want to be alone—we've been there." Her eyes became glassy as she stood and came around the table. "Thank you for allowing us to be a part of this."

Sara rose to embrace her, and both started crying. "Without you, we wouldn't be here."

Hope pulled back and wiped her face. "No, this is all you

and Jack. You two worked hard for this and didn't give up when you went through a difficult patch. Look at you now."

"Thanks, Hope," Jack said, embracing her.

Alex came around and pulled Sara into a hug.

"Oof!" she said. "You're as cuddly as a tree trunk."

He laughed. "I need to work out to keep up with your sister. Congrats, Sara."

"Thank you," she said, squeezing her arms around him.

Then he turned to embrace Jack. "Don't think this wedding stuff gets you off the hook from passing your IDC. I'm expecting a fully trained instructor in a couple of weeks."

Jack shook his head. "I'm not going to lie—It's gonna be a switch to go back to concentrating on diving after this." Then he gave Sara a small, private smile. "But now I have even more reason to look forward to getting home."

Will held his arms out to Sara, who entered them with a grin. "I'll say goodbye too, since leaving you two alone was part of the deal. But I have a feeling we'll be seeing a lot of each other."

Chapter Twenty-Three

SARA'S HAND was warm and solid inside Jack's as they walked toward the hotel. Above them, a vault of stars arced across the sky, and the faded sunset left a broad orange stripe on the horizon. A smile was fixed on his face as he ran through the day, and how Sara never ceased to surprise him. In the best possible ways. But his thoughts were now turning toward the coming night, and his smile took on an anticipatory cast.

They passed a nighttime craft market where a nearby stall had colorful woven blankets displayed for sale. Jack stopped cold as an idea flashed into his head.

The perfect idea.

He grinned at Sara, then turned to the shopkeeper. "How much for your blankets?"

"Twenty dollars each," the man replied.

Jack withdrew two twenty-dollar-bills from his wallet. "Great. We'll take two."

As the man handed him a canvas bag containing the two blankets, Sara smiled at him, her brow lined. They continued walking. "What are the blankets for?"

Jack looked up, and a soft breeze caressed his face. "It's

beautiful out, and I've got a better idea than spending our wedding night in a hotel. What do you say?"

"I say yes, of course."

"Perfect. Let's head back to the hotel to shower off the salt water. Then we'll grab a taxi."

IT WAS FULLY DARK when the taxi let them out at the side of the road. After showering, they had dressed in T-shirts and shorts, both wearing sport sandals. Jack carefully picked his way down a faint trail with Sara just behind. He turned on the flashlight on his phone to give them some illumination on the steep path. He grinned, remembering his last trek through the bush on St. Croix.

At least I have my flashlight this time. And in a much better mood.

He set a slow pace as the trail zigzagged down the sharp hillside. Twisting an ankle would not be romantic tonight. Holding a low-hanging branch aside, he made sure Sara passed under it safely before continuing.

"Jack, you've formed a habit of leading me through wild jungle trails. You didn't mention anything about expeditions."

"I know—sorry. The trail is steep, but it's worth it. I promise." The path finally opened onto a tiny crescent of sand. A nearly full moon hung before them, casting a pale, shimmering stripe over the rippling ocean.

"Kick off your shoes, and let's wade into the water," he said, setting the blanket-filled bag next to his sandals.

The newlyweds waded knee-deep into the warm water, which was nearly the same temperature as the air around them. They stood near one open end of an expansive horseshoe. Across the water, lights from houses twinkled all over the hillside.

Sara's head turned as she took in the nighttime scene, and she gasped. "This is magical!"

Jack came up behind her and slid his arms around her waist, pulling her back against him. "I've never been here at night. This is Magens Bay." He pointed to their left. "Over there is the main beach, considered the best one on St. Thomas. But we're on a special beach not many people know about."

Sara turned around in his arms, the moonlight reflecting in her eyes. "Oh? Another private beach?"

"Maybe not quite as private as ours, but we won't be bothered." He lowered his lips to hers, giving her a soft, fluttery kiss. He was already throbbing. "Which is good, because I don't plan on sleeping much tonight."

Sara pulled his head down, moaning as she kissed him deeply, circling her tongue around his. He slipped a hand under her shirt and slid it under her bra, cupping one large, delicious breast, and kissed her back harder.

Eventually, they pulled apart, both breathing hard. A slow smile spread across Jack's face. "Let's go back to the beach."

Returning to their sandals and the canvas bag, he picked them up and walked along the tree line. The moon provided ample light now that their eyes had fully adjusted. After twenty feet, he came across a recess in the vegetation. "Here we go."

Jack pulled one blanket out of the bag and spread it over the sand. Their alcove was slightly larger than the blanket, and dark trees arched overhead, giving them plenty of privacy. Taking both Sara's hands in his, he guided her down with him onto the soft surface.

They faced each other, each leaning on one hand. Sara stroked a finger down his beard. "What a great idea. I can't think of a better way to spend our wedding night."

"I thought it was appropriate to spend it on a beach."

He moved toward her, barely touching his lips to hers, then

sucked her lower lip into his mouth. Feeling her smile, he raised a hand to open the clip holding her hair. It tumbled loose, still wet, as a rich tropical scent exploded into the night. Breaking the kiss, Jack brought a handful of her hair to his nose, inhaling deeply. "God, I love the smell of your hair."

"Good, because my shampoo and conditioner cost a fortune."

He smiled and watched as he drew the thick strands across his fingers, wet and silky against his skin. "And not just the smell of it. It's so soft, so beautiful." He met her eyes. "Just like you."

Moving back, he kissed her again—hard this time, plunging his tongue deeply as his arousal ratcheted up. Sitting upright, he pulled her shirt off and unhooked her bra. Her full breasts were luminous in the moonlight. Pressing her down onto her back, Jack ripped off his own shirt before lowering himself, drawing one breast into his mouth. Her skin was hot and tasted slightly salty. Using both hands, he squeezed as he circled his tongue on its peak. Sara arched her back beneath him.

She traced her hand to the bulge in his shorts, then gripped, and he pressed back against her firm touch. Quickly drawing down the zipper, Sara slid one hand underneath. Jack moaned as she grasped him, moving her hand up and down in a slow, steady rhythm exactly how he liked it.

"Oh God, darlin'. That feels amazing."

Withdrawing her hand, she tugged on his shorts as she whispered, "I want you now. I *need* you now. Hurry, Jack."

They tore off the rest of their clothes and stretched out on the blanket, pressing their warm, naked bodies together. Jack traced his hand up her thigh and she opened her legs, drawing his hand between them. She did want him badly.

Jack kissed his way down her chin and over her neck. Goosebumps rose under his tongue, and she gave a long, soft groan, pressing hard against his hand. He darted his head to one breast, nipping and sucking it. When he resumed his movement down her body, kissing her navel, she grabbed both shoulders, halting his progress.

"Not now. I need *you*. Make love to me, Jack."

Quickly, he crawled up her body, pressing his cheek to hers as he positioned himself between her legs. With one deep, glorious thrust, he entered her, whispering in her ear, "Make love to me, Sara."

She enveloped him, encasing him in her warmth. The sensation was almost overpowering. They watched each other as they moved together, their lips inches apart and the air alive between them. Jack thrust deeper and she arched again, crying out softly.

Sara grasped both his shoulders and pushed, moving him onto his back as she rolled on top. They were still entwined as she took over the rhythm, going faster now.

He pulled her head toward his, kissing her deeply as he cupped her ass with both hands. Both of them were panting. Sliding his hand between them, he circled with his thumb, and a shudder ran through her body. He smiled against her mouth.

Getting closer now, he pushed harder, driving himself as deep as possible. Sara met him and gave back with equal measure. Finally, Jack broke the kiss to bury his head in her neck, trying to stifle a scream as they rode the wave together.

His Sara. The woman he'd wanted his whole life. The woman he'd almost lost but was now his forever.

His wife.

THE BIRDS WOKE HER. The sounds of morning songbirds filled the dawn air as Sara snuggled closer to Jack, warm and cozy under the second blanket they had pulled over the top of them.

The movement brought a twinge of soreness between her legs, making her smile.

Jack had been correct. They hadn't gotten much sleep.

A small blue and green bird landed on a shrubby branch above them. It looked down and chittered loudly.

"If I had a rock, I'd throw it at that damn thing," Jack muttered, drawing Sara tighter.

She laughed. "That's not nice. We're the ones invading its home."

"Not invading. Just visiting."

Sara breathed a long sigh. "Visiting. Ugh. Getting married definitely didn't solve one problem."

"What's that?"

"I came here because I missed you. Now how am I supposed to go back and wait again?"

Jack's chest shook as he laughed. "Yeah, I know. But we're over the hump now. In less than two weeks, I'll be home, and we can start our new life together."

"But for now, it's back to normal life. I fly home today, and you need to study for your exams." She frowned. "What if I kill George between now and when you get back?"

"It'll be all right. We're married now, so we get conjugal visits while you're in jail."

She dug her elbow into his ribs, and he broke into laughter. Sara raised onto an elbow. "Jerk."

Still grinning, Jack drew a finger down the side of her face. "Just call if you need me. We'll make it work."

"I know we will. We always do." She placed her hand over his, holding it against her face. "I loved every moment of yesterday. It was the best day of my life."

Jack's face stilled. "Mine too. But you know what? I have the feeling it was only the first of many best days for us."

Chapter Twenty-Four

APRIL...

Six champagne flutes clinked above the table at Marimba. Though the last of the day's light was fading, the sand was still warm under Sara's feet as she slipped them from her sandals.

"To Sara and Jack!" Hope called out, and they all drank. "I'm so sorry it took almost two weeks to organize this GNO, but trying to get this group together is like herding cats!" Hope gave Sara a quick hug.

"Don't worry about it. Best of all, Jack will be home the day after tomorrow!" Sara smiled as she panned her eyes around the table. Everyone was there. Heather had come straight from Ember, while she, Hope, and Selena had all carpooled. Cindy and April were already seated when they had arrived. Cindy now sported braided hair extensions, and the braids framing her face were a brilliant purple.

I have to get the name of her stylist!

But not tonight. Sara took a sip of champagne. "We sure

celebrate a lot here. We probably drink most of their champagne."

She had talked at length about her and Jack's improvised wedding with Selena and Heather. But she hadn't seen April or Cindy since the big event.

April waggled her fingers in front of Sara's face. "Come on! Let's see it."

Sara managed a demure smile as she placed her left hand in April's.

"Ooh, very nice!" Cindy said, peering closely. "I still can't believe you made that happen so fast."

"We had some help, but I managed to keep from letting Hope take over the whole thing."

Sara's sister dropped her head in both hands. "I'm sorry. I got a little carried away."

April inspected Sara's rings. "I really like this. It's different without being too flashy."

"Jack knows me well. His band is part of the same set." Sara studied April, who'd been more of a regular at Hibiscus lately. She'd given the divemaster darker highlights and a slightly shorter, blunt cut. "How are things with Brian?"

April's face lit up like the fourth of July. "Fabulous! We're going away for a long weekend to St. John and staying at a little B&B."

"I highly recommend weekend getaways around here," Sara said with a grin.

Cindy poked April in the shoulder. "Maybe you'll be the next to get married."

April's eyes got huge as she choked on her champagne. "Yikes! That's the last thing I'm thinking about. Though I'm not getting any younger either."

"Oh, please," Heather said. "How old are you?"

"Thirty-one."

"You've got plenty of time," the redhead said.

"Speaking of relationships..." Sara drawled, and everyone groaned. "What! We need updates, Heather! Are any wedding bells ringing for you and Robert?"

Hope buried her face in her hands again. "Sara, must you do this?"

She arched a brow at Hope. "Oh, that's rich, coming from you. You're the one who turned all dictator over my wedding." Then she turned back to Heather, who was a lovely shade of pomegranate.

"We've talked about marriage. But... marrying me is a complicated situation, guys." Heather twisted her flute in a circle on the table, then raised her eyes again and shrugged.

"You're talking about your family's money," April said.

Heather nodded. "We haven't discussed it outright, but Robert is a smart man. I'm sure he knows my father will insist on a prenup."

"Do you think that will be a problem?" Hope asked.

"I sure hope not." She exhaled forcefully. "But we're not at that point yet. We're just broaching the subject."

Cindy raised her glass. "Which means I'll have my roommate for a while longer."

"Absolutely." Smiling, Heather turned to Sara. "I have news for you! Your first royalty deposit should hit your account on Friday."

"Really?" Sara's stomach gave a fluttery little thump.

Hope tossed an arm over her shoulder and pulled their heads together. "My sister, the wunderkind. Freshly married *and* a professional artist."

More applause sounded around the table, and Sara did a little seated bow. "Now only if I could get Aqua finished and opened."

"We're getting there," Hope said.

"What's the latest?" Cindy asked.

"As of today, the feature wall is just about finished, and the floors are in all throughout the facility," Sara said.

Heather stared at her. "They're *still* laying stacked stone?"

Sara laughed. "No, that's done. If that wasn't installed by now, I'm not sure the crew would still be alive. Now they're attaching wooden shelves to the wall to hold potted plants."

"After that, we just need the inspector to issue the final permits, and we're open!" Hope said.

Sara breathed a deep sigh. "I can hardly believe the project is almost finished. After all the construction problems, at least the final permit should be a straightforward process."

JACK SMILED as a large midnight parrotfish swam lazily past him, then bit into a sponge, the crunch loud in the water. Its navy-blue and brilliant turquoise color shimmered as bright sunshine lit the seascape. Back kicking to slow his progress, Jack hovered motionless, just enjoying the sight as the three-foot-long fish ignored him, intent on its sponge. He was enjoying one final dive with Will before flying home the following day.

Well, mostly enjoying.

Jack was now a fully licensed dive instructor. His exam over two full days had been one of the most exhausting, mentally draining, and rewarding experiences of his life. He'd *earned* this title. Over the previous week, he had taught several classes, including two open water and three Nitrox courses. He couldn't wait to return to Half Moon Bay and get back to work, now fully confident in his capabilities.

If only I was as confident in Will.

Jack's brother appeared at his side, eyes wide at seeing the giant parrot fish. But he was coming in too fast and couldn't stop. Will reached out a finger, touching the coral to stop his forward progress, and startled the dark-blue fish. It darted over the coral hummock and disappeared. Will got himself back in control, then gave Jack an ok signal with both hands, his eyes still round. He craned his head, looking for any sign of the fish, which was now long gone.

Jack couldn't help flashing a smile in return. *At least he's enthusiastic.*

LATER, the two men sat at Amalie Grill, enjoying their last meal together. Jack's happiness and pride at his accomplishment was dampened by what he needed to say to Will before leaving.

"Gonna miss you," Will said. "At least we're close enough to visit now."

"I'll miss you too. Thanks again for the wedding. You did a great job."

Will grinned after swallowing his mouthful of French fries. "It went pretty well, considering there was exactly zero preparation. You sure you guys don't mind Robert sending me some stills and video?"

"Nah. Both of us are fine with it."

"I can use them to advertise my professional services. I'm on the schedule to lead dives every day for the next week." He frowned. "But I have to admit, the job is more daunting than I thought it would be. I got lost on a dive on Thursday. But I found my way back, and I don't think any of the divers noticed."

Jack heaved a deep sigh. He wasn't going to get a better opening than this. "How many dives do you have now?"

"I'm over sixty. Way over the requirement of forty, I'll have you know."

Jack pushed his plate away and stared evenly at his brother.

"Will, you're not ready to be a divemaster yet. You need a lot more experience."

Will surprised him by not immediately denying the point. "My boss says I'll learn as I go."

"And what if one of your divers runs out of air the next time you get lost? Will, your buoyancy sucks—you move around like a damn spaz down there."

"So you're saying I should just give up? Dammit, Jack. I think I just found out my purpose—a job where I can work outdoors, be with people, and be a pastor."

Jack held up a hand. "I'm not saying that at all." An idea had been niggling at him since the underwater wedding, and it was now or never. "I'm saying you need to be mentored before you lead dives alone. You have the training and the knowledge—now you need to get the experience and skills. And confidence."

Will watched him closely and cocked his head. "What are you saying, Jack?"

"How would you feel about working at Half Moon Bay?"

A crooked grin rose on Will's face. "Big brother's going to take me under his wing?"

Jack shook his head. "I've got my hands full. And I'm not experienced enough to mentor a new divemaster. But I know someone who is."

Will's lined forehead smoothed out. "Wait, are you talking about Alex? After that story he told over lunch, I don't want to get mentored by that guy, Jack. No way."

Jack laughed. "Yeah, that little anecdote surprised me too. But I had to prod him to tell the story—he doesn't flaunt his past. Most of the time, Alex is so relaxed you'd never know he used to be a SEAL. As long as you don't piss him off, anyway. You'll never find anyone better to learn under, Will."

His brother shrugged, picking at the label on his beer bottle. "Have you talked to him about this?"

"No, but I can after I get back."

Will met Jack's eyes. "What's in it for him?"

"He likes to teach, for one thing. And we need more dive-masters. If you impress him, I'd say you're virtually guaranteed a job there, since he personally trained you." Then Jack grinned. "And if you want to officiate underwater weddings, I can't imagine a better place to work than Half Moon Bay Resort. Do you have a contract with the shop you're with?"

Will shook his head. "They want me to work there, but I'm under no obligation to stay. I'm starting to think you were right about them putting me through the divemaster course in the hope I wouldn't realize how shitty the working conditions are. They aren't too concerned about how good their staff is."

"That's not uncommon. The first shop I worked for was similar."

Will tapped the side of his bottle absently before meeting Jack's eyes. "If I came to St. Croix, would the pay be decent?"

Jack shrugged. "It's very good for divemasters—if you get hired. Half Moon Bay pays more to get better staff. Frankly, I think you'd be lucky to get mentored by Alex for minimum wage."

"Then how am I going to afford a place to live?"

"You can crash with us until you get it figured out."

Will broke into his usual sunny smile. "Living with the two newlyweds? What would your wife think of that?"

"I haven't talked to her about it yet. But she likes you. I don't think she'll mind." Jack mentally crossed his fingers that his last statement was true, then straightened and pointed a finger at Will. "As long as it's temporary. Only until you get on your feet, ok?"

Will laughed. "All right. Ask Alex and see what he says. Just remember, if he breaks my nose, I'll be bleeding all over *your* house."

Chapter Twenty-Five

SARA TOSSED another log onto the fire, and a cascade of sparks rose into the night, briefly lighting up the ocean before her and Jack. Leaning back on the couch in front of their firepit, she eased into the hollow of his shoulder and placed her hand over his heart, feeling its calm, steady beat through his shirt. "This maybe isn't as romantic as our night at Magens Bay, but I daresay it's more comfortable."

Under her ear, Jack's chest shook with laughter. "And it ends in our room. You have no idea how much I've missed sleeping in my own bed."

Sara kissed his neck. "You have no idea how much I've missed you being in it."

"It's great to be home again."

"Sorry you had a list of chores to greet you."

He grinned. "At least that wasn't the only thing to greet me."

Sara had arranged to be off work, so she was there when Jack arrived in the afternoon. He'd briefly frowned at the bucket in the middle of the living room floor, but she'd distracted him with a kiss. Then further distracted him with the rest of herself.

After a leisurely couple of hours in the bedroom, he had climbed onto the roof to investigate the problem.

When he came back inside, she retrieved a beer for him. "Did you find the leak?"

"No, but I wasn't really expecting to. Water gets in the tiniest cracks. Next time it rains, I'll have a better idea. But I wouldn't be surprised if the entire roof needs replacing. Not that Calvin will do anything about it."

"I know the place has its problems, but I can't imagine living anywhere else now."

Jack sighed. "I know. It just feels like all we're doing is lining Calvin's pockets."

Point out the positive, Sara! "At least you got a decrease in rent."

He snorted, then took a long pull. "If he expects me to re-shingle the entire roof, we're renegotiating."

"I only saw the one leak, so hopefully it's not bad."

Jack stared at the brown wooden boards lining the ceiling. "We'll see."

Now, the fire popped again, bringing her back to the present and the request Jack had made earlier. "You're confident Alex will take Will on?"

"No, I'm not confident at all. But the resort is going to need more help, and Alex is smart enough to realize that. Robert's not working at Half Moon Bay much, and April works more at her other job. I wouldn't be surprised if Alex puts Zach through a divemaster course, but he won't be ready for a while. I really think Will just needs a month or so of solid, daily diving with instruction and he'll be great."

"You're a good brother."

He stroked one hand over her hair, twirling the locks around his finger, and she closed her eyes, enjoying the soft tug.

"I'm more interested in being a good husband. You sure you don't mind him staying with us for a while?"

Sara smiled, opening her eyes again. "I admit I wasn't expecting a new roommate as soon as I finally got you back. But yes, he can stay with us—for a while. I enjoy being around him. You think Will and Alex will get along? They're about as different as two men can get."

"I sure hope so. Will needs someone to help him, and he gets along great with people. Though he doesn't do real well with authority figures. That's when he tends to rebel, like with our dad when he quit the pastor stuff."

Sara burst into laughter. "Oh, they should get along famously then, since Alex isn't the commanding type."

Jack winced. "Yeah, I know. There could be some fireworks. I just hope Will listens to him. If he tries to get under Alex's skin, this could be a disaster."

"Do you think he would do that? I mean, Alex would be helping him. It would be pretty rude to be an ass and just throw it in Alex's face."

"I'm sure my brother will be on his best behavior. At first. But after he gets settled in... who knows?"

Sara took his hand, tracing her fingers over the back. "In other news, we're throwing the water switch at Aqua tomorrow. You want to be there to see it?"

Jack grinned. "The water switch?"

"That's what we've been calling it. The pumps and piping are finally complete, and George is ready to turn on the water features for the entire spa. He's tested them all separately, but this will be the big reveal."

"You want me there so I can restrain you if necessary?"

"An insurance policy never hurts. But each part has passed all its tests, so it *should* work." Sara ignored the lurch in her stomach. "I'll arrange the show for noon so it's between the two dive trips."

"I'll be there."

* * *

THE NEXT MORNING, Jack walked down the pier, amazed that everything at the resort looked the same, yet his life was completely different from the last time he'd walked these same steps. A grin lit his face as Alex and Tommy loaded *Surface Interval* with tanks for the morning trip. "Man, I never thought I'd miss looking at your ugly faces, yet here I am."

Tommy strolled over to shake his hand, his trademark smile cracking his face. "Congratulations. On both counts."

"Thanks."

Jack turned to Alex and laughed. "I just dropped off my big duffel in the gear room. What the hell happened? It looks like something exploded in there."

Alex raised his sunglasses onto his head, lifting a brow. "Well, that's because we're a *little* tight on space around here. I have plans to rectify that situation, but they depend on your dear wife opening her fancy new spa so we can use the second floor."

Jack laughed. "Touché. But we might get some news on that today. Sara invited me to see the completed water features at Aqua, and I'm sure she wouldn't mind you two coming along too. She's planning it in between dive trips."

"Can't," Tommy said. "I need to work on the engine."

"I'll pass too," said Alex as he slid two tanks into their white plastic holders. "Hope has kept me up to date on the progress, and I've got to get the class schedule ironed out. I'll probably have an advanced class for you tomorrow."

"Sweet!" Jack's heart leapt just at the prospect. But that

reminded him of the other subject he needed to bring up. He and Alex left the boat to retrieve the next round of gear.

"Scott had great things to say about you," Alex said, shuffling through the crowded gear room to grab some regulators. "Said he'd hire you himself."

Warmth spread through Jack's chest. "That's good to hear. You picked a great class. I feel confident about everything I was taught."

"That's the idea."

Jack took a deep breath as he folded a wetsuit over one arm. "I just wish I was as confident about Will."

Alex grinned. "I thought he did a good job with the ceremony. Once he figured out how to descend, that is."

"Yeah, that's the part that worries me. He got his divemaster license, and he's nowhere ready to lead dives."

They left the room and Alex was silent for a long moment before saying, "They passed him, huh? He talked with me about it during lunch. I could tell he was excited. And during the dive, I could see he had a long way to go."

Jack stopped on the pier and faced Alex. "I need to ask you a favor. It's a big one."

Alex arched both brows.

"Would you mentor Will? I think he'd make a great divemaster with some more experience. But he needs someone to work with him one on one."

"Why not you?"

"A lot of reasons. For one thing, I doubt he'd listen to his big brother. Something tells me it would be different with you."

Alex cracked a small smile.

"And I want him to learn from the best."

Alex laughed out loud at that. "Buttering me up pretty good, aren't you?"

As they began walking again, Jack said, "Maybe a little, but

I'm serious. I'm not qualified to mentor a divemaster—I know that. And Half Moon Bay could use another one."

"Yeah, I know. How many dives does he have?"

Jack tried not to wince. "Around sixty."

Alex snorted, watching the horizon. "Know how many Zach has now?" He looked at Jack. "Over three hundred. And I just recently thought he was ready to take rescue diver. Hope took the course with him while you were in St. Thomas."

"I'm sure Hope would like the idea of having someone on staff who can perform underwater weddings."

Alex's smile lingered. "She already has two. Though neither Tommy nor I want that job, so you've got a point there." He sighed. "All right. I can't pay him much, but I'll give him a chance. Where's he planning on living, anyway?"

"He'll be staying with Sara and I for a while."

The former SEAL threw back his head and laughed. "And she's ok with this?"

"Yes," Jack said, trying not to sound defensive. "They get along really well."

Alex stepped aboard, still laughing. "Well, sounds like Will's got some balls, and I like that. He's gonna get an earful of me during the day, then Sara after work. Your brother is a glutton for punishment, Jack."

AFTER A QUICK LUNCH in the restaurant kitchen, Jack and Sara made their way to Aqua. The sun beat down out of a cloudless sky, making Jack grateful for the protection of his long-sleeved rash guard. Sara wore a sleeveless sundress, but she was always liberal with sunscreen.

They stepped from the sand onto the brick patio. Jack opened the smoked-glass door, following Sara into the large open room. The ceiling, made of light-brown wood, soared above them.

The expanse was a pristine, stunning white—the floor was seamless white tile, only broken by the flattened river rock of the winding channel running through the lobby. Immediately to their right was an aquamarine glass counter with matching tables placed in front. Sara nodded at it. "That's the smoothie bar, and we'll have sandwiches and salads for sale also. We'll have both indoor and outdoor seating."

Jack nodded and turned to face the far wall. He hadn't been inside Aqua in months, and his eye was naturally drawn to the huge feature wall. They continued, stepping over a wooden bridge that matched the ceiling. Then they stood in front of the check-in counter—twenty feet of the same light-blue glass as the smoothie bar. It almost glowed against the dark stacked-stone wall. Random placements of light and dark gray stone gave the wall a remarkably homogeneous appearance.

Shelves made of the same wood as the bridges and ceiling were spaced over the wall, and each held a potted plant in a large white ceramic planter. Snake plants, ferns, and others Jack couldn't name gave life to the undeniable focal point of the lobby.

George stood in front of the wall with several other men in fluorescent yellow construction vests. He looked up at their approach. Jack kept a straight face when the big man swallowed hard at the sight of Sara. "Here for the big show?"

"We are," Sara said. "Jack hasn't seen Aqua in a while, and today was perfect to get caught up."

"What do you think?" George asked.

"It's beautiful. Exactly the way I pictured it when Sara first described her idea." Jack nodded at the wall. "As long as that works, anyway."

"It'll work," George said. "I've tested it every way to

Sunday." He turned to Sara. "You want to throw the master switch?"

"Yes!"

She almost vibrated as she rushed around the empty basin at the base of the stacked stone monolith, opening a hidden panel in the white wall next to it. A large green button was inside, which lit up when she pressed it. She hurried back to Jack's side and the room became silent as everyone lifted their eyes to the top of the wall.

"I don't hear anything," Jack murmured.

"The whole pumping system is nearly silent, so that's a good thing," George said.

Movement appeared at the top layer of stone. A delighted smile rose to Jack's face as water slowly trickled down the entire face of the wall, slowly increasing in volume as the pumps warmed up. Within seconds, the wall was alive with water, gently cascading downward and emitting a soothing whispering sound. The water passed through a narrow gap between the stone and the wooden shelves with their plants, finally collecting in the rectangular pool below. It quickly filled.

With his eyes, Jack followed the meandering channel to where it met the pool, but there was a solid white barrier between the two. "How does the river get filled?"

"It's automatic," George said. "Once the pool gets three-quarters full, the panel in the canal will open and it will start filling. Once everything reaches equilibrium, the water recirculates back up to the top of the wall."

Sara ambled away, following the channel. She re-crossed the bridge to the edge of the salon and looked over what would be her primary domain.

George edged closer to Jack and grinned. "She bring you along for protection in case things went sideways again?"

Jack stared evenly back. "I'm here for your protection, not hers."

He had to work to keep from laughing when George's smile disappeared. The project manager darted a wide-eyed glance at Sara. "It'll work."

"I sure hope so."

As Jack completed the sentence, a *shush* sounded from the front of the canal and the panel slid back. Water ran into the channel, gently trickling as it washed over the flattened river rock lining the small river. Jack followed Sara into the salon. They crossed over two bridges until the channel ended at the end of the room in a small pool, ferns arching over it.

"This is where we had the big flood, but it's holding this time." Sara was bright-eyed, and Jack couldn't keep the smile off his face as he watched her. She grabbed his hand. "Come on! Let's head to the other side."

They returned to the lobby, hurrying through it and past the cluster of men still studying the feature wall. The other wing of Aqua contained the same opening as the salon, leading to the massage area. They followed the small river as it slowly filled. Treatment rooms with closed dark-gray doors lined each side of the wide hallway, tall potted palms and bamboo plants adding to the tranquil scene. After traversing several more wooden bridges, they stopped at the end of the hallway.

A larger pool, also lined with river rock, filled the area on this side and butted up against the white wall. More greenery surrounded the far side.

"I'm going to put goldfish in here," Sara said. "I wanted koi, but the pool isn't big enough for them."

"Maybe the one under the wall is."

Sara nodded, her face lit from within. "It is. I'm planning on having several good-sized ones in there." She glanced back down and clapped her hands. "It's all holding! This was the final test, Jack!"

She threw her arms around his neck and kissed him. Jack laughed, then kissed her thoroughly back.

"Let's head back to the lobby." Sara took his hand and led him back. The large room was mostly bare except for the two aquamarine glass counters.

"This is awfully bare. Are you putting furniture in here besides the tables for the café?"

Sara nodded. "There will be two seating areas where clients can wait for their treatments. We'll have gray couches and chairs to match the stone, with wooden tables to match the bridges and ceiling. Everything coordinates!"

George leaned over the pool in front of the big wall, poking and prodding with his finger.

"Everything going as planned?" Sara asked.

The supervisor broke into a wide smile. "Exactly as planned. You can set up the final inspections with the county. They won't care about the furniture. I'll be here to go through it with you."

Sara's face became even brighter. "Finally!" Then her smile faltered. "You're not expecting trouble with the permit, are you?"

"No. You never can tell with these guys, but we've done everything by the book. He shouldn't find any deficiencies."

"I'll call today."

Jack glanced at his watch and led Sara back to the door on the beach side. "I'd better get back to work." He cupped her face and gave her a soft kiss. "I am so proud of you. You persevered and now it's paying off."

She glanced at the space around them, grinned, and bounced on her feet. "Thanks. I'm so excited!"

Jack laughed. "You'd never tell by looking at you. See you tonight."

As he walked back to the pier, a soft breeze caused a light chop on the ocean. The northern bungalows were modern, yet elegant, with their newly finished outdoor, Bali-style showers. The wooden structures stood in the bright sunshine, the pier reaching out to sea behind them. Jack took in the beautiful scene, then nearly staggered as an incredible sense of gratitude overcame him.

I'm a dive instructor, Sara's dream is coming true, we're married, *and now Will's going to move here. She and I didn't have the easiest road to get here, but look at us now!*

Regaining his footing, Jack let a smile crack his face as he climbed onto the pier, ready for the afternoon's adventures.

Chapter Twenty-Six

A WEEK LATER, dappled morning sunshine filtered through the canopy of trees as Sara drove her RAV4 down the Half Moon Bay access road, tapping her fingers on the wheel. Instead of heading to the sand parking lot of the resort, she turned right onto a newly paved lane running behind and parallel to the row of rainforest bungalows. A thick strip of vegetation screened the bungalows from view, and the lane ended in an asphalt parking lot.

Exiting her car, the pungent smell of fresh tar met her nose. The official front entrance of Aqua lay in front of her. The smoked glass here was smaller than the beach side, just two entry doors. Above the doors, the four letters of the spa's name were spelled out in a large block font. They were made from the same turquoise-colored glass as the counters inside, contrasting vividly against the white building. The letters were anchored to a smaller stacked stone wall behind them. This feature also had a waterfall spilling down it, though it was currently turned off.

With a gleeful smile, Sara unlocked the front door and entered the silent building, eager to complete the final major task. She slid through the area between the check-in counter and the large pool at the base of the rock wall. Reaching the main control panel, she turned everything on, including the sign out front. It was 8:55 a.m., and she ran an eye over the lobby, ensuring nothing was out of place.

Five minutes to spare, and George should be here any moment.

She returned to the check-in desk and ran a hand over the cool, smooth blue glass, delighting in the feel of it. Her phone rang and she dug it out of her purse, frowning when the supervisor's name flashed on her screen.

"Hi, Sara," George said. "I'm sorry, but I can't meet the inspector with you this morning. I've got an injured worker on another job, and I'm on my way to the scene now."

The irritation that had risen at his first sentence disappeared at the second. "Oh, I hope it's not serious!"

"I'm not sure yet. Listen, the inspector assigned to your job is Mr. Janssen. He's a stickler for doing things by the book, but we shouldn't have any problems. Just give me a call if you run into any issues. I gotta run now."

George hung up and Sara stared at her dark phone, a line forming between her brows. "Why do I feel like he was trying to warn me?"

The front door opened, and she didn't have time to ponder the mystery further. A middle-aged bald man in a tan tweed suit and red bowtie crept into the building. He held a leather satchel in both hands and darted his eyes all over the room before finally locating Sara behind the counter. He moved toward her, moving with diffident steps, still craning his neck around the room. Sara was only 5'3", but the man couldn't have been more than an inch taller.

Finally, he focused on her. "Hello, are you Ms. Sara Collins? The manager?" The man spoke with a European accent and had close-set, beady eyes and large protuberant ears.

His wispy light hair was styled in a truly unfortunate comb-over that had Sara itching for her clippers to rectify the situation.

"Yes, manager and part owner, though it's Sara Powell now." Delight rolled through her just saying the words. "Are you the building inspector?"

His eyes had been darting around yet again, but he jerked them back to her and bowed slightly. "Yes. Henrik Janssen, at your service. Powell, you say? I wasn't informed of the change." He shook his head, correcting the entry on a clipboard he carried, muttering under his breath. Then the small man dug into his satchel and handed her a business card. He moved to the end of the counter, bending down and staring closely at it.

"Yes, I was recently married."

Mr. Janssen ignored this, instead studying the glass counter. Sara stared at the business card, now confused. His name was listed, but the rest didn't make sense. "Colonial Insurance Company?"

Janssen whipped upright, then scowled as he rummaged through his satchel on the counter. "No, no!" After producing another card of a different color, he hurried over to her. "I have two professions, you see," he said, still frowning as he handed over the second card. It read *St. Croix County Code Inspection and Enforcement,* reassuring her he wasn't lost. He was a truly bewildering man. He'd looked frightened when first entering, but now was fussily irritated.

Janssen turned around in a slow circle, craning his head all over. Sara just stared at him. Finally, he met her eyes once again. "Will anyone else be joining us this morning?"

"No, my construction project manager was called away on an emergency. Is there someone you're looking for?"

Janssen jerked. "Not at all, not at all. Shall we begin?" He removed a clipboard with several pages of text attached, each page full of multiple rows of checkboxes and blank lines for notes.

"Of course. This is the main lobby of the spa..."

An hour later, Sara was ready to throttle Janssen, and George's vague offer to call if she needed help made more sense. The small man found fault with *everything*. It had started with the potted plants on the feature wall.

Mr. Janssen had frowned direfully at them. "I'm not sure water splashing on those pots is proper."

Sara stared at them. *What is he talking about?* "There's a tiny bit of water on the back of the pots, but it isn't even visible from the front. Is that against code somehow?"

The man tut-tutted and wrote on his clipboard. "I'll have to check the regulations when I return to the office. Let us move on for now."

Then he hadn't liked the width of the channel and potential danger if someone fell in.

"Well, that's why we have bridges," Sara said, using her best fake professional voice. "And the channel is only two feet deep, just in case."

He scowled at the canal. "Still... highly irregular. I really can't say if this is a code infraction or not... yet another item to investigate." He scribbled on his clipboard.

The final straw had come when they stood in the massage wing hallway. Mr. Janssen bent over to peer at an outlet, then hurried down the hall to peer at the next. Removing a tape measure from his pocket, he dragged the tape between them. Then the small man repeated the process with the next two outlets, scribbling some more.

Dotting his final entry with a flourish of his pen, Janssen stopped before Sara. "I suggest you call your contractor. This won't do at all. The St. Croix County building code clearly states there must be six feet between GFCI outlets in commercial buildings with nearby water features. These measured an average of 5.97 feet. Most irregular. It won't do at all, Mrs. Powell."

Without waiting for a response, he marched back toward the lobby.

Panic fluttered through Sara's entire body as she hurried to catch him. "Wait! What are you saying?"

Mr. Janssen stopped at the check-in counter and slid his clipboard into the satchel before zipping it closed. "I'll have my primary findings to you by the end of the week. You will need to call your project manager immediately to inform him of the deficient GFCI outlets. They must be rectified before proceeding any further. That is the most pressing failing, among the many others we discussed. Good day, Mrs. Powell."

After a small bow, he turned and walked out the door.

Sara stood motionless—and speechless. She stared at the door as her breath steadily spooled upward, like a plane preparing for takeoff. Grinding her teeth, she stalked to her purse still sitting on the counter, dug out her phone, and stabbed her finger on the screen to place the call.

George sounded tired when he answered. "What's up, Sara?"

She took a deep breath, trying to keep her voice even. "The inspection didn't go so well, George. And I'm not very happy right now."

A deep sigh came through the phone, and Sara remembered the emergency. A pang of chagrin rolled through her. "How is your worker?"

"He'll be all right. He fell off a ladder but didn't hurt himself too bad. What did Janssen say, exactly?"

Sara couldn't keep her voice from rising, and it echoed

around the silent lobby. "He said pretty much the whole project is screwed up! The GIF outlets are too close together or something."

There was a pause. "Do you mean GFCI?"

She slammed her hand on the counter, then flapped it back and forth to ease the sting. "I don't know! I'm not the contractor, am I?"

George groaned. "We put those in exactly to code—every six feet."

She paced back and forth behind the counter. "He got out his measuring tape and said they were 5.96 or something like that."

Another, longer pause. Then, "He wants a bribe, Sara."

She froze. "What?"

"Everything on this project is to code. Every single item. Of course there's going to be slight variance, but that's allowable." George sighed heavily. "Janssen can be like this. He has short-man syndrome and likes to throw his weight around—such as it is. Usually it's big, brawny guys he likes to mess with, and I thought things might go better without me there. Maybe he was in a bad mood or something. But the bottom line is you need to bribe him, or you won't get your permit."

Righteous indignation flooded through every cell of Sara's body, making her so angry she could hardly speak. She resumed her pacing, stomping loudly. "I'm not paying him off!"

"You will if you want a spa."

Motes danced in front of her eyes, which probably wasn't a good sign. She took a deep breath. "Are you serious right now?"

"Sara, it's how things get done down here. Not all the time, but some officials expect to be... uh, tipped."

"No way. I'm not bribing that officious little prick. I'll figure something else out." Then she sighed, getting a hold on her anger. "Thanks, George. I'm glad your guy is going to be ok."

Sara hung up the phone and glanced around the lobby, the only noise the gentle sound of trickling water. Tears filled her eyes. "No!" She blinked rapidly, fighting them back. "There's got to be another option."

After scooping her purse up and locking the front door behind her, Sara made the grim march toward the resort lobby. She stomped up the steps, making front-desk clerk Martine look up, wide-eyed, when she entered. Recognizing Sara, she dropped her shoulders, but her caramel-colored brow was still lined. "You ok, Sara?"

"I'm not sure yet. About to find out though."

Sara moved to the office behind the front desk. Patti and Hope were both behind their desks. She entered and shut the door before leaning back against it. "I am officially at the end of my rope, guys. This is it. You can't see the rope, but I'm holding it in my hands right now. It's ugly, frayed, and smells bad."

Patti and Hope shared an alarmed glance before Hope spoke in a calm, soothing voice. "Was there a problem with the inspection?"

"You could say that. The guy found fault with just about everything in the building. After he left, I called George and laid into him. I'm still trying to process what he said."

"What was that, child?" Patti asked in the same tone Hope had used.

Sara stared between the two women. "George thinks the inspector wants a bribe. A *bribe*. I've already hired most of the Aqua staff! We can't afford any more delays. Can you believe this?"

Patti sighed and rested her head in one palm. "Yes, unfortunately. I'm surprised we haven't run into it more with all the construction that's happened."

Sara was floored. "Really?"

Hope shrugged. "As a general rule—especially in one very

specific instance—I won't play along. But sometimes you have to get things done. We paid a *processing fee* to get the lumber so the last of the southern bungalows would be finished on time."

Sara glowered, straightening from the door. "I am not giving that little..."—she glanced at Patti—"jerk a bribe! Can't we report him or something?"

"Then it will only take longer to get your permits," Patti said, then turned to Hope. "I don't like the process either, but with the spa already so far behind schedule, maybe we should pay him off."

Sara crossed her arms. "Now that I think about it, I'm pretty sure George is right. The inspector didn't bring up any major infractions, just tons of minor, meaningless things. In fact, he made the biggest stink over some outlets being a tiny bit off. It makes no sense."

"And if George somehow got those corrected, the man would likely find something else," Hope said, twirling a pen in her hands. "He has the power and wants to flaunt it."

Sara flopped against the door again, tapping the back of her head against it. "Ok, I see your point. I'm not happy about it, but I'll call Mr. Janssen tomorrow and see if I can pay an additional fee to *expedite* the permit."

Hope dropped the pen, becoming completely still except for her mouth hinging open. She closed it with an audible snap of teeth as her gaze narrowed on Sara. "Wait a minute. Did you say his name was Mr. *Janssen?*"

Chapter Twenty-Seven

BLOOD RUSHED to Hope's face, and her lean, attractive face morphed into a visage of tight anger. Sara blinked at the change but answered readily enough. "Yes."

Hope's low, husky voice took on a strained tone. "Was he short, bald, and looked like he should be living under a bridge?"

Sara blinked for a moment. "Now that you mention it, that's a very good analogy."

Hope's breath exploded out, and one hand balled into a fist. "Janssen is my insurance troll! Why is he doing building inspections? We've never run into him during the construction on the bungalows."

Sara raced a hand to her front pocket and pulled out the business cards. "He gave me the first card by mistake and said he worked two jobs." She handed the card to Hope. "Here—Colonial Insurance Company."

Hope yanked open her top desk drawer and riffled through a pile of business cards. Stopping, she pulled one out and set it next to Sara's. They were identical.

She raised her head to Sara, who asked, "Your insurance

troll... is he the guy whose office you camped out in when the boat sank?"

Hope slowly nodded her head as Patti broke into loud laughter. "Oh my! Now there's a coincidence." Then she shrugged. "Though it is a small island, isn't it? Lots of people work multiple jobs."

Hope drummed the fingers of her right hand on the desk. "This changes everything."

"Why?" Sara asked.

Hope gaped at her. "Why? Because he's a malignant little troll!"

Now Sara joined Patti in laughter. "You don't want to bribe him anymore?"

A slow smile rose to Hope's face, and it wasn't pleasant. "Oh no. This calls for a different plan of action. When I mentioned the one major exception to the bribery rule? We're talking about him. When do you get his report?"

"He said he'd have it to me by the end of the day."

Hope snorted but only said, "Since he's expecting money, he likely *will* get it done as soon as he can. When you get the report, wait a couple of days, then call him back. Tell him George fixed all the deficiencies and you want him to come back for a reinspection. Leave my name out of it, though. When he returns, we'll face him together."

Sara frowned. "So he can find something else to pick apart?"

"That won't happen. I assure you, this second visit will go completely differently."

SARA RETURNED to Hibiscus to work for the rest of the morning, letting the familiar motions ease her worried mind. By the time she finished with her final morning client, *Surface*

Interval was tied up at the dock, and her mood was much better. As she descended the stairs, she shaded her hand against the sunny glare, but the boat was empty. Entering the dive shop, Sara nodded to Zach, who was assembling a display rack. She proceeded into the classroom, where Jack's and Alex's voices could be heard.

Alex sat on the front table, facing Jack, who reclined in his chair with one leg tossed over the end of the table in front of him. "To start," Alex said. "I'll give him one task every day to focus on, starting with buoyancy drills. Three dives every day—I want him in the water as much as possible."

Sara leaned against the doorway. "Sounds like you got your update on Will's arrival, hon."

Jack turned to her, breaking into a smile. "He'll be here in a few days."

She moved her gaze back to Alex. "Planning on breaking out the rubber duckie?" Alex had used the prop to reassure her during her scuba class, and it had made a huge difference, relaxing her immensely.

Alex grinned. "If I have to, but I don't plan on putting him in the pool. I want to make sure he can handle himself in open water." He turned back to Jack. "And that couple who wants the open water class will be here a few days after Will."

Jack nodded. "I look forward to certifying them. My first full certification at Half Moon Bay!" He narrowed one eye at Alex. "You said they're returning guests. Sure they're not going to be disappointed you're not teaching them?"

"I didn't specify it would be me. I'm sure they'll be fine."

"They'll be lucky to have you as their instructor," Sara said to Jack, giving him a slow wink.

Jack grinned, then held up a hand. "Enough about diving. How was the inspection? Is Aqua ready to go now?"

Sara felt like all her bones drained out her feet. It was a tremendous effort just to stand up. Jack immediately vaulted to his feet and took her into his arms. "That doesn't look good."

She leaned her head against his shoulder. "I'm so glad you're home."

"What was the issue?" Alex asked. "The delays have been a nightmare, but the quality of construction has been excellent. At least that's what Hope told me."

Sara turned around in Jack's arms and nodded, bones restiffening. "The problem isn't a what, it's a who."

Alex twitched the corner of his mouth. "The inspector?"

"Yes. He wants a bribe. Sounds like you're familiar with him."

Alex straightened. "I doubt it. I don't know any building inspectors."

"He also has another job. Hope went through the roof when I told her what happened. She calls him her insurance troll."

A strange look crossed Alex's face, like he didn't know whether to flinch or laugh. Laughter eventually won. "I thought we'd heard the last of that guy. Guess not."

"Wait a minute," Jack said, squeezing her shoulders. "He expects to be bribed?"

Sara couldn't help laughing. "Yes. Both Hope and Patti were leaning toward doing just that until Hope put the pieces together about who he was. I thought steam was going to come out her ears. I'm going to call him back, and Hope and I will face him together."

Alex's smile softened. "Hope really put the fear of God into him when the boat sank. Then he was meek as a lamb after the hurricane, signing off on everything right away. Since he was dealing with you this morning, maybe he thought Aqua wasn't affiliated with the resort, and he was safe from her."

Sara paused as a thought occurred to her. "You know, you might be right about that. When he first arrived, he acted scared to death, and actually asked if anyone else would be joining us. I think he meant Hope!"

Alex's grin got bigger. "I almost feel sorry for him."

Jack tightened his hold on Sara. "Wait a minute. Should we be letting them face this guy alone? He's obviously sketchy as hell."

Sara scowled. "We're not some fainting, corset-wearing debutantes, you know!"

Even before Sara's answer, Alex had started laughing again. "Jack, you've never been on the receiving end of a double-barrel blast of Collins sisters, have you?"

"Uh, no."

"Trust me, we don't want to be anywhere near the place. And this guy isn't dangerous, just full of himself." Still smiling, Alex shook his head. "But I'd sure love to be a fly on the wall for this conversation."

FIVE DAYS LATER, Sara stood alone inside the lobby of Aqua once again. Mr. Janssen, dressed in a different rumpled tweed suit, and with a blue bowtie this time, arrived and removed his clipboard from the satchel. She and Hope had come up with a plan, and Sara actually looked forward to it.

Janssen attached blank report sheets, frowning at them. "I very much doubt your contractor could have corrected so many deficiencies in such a short amount of time. Perhaps it would be a better use of our time if he could call me and discuss how to rectify the situation."

"I can assure you this project is completely within code.

Though I'm sure a stylist like myself couldn't possibly understand something as complicated as building codes."

He gave her a long side-eye, but tucked his clipboard under one arm. "Let's proceed to the hallway with the outlets. If they aren't precisely six feet apart, we are both wasting our time here."

So cranky today! You really want your money, don't you?

Janssen marched to the massage half of Aqua and once again measured the distance between the two outlets. Sara followed at a leisurely pace. After letting his tape measure snap closed, he harrumphed and turned toward Sara, who stood a few feet away with a bland, pleasant smile on her face. "Mrs..." He glanced at his clipboard. "Powell. There has been no change here! I am most upset, and really must insist that you have your contractor contact me directly. I'm afraid you don't understand the situation at all."

Sara hardened her expression, stepping nose-to-nose with the small man.

You little shit!

She kept a firm grip on her temper, but let her steel show. "Oh, I understand perfectly. Far better than you do, Mr. Janssen. But I think you're about to get caught up."

He took two steps back, his mouth forming a snarl. Then his face instantly changed to slack-jawed shock.

Hope breezed into the room. Dressed in a tailored gray power suit and wearing three-inch pumps, she looked just like she had when gracing the cover of *Entrepreneur Today* magazine. "I'm terribly sorry I was delayed! Mr. Janssen, it's *so* lovely to see you again." Breaking into a wide, sunny smile, Hope marched up to him and stopped mere inches away. She grabbed his limp hand and pumped it several times. Hope wasn't particularly tall, but in the high heels, she was a good four inches taller than Janssen.

Sara could barely keep a straight face. Janssen's eyes were bulging and a fine sheen of sweat dotted his forehead. He stood frozen, his eyes widened in horror as he stared up at the woman in front of him.

"I'm sure there has been a misunderstanding here, so I wanted to come down personally. I explained to my sister Sara —you do know she's my sister, right?—that we could straighten out this confusion right away. I can't believe you came all the way out here and I didn't even know about it! It's been too long since we've had a chance to catch up."

Janssen blinked several times, then recovered somewhat. "Very nice to see you again, Ms. Collins."

"Oh, it's Mrs. Monroe now. You remember my husband, Alex? He's the one who knocked out that thug during a mugging we were involved in. But I don't think he needs to be involved here, do you?"

Janssen had become even paler, stammering, "N-no. But building code violations are an extremely serious issue, Mrs... Monroe."

"We agree one hundred percent," Sara said, moving to stand at Hope's side. She spoke in a firm, even tone, opposite to Hope's jocular approach. "Which is why I have been involved in this project every step of the way, verifying that every phase was constructed to the highest standards."

Janssen drew himself upright. "Nonetheless, I cannot approve the final permit simply because you wish me to! That would be highly irregular, and I have more important things to do than stand in this hallway with you two." He tried to move around them, but both sisters stepped sideways in unison, blocking him again.

"Oh!" Hope said, clasping her hands together as she gave him a pleasant smile. "I take it you'd prefer to continue this conversation in your office, like we did on our initial visit?

Which office would you prefer? I'm rather partial to your insurance office, as you know."

Janssen gasped and stepped back again.

"Do you still have that lovely painting of dogs playing poker on your wall?"

Sara almost laughed when Hope turned to her, acting her part perfectly. "You would love it, Sara. The colors are so vibrant!" Then she turned back to the horrified Mr. Janssen. "My sister is the most amazing artist. Wait—I know! She can bring her easel and supplies and join us. That way she can paint while you and I have another nice, long visit. Sara's a professional artist, you know. She might even sell you the painting!"

Janssen's head whipped back and forth between the two women. "This is... absurd!"

"Oh, dogs playing poker!" Sara exclaimed, now matching Hope's tone. "I'd love to do my own spin on that. I'm a rather slow painter, but Hope tells me you two can while away hours together, so I'm sure I'll fit right in!"

"You will *not* invade my office, madam!"

Hope dropped the act, hardening her face as she stepped up to the inspector once more. "Then I suggest we take care of this right here and now. I'm sure you've got a laptop in your bag. Please enter your inspection findings again—correctly this time —and process the permit. You can email it to us right here, and we can be finished in minutes, Mr. Janssen. Or we can follow you back to your office. I've cleared my schedule. How's yours looking?"

She arched a brow.

"I've got all the time in the world too," Sara said, eyeing him intently.

Janssen's face was bright red, his lips pressed into a white gash, and Sara really wasn't sure how he was going to respond. She spun around, walking toward the lobby, and called back over her shoulder, "I'll get my painting supplies. It will only take a moment. Mr. Janssen, do you have room in your car for my easel, by any chance? And do you have a drop cloth? I'd hate to spill paints all over your floor."

"All right! All right!"

Sara stopped dead, then slowly turned around again. Hope still stood in a power pose in front of the man, her arms crossed and her feet spaced evenly apart.

Janssen glared at Hope, one hand clutching his clipboard and the other bunched into a fist at his side. She stared straight back, then said, "Shall we return to the lobby?"

Without a word, Janssen stepped around her and stalked back through the hall, his footsteps echoing around them. He eyed Sara narrowly as he passed. Hope waggled her eyebrows as she approached Sara, giving her a triumphant smile before returning to a somber, professional expression.

Sara looped her arm through Hope's elbow, and they followed the inspector silently.

Ten minutes later, Janssen hit *enter* on his laptop with more force than necessary. "There. Your permit has been emailed."

Hope pulled out her phone. "I've got it here. Sara?"

"Not yet." Sara refreshed her screen, but the permit still hadn't arrived.

"Really, ladies," Janssen said, his jaw tight. "Clearly you have it in your inbox, Mrs. Monroe. I think we're finished here."

"Not until my sister has it." Hope's voice was low and firm. "This is her project, not mine. You should have sent it to her first."

"She's right, Mr. Janssen," Sara said. "I'm in charge of this spa, and you should realize that by now."

"Fine. I'll send it again."

Janssen was attacking his keyboard with furious fingers when Sara's phone dinged. "Oh, look at that. Got it!"

He froze again, fingers curled in mid-air.

"Does it look ok?" Hope asked without taking her eyes off Janssen, who had a large sweat stain under the collar of his shirt.

How the hell should I know?

But Sara dutifully scrolled through the attachment, which looked like every other incomprehensible government document she'd ever seen. But at the bottom was a red electronic sticker reading *Approved*. "Yes, the permit looks fine." Elation rolled through her at the words, and Hope returned to the happy, glad-to-see you face she had started with.

Janssen slid his laptop back into the satchel and nodded stiffly. "The official paper copy will be mailed within thirty days. I must see to my next appointment."

"Thank you for stopping by," Hope said warmly. "I'm so glad we could get this straightened out. We hardly had a chance to catch up! Maybe next time."

"I'll bring my easel!" Sara said with a jaunty wave.

Janssen zipped up his bag and glared at Hope. "I doubt there will be a next time. Perhaps a different inspector would suit your needs better. Good day, ladies." He spun around, slamming the door open so hard it rebounded off the wall before whisking to a close.

"Good thing the door has a soft-close mechanism, or that little bastard would be paying for a new door," Sara said.

Hope shook her head and leaned against the counter, grinning.

Sara stared at Janssen's rapidly retreating form. "Thank God that's over. Was it that hard to get the approval when your boat sank?"

Hope finally laughed, slapping her hands on her tailored skirt. "This was much easier. He gave in much quicker than I thought. Last time it took me *hours* to wear him down, and I fully expected to crash his office today. Maybe our Mr. Janssen is learning."

Sara moved to wrap Hope in a big hug, leaned into her strong, reassuring presence. "Big sister, you and I are a force to be reckoned with."

Hope patted Sara's back. "Oh yes. Malignant trolls all over the world better look out."

Chapter Twenty-Eight

JACK SAT on the back porch, his feet resting on the railing and crossed at the ankles. He wiggled one shoe, relieved the wooden railing didn't move.

At least that repair is holding.

Beside him, Will breathed a relaxed sigh and set his empty Leatherback bottle on the coffee table. The sight distracted Jack from his worry about the reinspection at Aqua. Not to mention his troublesome students. The sound of tires on gravel drifted back to them, letting Jack know one of his mysteries was about to be solved.

"You've got a great place to unwind at the end of the day, I'll say that," Will said.

"Like you need to unwind. You hardly did anything all day."

"I'm *learning*, remember? Your boss is a serious guy, but he knows his shit."

Jack hadn't been on the boat that day and was curious how Alex and Will had gotten along. "What was Day Two's major skill?"

Will scratched his head. "Trying not to use my BCD during

the dive. It was weird. I've never paid that much attention before, but your lungs have a big effect."

No shit, sherlock.

But he didn't want to discourage Will. "Using your lungs efficiently also stretches out your air supply."

Will rolled his head toward Jack. "Is it true that Alex conducts rescue clinics for staff every year? My shop on St. Thomas never did that."

Jack stared at him. "You do realize people can *die* scuba diving, right?"

"Yes, *Dad.* And I want to be prepared. I just think you can have fun with it and not be serious all the time."

"I like that Alex makes sure our skills are sharp. You're right though, not many shops do drills like that. And he isn't serious all the time."

Will snorted. "He is with me."

"Then maybe he has a reason."

"Whatever. He's a good teacher—I don't have to love the guy to learn from him."

Sara pushed through the back door and twirled around with her arms out, a giant smile plastered across her face. "You gentlemen are now looking at the manager of an officially licensed spa!"

Both men applauded and Will threw in a shrill whistle for good effect.

"You two talked him around, huh?" Jack asked.

"He didn't stand a chance against Hope and me combined," she said with a sly smile, and took a seat across from Jack. "Now I can get busy getting everything set up and plan the opening."

"When will that be?" Will asked.

"A few weeks. Since we've been delayed so much, I want to get going as fast as possible, so it won't be a huge gala like Ember's. We'll have a Grand Opening with some giveaways, discounted packages, and tours." Sara leaned her head back and closed her eyes. "I am so glad to have that over with!" After a long breath out, she raised her head and stared at Jack, as if sensing his mood. "How did it go with your students?"

Jack tried to smile, but it was forced. "Remember when I asked Alex if they'd mind that I was teaching instead of him?"

She nodded. "He said they wouldn't care."

"He was wrong."

The whole frustrating day rushed back. The couple wanted a condensed scuba course, which consisted of morning classrooms followed by afternoon pool sessions for two days, then two days in open water for the final test. Jack had taught open-water classes at Seascapes, so he had honed his routine. But he hadn't been prepared when he'd introduced himself that morning and the husband, a bull-necked, buzz-cutted specimen naturally named Butch, had thrust out his chin and asked, "Who the hell are you?"

Butch had made it clear he wanted to be taught by the ex-SEAL, not "some Joe Shmoe." His wife Gina was palpably nervous, wringing her hands together and wanting the support of an expert instructor. Jack had reassured them of his experience—without mentioning he was a new instructor—and they had proceeded with the day, though there had been plenty of grumbling from Butch.

"I'm not sure they're going to finish, to be honest," Jack said as he rolled a cold beer bottle over his forehead. "Maybe I should just turn them over to Alex."

"You can't," Will said. "He's on the boat the next few days."

Jack nodded, accepting the inevitable. "And he wouldn't undermine me anyway. I'll either succeed with them or I won't."

"They're idiots," Sara said.

Jack laughed. "I'll tell them you said that."

"You'll do fine." She leaned over and stroked a hand down

his arm, bringing him a sense of peace. They had been married over a month now, a fact that still amazed him.

"I'm sure you'll give them a better class than the place where I took my divemaster," Will added.

"I will if they'll let me, but I'm really frustrated."

Sara cocked her head. "You've already taught several classes since you returned. Why is this one so important?"

"Alex has been easing me into the schedule. So far, the classes I've taught have been to certified divers—continuing education. This couple is the first open water class I've taught here, to people who have never dived." He raked a hand over his head. "I just wanted to prove to Alex that I can do a good job."

WILL HAD his own room at the end of the hall, well separated from theirs. And he was sensitive to the fact that Jack and Sara were newlyweds, trying to give them plenty of space. Jack was glad his brother was there, but there was no denying the relief of being alone with Sara as they got ready for bed. Jack stripped off his shirt and threw it into the hamper, his mind still on his current class. "I feel like a failure."

Sara approached and gently clasped his face between her hands. "Why? If you're that concerned about it, talk to Alex. He could give you some ideas."

Jack sighed, leaning against the dresser. "That's what I'm trying to avoid. I need to figure this out myself. Butch and Gina are being evaluated by me all the time, sure. But I am too. By Alex."

Sara inclined her head. "I'm sure you're right about that. Alex is good at hiding his thoughts, but not much gets past him."

He took her in his arms, holding tight and drawing strength from her, like always. She never failed to rejuvenate him. "I need to make this work."

"You will. You're an amazing teacher."

She nestled closer into his chest, relaxing against him. He stroked her back as the afternoon replayed in his head for the thousandth time. Then Sara became heavy in his arms, her breath deepening.

Jack grinned, fully brought back to the present as he shook her gently. "You're falling asleep on your feet, darlin'. Let's get you to bed."

She yawned hugely. "Sorry, all the stress has caught up with me. I'm so tired I could sleep for a week."

They crawled into bed, Sara settling into his arms and falling asleep immediately. Jack tried to invite sleep in, listening to the deep regular rhythm of her breaths, but it didn't work. He was awake long into the night, trying to think of ways to engage Butch and Gina. And dreading meeting with them again.

THE NEXT AFTERNOON, Butch and Gina grinned at him as they all stood in the shallow end of the pool. "What on earth did you do?" Gina asked.

Jack laughed and shook his head, relieved his plan was paying off. Since the couple wanted assurances that he was experienced enough to teach them, Jack had decided to regale them with stories of when he'd divemastered at the diver-mill shop in St. Thomas. "I ran to the gear room and grabbed all the equipment I could find. The equipment these two had brought was forty years old at least, and belonged in a museum, not on a dive boat. It would have been a disaster if they'd tried to use it."

This story had been his third or fourth over the morning, and the tactic had broken the ice like he had hoped. "All right, let's get back to it. We'll submerge and remove our masks for a full minute."

Gina breathed out a nervous sigh and shook her hands out, then nodded. "You'll do fine," Jack said, his voice warm. "Just keep your eyes closed and relaxed. And *breathe.* I'll tap you on the shoulder when it's time to replace your mask."

She performed the skill excellently, her face unlined and calm as she breathed in long, easy lungfuls, and satisfaction rolled in a long wave through Jack. After Gina replaced her mask and grinned at him, he turned to Butch, who was staring at the side of the pool.

Jack rapped his tank to get Butch's attention, then indicated it was his turn. The large man proceeded to do the skill adequately, but his face was scrunched up as Jack counted the minute down. When he got to fifty-eight seconds, Butch replaced his mask of his own accord. This time Jack felt irritation rise instead of satisfaction.

Figures... this guy has to make an issue of it and do things his way.

Jack considered making Butch repeat the maneuver, but didn't want things to deteriorate when he'd finally begun to make progress with the couple.

An hour later, they finished their final pool session. "Tomorrow, you guys graduate to the big pool. We'll meet on the dock at 9:30 and you'll do many of the same skills, but this time in the open ocean."

"Good!" Butch said. "I'm tired of looking at the bottom of the pool." But at least he was smiling.

"The next two days will be the real deal, so get a good night's sleep."

THE PIER WAS SILENT, *Surface Interval* off on the morning trip, when the trio reassembled the following morning. Jack studied

Gina closely, but she watched fish milling about under the pier, excited at the prospect of joining them.

As soon as they descended, it became obvious Gina wasn't going to be the problem. When they settled on the sand in twenty feet of water, Butch was red-faced and chugging air like a train rolling down the tracks. Jack moved in and raised his brows, gesturing with an ok signal. Butch whipped his head back and forth, pushing off the sand as he bolted for the surface.

Oh boy, here we go.

Gina's brows were drawn together, and Jack signaled her to wait there. Then he headed for the surface, where Butch struggled to stay afloat.

"Add air to your BCD," Jack said calmly.

Butch fumbled for his inflator and added air, then calmed as soon as he floated easily.

"Better?"

The big man's face was still red. "Yeah. Thanks, I don't know what happened. The wetsuit just felt tight, and I couldn't get enough air."

"It's ok. You're in open water for the first time—that's a normal reaction. We'll descend again together. Keep your eyes on me, ok?"

This time, Butch made it to the bottom and settled successfully, breathing more calmly. Gina performed all the skills well, including the emergency procedures and towing her much larger husband. Jack was surprised at how much more difficulty Butch was having when he'd been fine in the pool. The mask flooding was scheduled for the following day, but Jack decided to do it both sessions, wanting to make sure Butch could do it confidently.

They floated on the surface when Jack explained this, and Gina frowned at him. "Do we have to remove our mask completely, like yesterday?"

"No, that's only in the pool. But you do need to flood it and clear the water out successfully."

Husband and wife looked at each other and shrugged. "Ok."

Once again, Jack was proud of how well Gina performed the skill. After her mask was clear again, she squinted her eyes and scrunched her face up, a common result of the stinging salt water. Butch was another story. It took him four tries before he could perform the skill successfully, bolting again for the surface the first time.

Jack gave him another pep talk and made him repeat the skill twice more. The final time, Butch cleared his mask, then smiled at Jack, pride showing through.

After they returned to the pier, Jack had the couple break down their kits, another course requirement. "Ok, I'll give you a choice for your final day. Would you rather stay here in the bay or go out on *Surface Interval?*"

Both were enthusiastic about their first boat dive. "Will we be with one of the main groups?" Gina asked.

"No," Jack replied. "We never mix students with certified divers. The three of us will be a separate group."

"Good," she replied with a laugh. "I'm not sure I'm ready to be one of the guys just yet."

As the pair walked up the pier, a faint sense of optimism rose in Jack. Then he frowned. "Don't get overconfident. Butch will probably be back to hating me by tomorrow."

Wondering what challenges open water would bring, Jack picked up a tank in each hand and headed for the gear room.

Chapter Twenty-Nine

THE NEXT MORNING, Jack was partway through the second dive when he held up his slate to Butch and Gina, smiling around his regulator.

Finished! You're officially certified divers.

He shook both their hands, and they returned the gesture enthusiastically. The final half of the dive would be a tour of the reef. At the beginning of the first dive, Butch had been uncomfortable again, red-faced and breathing hard, but Jack worked with him until the large man relaxed. Now he was a model new diver as he swam beside a ridge—slightly bumbling and clumsy with his equipment. But he used care as he swam along, careful not to make contact with the fragile reef.

Jack was damn proud of himself.

As they neared the boat, he caught sight of Alex's group and spotted Will immediately. He was perfectly horizontal in the water, arms in tight, and looked like a completely different diver than the clueless, lumbering mess from St. Thomas. He swam next to Alex in the lead but was absorbed with something in his cupped hands. The posture was odd, and Jack needed a moment to realize Will was concentrating on his compass as the group maneuvered back to the boat.

As Jack's pair ascended to do their safety stop, he watched Will swimming toward them. Soon Will diverged from Alex, who wasn't using a compass at all. Still laser-focused on the instrument, Will angled off from the group. Alex hurried over and tugged on his fin, beckoning him back.

Jack's stomach clenched. *He still can't figure out his compass?*

A divemaster who couldn't navigate wouldn't hold a job long.

Alex took Will's compass and their heads bent over it as they continued toward the boat. Eventually Will nodded and took the compass back.

His buoyancy is a thousand percent better. Maybe he just needs more time with the compass too.

Turning back to Butch and Gina, who were hovering nicely as they counted down their safety stop, Jack was ready to bask in his own victory.

Will would have to overcome his own challenges.

After *Surface Interval* returned to the resort, Jack accompanied Butch and Gina into the dive shop. He was surprised when Hope smiled at them from behind the counter.

"Zach off today?" he asked.

"Yes, he's a little under the weather and wanted to stay home. I'm filling in for him."

Hope gave Jack a long look and he nodded back. There was a flu bug going around the resort staff, which they had come to call *the plague*. The dive staff was particularly careful to stay isolated since a head cold could stop a dive guide in their tracks. Diving was impossible if you couldn't clear your ears.

Hope turned her attention to Butch and Gina. "How did it go today?"

"Fantastic!" Gina said. "We passed."

"Of course you did," Hope said with a delighted smile. "You couldn't lose with Jack as your instructor."

Jack grinned and turned to the couple. "I can sign you up for the morning trip tomorrow, and you can experience your first real dives. Both Alex and I are leading, so I can put you in his group. I know you were disappointed he couldn't teach your class."

Butch shook his head. "No, we'll stick with you. No reason to break up a great partnership now."

As Jack came around the counter and woke the computer to add them to his group, Hope gave him a pat on the lower back and winked at him. A happy warmth spread through his midsection. As an instructor, Jack would undoubtedly face other challenges, but he'd just learned another way to overcome them.

And figured it out for himself.

The pier was quiet when he stepped back outside. Will and Alex stood in the stern of the boat, and their posture brought Jack's feet to a screeching halt. Alex stood over Will, hands on his hips and his face hard. Jack was too far away to hear the conversation, but it obviously wasn't a pleasant one.

His first instinct as the older brother was to rush to Will's aid. His feet had already started moving when he brought them to a stop once again. He'd seen with his own eyes that his brother was learning, but still had a way to go.

Let them work it out. After all, that's what I asked for.

Alex took a step back, then stalked off the boat. He gave Jack a long look as he passed by toward the resort but didn't say anything.

With a long sigh, Jack stuck his hands in his pockets and

headed toward the boat, where Will was preparing for the afternoon trip.

"That didn't look like a fun conversation," Jack said.

Will glanced up, his face drawn. "Not particularly."

"I saw you on the second dive. You looked great in the water. Big improvement."

Will hesitated, then said, "Thanks. I have improved. Not that Mr. Perfect will acknowledge that."

"He hasn't given you any encouragement?"

Will sat on the side bench with a thump. "Yes, but everything has to be his way. I get no input whatsoever. I feel like an indentured servant."

His lips curving into a reluctant smile, Jack sat next to him. "You pretty much are. What was Alex getting on you about?"

"Navigation. I know how to use a compass—I just get turned around sometimes. He thinks I need to work one on one with him. I disagreed. It didn't go over well."

"Little bit of oil and water going on, huh?"

"You could say that. He's not giving me any credit for the training I already have. I told him I'm already a licensed divemaster." He turned to Jack, his normally calm eyes full of anger. "You want to know what he said back?"

I can hardly wait... "What?"

Will's face hardened. "'Wrong, Will. You're an open water diver with a piece of plastic that *says* you're a divemaster.'"

Jack thought Alex's observation was spot-on, but now wasn't the time to say so. "You admitted you need more time in the water, and I could see the difference since you've been here. I'm sure he could really help you with the compass."

"So what? The water's clear. I just need to memorize the landmarks, and I can find my way around just fine."

"What about at night?"

Will's jaw dropped open. "Uh, I didn't think of that."

Jack nodded. "At first, I used my compass a lot. Everything's different in the darkness."

Will rubbed his face. "Shit. All right, I'll sign up for Remedial Compass 101. Though if Alex acts like a dick, I might tackle him."

Jack burst into laughter. "Good idea! That worked so well when the other guy tried it."

Will laughed begrudgingly. "You know, I'm mostly doing this for you."

Jack clapped him on the back. "Yeah, I do. But I have to say —it wouldn't hurt to show a little appreciation to Alex. You can cop an attitude when you get defensive."

"I'm not kissing his ass."

"I'm not asking you to. Just try to work *with* him, instead of against him."

Will heaved a big sigh. "I never could resist those big brown eyes of yours. At least I got all the charm."

"So put some of it to use."

WHEN JACK WALKED into the restaurant kitchen, Alex sat at the employee table devouring a hamburger. Jack took another for himself and sat across from him. "I just talked to Will. He'll do a private compass session if you think he needs it."

Alex eyed him steadily as he swallowed, wiping his hands clean with his napkin. "He needs it. I can build his skills no problem. But I can't fix his attitude."

Jack sighed. "I know. He really wants this, but he can't help rebelling when someone puts their thumb down."

"Jack, I've been doing this a long time. The only type of diver I can't work with is one who thinks he already knows everything and won't listen. There's only one solution to that situation."

"What's that?"

"They have to learn the hard way. I've been trying to prevent that, but I don't think it's working."

"Will appreciates what you've done, even if he won't say so. I do too, and I'm sorry he's being such a giant pain in the ass."

Alex burst into laughter, leaning back in his chair. The change made Jack blink.

"On the pain-in-the-ass scale, Will barely even registers," Alex said, still smiling. "I spent almost twenty years with SEALs, remember? I was *much* higher on the scale myself. Will's a challenge, and that's good. But he's not a SEAL, and maybe I need to remember that. I'll lighten up on him a little."

His smile faded. "But I meant what I said. I think he might have a reality check coming. I just hope no one else gets caught in the crosshairs."

After finishing lunch, Jack returned to the pier and climbed the stairs up to the spa. When he entered, Sara and Selena were hovering in front of the computer screen. Sara typed on the keyboard. "There. Everyone's rescheduled. Head home and get some rest, Selena." She saw him and held a hand toward him. "Hold there and let Selena go by. She's got an upset stomach."

Jack quickly moved to the side, crossing his fingers behind his back. Selena slouched out the door, tossing him a wan smile as she went.

He walked behind the counter and confirmed they were alone before wrapping Sara in his arms. When he pulled back, he darted his eyes over her tired face, noting the smudges under her eyes. "You're not getting sick too, are you?"

Sara's shoulders fell. "I hope not. I was a little off earlier, but

I'm doing better now. I'm still working on the Aqua schedule in the evenings, but will head to bed early tonight."

"Good. I don't want you getting the plague."

"Or you, especially. How was your morning?"

He laughed, telling her the highlight of his couple completing their class with top marks, then preferring him over Alex for their first regular dives. But his euphoria dimmed describing the tension between Will and Alex. He drew her tight against him, taking a deep breath of her hair as his stress melted away. "I can't do this without you."

"I hope you can't do a lot of things without me."

He laughed. "I thought everything would be smooth sailing once I became an instructor, but it's been the opposite."

"We can commiserate together."

"At least things are finally coming together at Aqua."

"Don't say that! You'll jinx it."

Jack drew his thumb and forefinger over his lips, zipping them shut. Then he kissed her, taking care to press his lips to her forehead. "Take off early if you start feeling worse. I need to get ready for the afternoon trip. See you at home."

Chapter Thirty

SARA LET the hot shower beat down on her face, eyes closed. She was still drained and wiped out this morning, and her stomach wasn't feeling so great either. Jack and Will had left for the resort early, so she was on her own to wake up.

"I don't have time to get sick," she whispered, as if stating the intention would make it true. Her only client for the day was scheduled at ten, so at least she had plenty of time. The guest wanted a complicated ombre coloring, so Sara had scheduled her for several hours and given herself the rest of the day off.

The water cooled quickly, so she turned off the faucet and toweled herself dry. She stood in front of the mirror, evaluating her body. *At least I haven't gained any weight since I moved to St. Croix.* A tiny smile graced her face as she looked at her full, shapely breasts and wide hips. At her round curves. Jack loved her—exactly the way she was. Her eyes widened in the mirror at the realization that she was *happy* with her body.

For the first time ever.

Because she'd found a man who made her feel completely accepted. Sara closed her eyes again as Jack's bearded face flashed into her mind, and a deep welling of love rose within her. Alongside it was gratitude—for all they had received and accomplished since becoming a couple. She opened her eyes to stare at her left hand, at the ring she had never expected to wear.

Her gaze shifted to the soft curve of her hip, appreciating its contours. Then she caught sight of the birth control patch on her lower abdomen. Sara's gaze narrowed on it.

More specifically, on the frayed, raised edges of the patch.

Another wave of nausea rolled through her like an oily wave, saliva flooding her mouth. Her heart raced. She rushed a hand to touch the patch. All four beige edges were slightly curled and coming loose, the strands unraveling.

"Oh my God! When was the last time I changed my patch?"

Her knees weakened as she thought back week by week. "It was before I went to St. Thomas. With the problems at Aqua, then the trip and the wedding, I never even thought about it. Then I had to deal with the Aqua construction and Janssen after I got home." She swallowed hard, trying to dislodge the heavy lump now lodged in her throat.

In the mirror, she met her eyes once again. They were enormous, her face pale.

"What if I'm not sick? What if I'm pregnant?"

Her breathing increased to match her pulse and she leaned both hands against the counter, dizzy now. Breathing through her nose, she forced her lungs to slow, and the wave of dizzy nausea passed. Straightening, she marched to the closet to dress.

"Drugstore, *now*!"

AN HOUR LATER, Sara was back in the bathroom. She had bought two pregnancy tests.

Just in case.

After peeing on the wand, she set it on the counter and set a timer on her watch, refusing to look at it. "It's just a coincidence. Everyone at work is sick. That's all it is."

And what about the fact that I haven't had my period, either?

"Stop being ridiculous. I can't be a mother. I'm not cut out for it."

She left the bathroom and paced in the hall for the required minutes. Her phone alarm went off and her heart hammered once again.

Slowly, Sara crept back to the bathroom, craning her head around the open doorway.

Swallowing again to ease her parched throat, she shuffled forward to the vanity and the white flattened wand laying on top. Taking a deep breath and holding it, Sara looked down.

Both windows held a pink line.

Oh my God. Oh my God. Oh my God.

She was starting to hyperventilate, so she forced her breath to slow.

In through the nose, out through the mouth. Repeat.

"Calm down. I bought two tests for a reason. Maybe it was a bad test. Do it again."

The second white wand was the same.

She was pregnant.

"A *baby*? How is this even possible?"

A weak laugh escaped that turned into a sob. *I don't really have to answer that, now do I.*

It was now 9:30 and she braided her hair since she didn't have time to style it. As she drove to work, her head felt stuffed with cotton. She fixated on the empty ocean behind the palapa as she walked down the wooden pier, her sandals clicking on the boards.

I can't just ambush Jack when there's a bunch of people around. I need to think about how to get him alone.

Her client was right on time, and the soothing, familiar

routine eased Sara slightly. Fortunately, the woman wasn't the chatty type because she couldn't have kept up her usual banter. Coloring hair, even a multi-stage series of colors like her client wanted, was so familiar to Sara that her mind was able to turn over her predicament for the four hours it took to finish the woman's hair.

By the time she descended to the pier again, the afternoon dive trip was long gone. She made her way to the kitchen for a late lunch. Though not terribly hungry, she had ample reason to eat well now. Gerold was cooking and whipped up a chicken sandwich for her. She sat at the table, mindlessly scrolling on her phone.

"You ok, Sara?" Gerold asked as he set down the plate in front of her. "You're bein' awful quiet today."

Oh boy, Gerold. I am a long way from being ok.

She smiled at the chef. "Didn't sleep well last night. Just a little tired."

By the time Sara finished, it was close to four. As she returned to the pier, the sight of the dive boat tied up sent her stomach into gymnastics again. Jack and Will were both aboard, laughing, but she didn't see Alex or Tommy anywhere. "Are the two mice playing while the cats are away?" she asked, stepping aboard.

Jack brightened and gave her a quick kiss. "They're taking care of some boat paperwork, leaving all the hard work to us."

Sara turned to Will. "Can I borrow Jack for a second? I need help with something." *Understatement of the year.*

Soon she and her husband were walking back up the pier.

"What's up?" Jack asked. "It can't be a repair at Hibiscus, or you'd ask Tommy to do it."

"No, everything's fine at the spa." Then she remembered her hot shower that morning. "I think we may need a new water heater though. I ran out of hot water during my shower."

They stepped off the pier and turned north, walking along the beach above the high-water line. Jack snorted. "That's something Calvin can take care of. I'm not about to spend our own money buying a new water heater." He took her hand and gave her a crooked smile. "We weren't quite so comfortable the last time we walked on this beach, were we?"

She couldn't help smiling at the memory. They had broken up, and both were miserable when Jack had followed her onto the beach, announcing he was in love with her during a fight.

"A lot's changed," she said. "Everything's changed."

He gave her hand a quick squeeze. "What's going on? I doubt you pulled me off the boat to walk along the beach."

Sara stopped.

Now that the moment was here, her nerves had settled. Jack wanted children—she wasn't worried about him being upset.

But their lives were about to change forever.

"No, you're right about that." She met those big brown eyes, full of concern. "I've been so wrapped up with Aqua, and our wedding, and finally the insurance-inspector troll, that something major slipped my mind."

"What?"

She took a deep breath and opened her mouth, but no words came out. She just stared at him.

Jack gazed back, concerned. He lifted a hand to cup her face. "What slipped your mind?"

"My birth control patch. I'm pregnant, Jack."

For a long moment he just stared at her.

Then a tiny smile cracked the corners of his mouth. It grew wider, then wider again, until his entire face was beaming. "Really? Are you sure?"

Sara smiled. It was shaky and halting, but she tried. "Positive. I took two pregnancy tests this morning. And it explains why I've been feeling so lousy."

Jack pulled her to him, wrapping her in his arms. "We're gonna be parents? For real?"

She burst into tears.

JACK PULLED her tighter as his throat constricted, elation filling his chest. "Don't cry, Sara. This is the best news ever!"

She snuffled and pulled away, turning her wet eyes to him. "How am I supposed to be a mother? I'll be terrible at it."

Jack smiled softly and pulled her braid over her shoulder. "I imagine a lot of women feel that way at first. And you won't be terrible—that's not possible." He wanted to jump for joy, but Sara was clearly in a fragile state. "How far along are you?"

"I need to make a doctor's appointment to find out for sure. But I missed my period, so at least four to six weeks. I've been so distracted I didn't even notice!"

He watched her carefully. "I know this is a huge shock for you. But... you do want this, don't you?"

She met his gaze. Her eyes contained fear, but also certainty. "Absolutely. This baby is a part of us. I wish it hadn't happened right now, but it did. Good thing I have seven or eight more months to get used to the idea. I can't believe I forgot all about my patch! I'm such an idiot!"

"No, you're not. You've been completely frazzled for months." He took her in his arms again, and she held him tightly back. At least she wasn't crying anymore.

Jack kissed her forehead. "Well, we're married, so this *is* kind of the next step, right?"

"We hardly even got to enjoy being newlyweds. And you're finally an instructor and Aqua will need a full-time manager. What are we going to *do*?" She started breathing hard again, cycling up.

"Figure it out one step at a time. Together." He grasped her upper arms and stepped back to look at her. "Do you want to keep the news quiet for now?"

Her eyes became round. "Yes! At least until the doctor's appointment—I'm not quite ready to face this reality yet. You'll be a great dad. I'm not even remotely worried about that." She groaned. "What if I drop the baby on its head?"

Jack burst into laughter. "If he—or she—takes after me, it won't matter. You'll be a great mom, Sara."

Her eyes filled with tears again, and she spoke in a near whisper, "What if I can't do this? What if the kid hates me?"

"You're Hurricane Sara. Nothing stands before you. You're also tender and loving. That baby and you are going to get to know each other pretty well in the next eight months. When it's born, it will already love you."

She sniffled. "We're calling our child an it."

"That's easier than he or she every time."

Sara frowned. "Doesn't seem very parental."

"What would you rather call... him or her?"

She giggled, and he pressed her head to his chest. "Let's call the baby Bump. For now."

"Gender neutral. I like it."

She burrowed tighter against him. "I was just thinking this morning about how I've finally come to appreciate my body and not be as self-conscious about it. Now I'm going to get as big as a house."

"You should appreciate your body. I certainly do." He traced a hand over her ass, making her laugh. "And even more so now. What you're going to accomplish in the next several months is about the most incredible thing in the world."

She sighed deeply, making the circle of his arms expand. "I hope I'm up to it."

"We'll do fine, Sara. *You'll* do fine."

· · ·

JACK RETURNED to work after Sara left for home, a live current running through him. He was bursting to tell Will the news but stayed silent.

Probably need some time to get used to the idea myself.

Sara was right that the thought of having a child was a daunting responsibility. But it was one he'd wanted for years.

Jack shook his head, grinning.

In less than two months, we've gone from two single but committed people to married and expecting a baby. And my folks will be happy it was in that order.

Chapter Thirty-One

MAY…

Sara sat in a comfortable armchair inside Dr. Susan Granger's office. She picked at her shirt, making sure she was properly redressed after the longest examination of her life. Nearly two weeks had passed since her home pregnancy test, and the doctor had quickly confirmed she was pregnant. Dr. Granger's blonde hair lay in a flat sheet halfway down her back as she sat behind her giant wooden desk.

She gave Sara a reassuring smile. "Your lab work looks good, and we'll send off genetic studies just to make sure nothing's off there. But since you said neither you nor your husband have any history in that area, I'm not expecting any problems." Tenting her fingers together, the doctor leaned forward in her chair. "The only area of concern, and I'm just mentioning this to be thorough, is that you're older than most for your first pregnancy. So listen to your body as you move along."

Sara nodded, not exactly thrilled at essentially being called old at the ripe age of thirty-four. "So when's the big day?"

"Since you could narrow down the date of conception, you should have this baby around December 11th. For record-keeping purposes, I noted the date of conception as March 20th."

Sara smiled, and the cold, hard knot in her stomach loosened. "That was our wedding night."

Dr. Granger laughed. She was warm and comforting, exactly what Sara was going to need for the next seven-plus months. "Very appropriate! If your morning sickness becomes a problem, call the office."

"So far, it's been tolerable. I have to pee all the time, though."

The doctor smiled again. "I'd like to tell you that will pass, but it's only going to get worse as the baby grows and presses on your bladder. Sorry."

Sara blinked, her head still spinning.

Dr. Granger's eyes softened. "How are you feeling about all this?"

"Terrified. And... excited. A little."

"That's very normal—and expected. You and the baby will have plenty of time to learn about each other before you meet face to face, which helps. I can give you some support resources if you'd like."

Sara shook her head. "I don't think that will be necessary. I have lots of support around me, and my husband is beyond happy about this."

Sara left the office with a prescription for prenatal vitamins and a printout of upcoming appointment reminders. Thirty minutes later, she parked in the lot in front of Aqua. Inside was a busy hub of activity as they prepared for the opening. Sara surveyed the lobby, now full of couches and chairs. The café was in the corner, with its blenders and refrigerators ready to go.

Sara approached the full-time receptionist she'd hired.

Violet, a polished, elegant woman with a tall, willowy figure, stood behind the turquoise counter. Since they weren't open yet, she was dressed in street clothes.

"How are the bookings looking?" Sara asked.

Violet typed on one of four terminals lining the long counter. "We're nearly full the first two days," she said, her Caribbean accent crisp.

"That's all we can ask for, isn't it?" Sara had the strangest sense of dislocation. What she had worked so hard for was finally in grasp. Her dream was about to become a reality.

Except it wasn't the most important thing in her life anymore.

It wasn't even in the top two. But a great wave of pride and satisfaction still rolled through her as she looked around. She had fought like hell for this, and seeing it finally come together was more than a little gratifying.

Selena watered a large potted palm next to the counter and looked up as Sara approached. "Do you have anyone hired to look after all these plants?"

"Not yet. I'll probably get a service to do it."

"I'd be happy to. I love to garden and look after plants." Selena frowned at the moving wall of water behind the counter and its arrangement of greenery. "I'll need a ladder for those."

"You're hired! And those pots are self-watering, so we don't have to worry about them." Sara glanced around, but one person was conspicuously absent. "Where's Hope?"

"She was here most of the morning but was called away to deal with a problem with one of the new bungalows."

Sara nodded. She wanted to tell Hope about her pregnancy, but she wasn't quite ready to share the news.

I won't show for a while yet, so there's no rush.

· · ·

That evening, Sara and Jack sat around their firepit, unlit in the warm evening. The ocean provided all the ambience they needed. "I'm glad tonight Will is working his first night dive alongside Alex," Jack said. "Now we can celebrate alone." He poured out two glasses of sparkling cider, handing her one.

She accepted it, then frowned. "You can have a beer, you know."

He leaned in and gave her a soft, feathery kiss. "Nope. If you're not drinking, I'm not drinking."

"You're a sweetie, you know that?"

He shrugged. "My part in all this was over pretty fast. You're the one doing all the work. I'll support you however I can."

The sun had just set, casting a crimson glow over the horizon. "I hope Will's dive goes well tonight," she said. "Are he and Alex getting along better?"

"Yeah, but Will is still a little careless. He's learning though, and is worlds from where he started."

"As much as I like having him around, things are going to get rather cramped here in about seven months. And we need to prepare."

Jack set his mostly full sparkling cider on the coffee table. "Yeah, the room Will is using is the natural choice for a nursery. You still want to keep quiet about Bump?"

"For a little while longer. I'm getting used to the idea, and I kind of like that it's our secret."

"I was hoping Will and Alex would be getting along better by now. I really want Will to get hired and get a decent paycheck. Then I could kick his ass to the curb without feeling guilty about it."

Sara grinned and took a sip of cider, enjoying it more than Jack apparently had. "You're such a kind brother." She ran a finger over the faint scar below Jack's jaw, just below his beard. "Was Will the brother who pushed you out of the tree?"

Jack laughed. "No, that was Henry. I would have beaten the shit out of Will if he'd tried anything like that."

"You don't want six kids, do you?"

He kissed the top of her head. "No, that's a bit much. Five will be plenty."

When she narrowed her eyes at him, he burst into deep laughter again.

"Nice try, mister. Let's just take this kid thing one at a time, ok?"

"Deal."

SEVERAL DAYS LATER, a knot twisted in Jack's stomach as he stared at the ocean surface fifteen feet above. He was finishing the final dive of an advanced class and teaching two sisters. The weather had been good for a learning experience.

But not much else.

A low-pressure system was stalled over the island, and conditions were worsening. Jack watched the bottom of *Surface Interval* as it rolled over the waves. Two ladders were attached to the stern platform, and as a wave swept under, they rose completely above the surface before crashing down in a froth of agitated water. Before the dive, Tommy had given strict instructions on how to reboard the boat, his usual jovial attitude completely absent.

Jack indicated to the two women to surface, and the three divers bobbed in the six-foot waves. Robert's group was already on board, with Alex and Will's group approaching the rocking boat. Two tag lines trailed behind the stern, so divers could hold on in the challenging conditions. On board, Alex quickly rose after removing his tank, lending a hand to his group from above while Will stayed in the water to remove diver's fins.

Jack turned to his two students. "Ok, remember! Hand me your fins, then time it so you *do not* approach the ladder when it's at the top of its roll! Mask on and reg in your mouth! Don't let go once you're on the ladder. Cate, you go first. Jen, you next —and make sure you give her plenty of room! Do not approach until she's completely up."

Both women nodded and replaced their regulators in their mouths. He didn't need to tell them getting back on the boat was by far the most dangerous part of diving. Especially in conditions like this. Alex and Tommy were helping divers up on the right ladder and Jack moved his divers, their eyes grave and intent, to the left tag line.

The two women performed the procedure like pros, both getting back on the boat without incident. Jack followed, shrugging out of his tank quickly so he could help the remainder of Alex and Will's group.

Alex and Tommy were on each side of a frail man, helping him back to his seat as the boat rocked beneath them. Jack hurried toward the platform, shocked to see Will coming up with one diver still in the water behind him.

Why the hell are you coming up before that guy?

But there was no time to reprimand his brother. Jack just wanted everyone back on the boat as soon as possible. Will clung to the ladder and met Jack's gaze as the stern lifted over another wave. Will's eyes opened wide as his foot slipped off the rung.

Jack knew what was about to happen, but was helpless to stop it.

He lunged for Will but was too far away. The wild motion of the boat threw Will's center-of-gravity backwards. With the extra weight of his tank behind him, he lost his grip on the ladder and crashed into the ocean.

Right on top of the diver behind him.

"Oh, *shit!*" Jack hissed.

Both divers soon surfaced. Will sputtered, the reg dislodged from his mouth, as he frantically grabbed the line to keep from being swept away.

"Get your reg back in, dammit!" Jack turned his attention to the other diver, who was bobbing upright on the surface with blood running down the side of his face. He wasn't moving and his eyes were closed as he quickly drifted away from the boat, head lolling.

Chapter Thirty-Two

JACK IMMEDIATELY DOVE into the water. A surface rescue throwing a life ring was impossible with an unconscious diver. He swam with powerful strokes to the man. The diver's BCD was fully inflated, so there was no danger of him drowning. When Jack reached him, he was already coming around, moaning and slowly blinking his eyes.

"Is he ok?" Will yelled, his voice panicky.

Jack evaluated the diver quickly. His eyes were dazed, but both pupils were the same size. "Keep your reg in your mouth and listen to me. Do you understand?"

The man focused on him, slowly nodding his head. Jack turned toward Will. "Yeah, I think so. Put your reg back in and help me out here."

Will came toward them, still holding the tagline. They all rose, then fell as another large wave swept beneath them. Still wearing his wetsuit, Jack had plenty of floatation.

"Can you hold on to the line?" Jack asked the diver. The man made a feeble grab for it but missed. "Don't worry, it's ok. I've got you."

Jack grabbed the line with his left hand while holding the man's tank valve with the other. Facing backwards, he towed the diver toward the boat. They were over twenty feet away and it was difficult, slow going in the rough water.

A glance behind him revealed both Tommy and Alex standing on the stern platform. Alex yelled to the divers clustered on the main deck, "Everyone stay back! Give us room to work."

When Jack reached Will, he handed the diver off to him and briefly submerged, removing the man's fins. Then he linked his arm through the man's free one. On each side, Jack and Will kicked hard to get to the boat. When they neared the ladder, Jack pulled up and faced Will. "We need to get his tank off. He'll never be able to climb that ladder with all the weight." He turned to the man. "We're going to take your BCD off so you can move easier. I'll get you to the ladder. Alex and Tommy are both at the top, ready to pull you up. All you have to do is grab hold of the ladder. Can you do that? Just nod or shake your head."

The man's eyes were clearer now. Swallowing hard, he looked at the wildly bucking ladder with Tommy and Alex standing by. Then he nodded at Jack, who clapped him on the shoulder. "Good man. You'll be fine, ok? Once we get your tank off, we're gonna move quick."

Jack met his brother's eyes. "Once we get his gear off, you hold on to it. I'll get him to the ladder."

Will jerked a nod, his regulator still in his mouth. They quickly unbuckled the diver's BCD and removed it and the attached tank. Will slid both arms through the arm straps, securing it as Jack looped an arm around the man's shoulder and towed him toward the ladder.

He watched the ladder, waiting. As it crashed into the water, Jack surged forward, just as Alex yelled, "Now!"

Jack pushed with everything he had in him, and the diver reached for the ladder with both hands. Jack let go and bolted to the side, out of the way of the thrashing ladder but ready to swim back if the diver fell.

But he didn't.

The man firmly clasped the ladder as Tommy and Alex both grabbed his upper arms, hauling him onto the stern platform in one smooth motion. A loud round of cheering went up from the watching divers as Tommy helped the man to his seat. The diver was walking fine, though it was hard to tell if he was woozy, since everyone was having a hard time moving on the rocking boat. Alex remained at the stern, watching Jack and Will.

Breathing a big sigh, Jack swam back to where Will still held the line, the man's tank secure in his arms. "Give me the tank and get back on board."

Will spit out his regulator. "I want to help. I can carry it up."

Anger welled inside as Jack snapped, "Alex and I will take care of it. Just get your ass back on board. Now!"

Mortification flashed in Will's eyes as he gave another shaky nod. "Ok."

Will didn't have any difficulties boarding the second time. Alex gave him a long stare as he stepped aside to let Will pass. Jack swam the scuba kit back to the ladder as Alex descended several steps, submerging to the waist. In one lightning-fast movement, Jack thrust the tank at him, and Alex looped one arm through the shoulder holes. Then he scrambled back up the ladder and handed the BCD off to Tommy. Turning back, he helped Jack climb the ladder. Their eyes met, and Jack blew a giant sigh when both feet were solidly on the fiberglass deck.

"Thanks," Alex said as they pulled the ladders out of the water. "I saw the whole thing happen but was too far away to help. You ok?"

Jack nodded before casting a dark look at Will, who sat on the bench with his head down. His anger diminished a bit. "I think Will just got the hard lesson you were talking about. And I'm pretty sure he knows that."

Tommy walked over, moving with practiced ease over the deck.

"Is Rob ok?" Alex asked.

"Seems to be. He got knocked on the head. I gave him an icepack and the cut has stopped bleedin'. Doesn't look like it needs stitches."

Alex nodded, already moving. "He's in my group. I need to make sure he's ok." The tall man walked over to the diver, who had a cluster of people around him, and sat down. Alex grasped Rob's head and examined the cut, then looked closely at his eyes.

Tommy looked at Jack, speaking softly. "Why the hell was Will comin' up the ladder?"

"I have no idea."

The captain clapped Jack on the shoulder. "Good job. We're lucky you were there. Let's head back." Tommy climbed to the wheelhouse as Jack sat down, just now noticing how hard he was breathing.

His two students came back. "Are you ok?"

Jack worked up a smile for the two women. "Fine. That was a perfect example of why we harp on procedures so much. You two were fantastic. Congratulations on being advanced divers."

Tommy called the resort office on the trip home. Hope and Patti stood under the palapa when they returned, boarding quickly as the other divers disembarked.

Rob's face was the color of a tomato. "I'm ok, really. Just a little headache and a bit dizzy. The whole thing was my fault, not Will's. I should have been further away from him."

Hope wrapped an arm around him and led him toward the

side of the boat. "It was an accident, but we need to make sure you're ok. Patti will drive you to the medical clinic in our van."

"It's really not—"

Patti flashed her warm, brilliant smile. "Maybe not necessary for you, but it is for us. Accidents happen, but I won't be able to sleep tonight unless I know you're ok."

The man finally gave in and let Patti lead him off the boat and up the pier.

Hope exhaled as Alex moved toward the cooler and removed an armload of sodas.

"It sounds like you guys had an exciting morning," Hope said

Will stood to unscrew a regulator from its tank, not looking up. "Yeah. Let's get the gear off the boat."

"Not yet," Alex said, handing a soda to everyone. "Have a seat. We need to debrief that accident."

Will flopped onto the bench. "I screwed up. That's all anyone needs to know."

"This isn't a blame session, Will," Alex said. His posture and voice were calm and reassuring, with no sign of anger. "That doesn't help anyone. But to prevent further accidents, we need to unpack this one and figure out what we did wrong and what we did right."

Jack took a seat next to his brother, relieved Will understood he was the cause, but still confused. "Why were you climbing the ladder before that diver?"

"Rob said he wanted to be last so he could study the ladder more before attempting it."

"That's common with a nervous diver," Alex said, sitting next to Hope on the opposite side bench and opening a Coke. "But that left an insecure, nervous diver alone in challenging conditions. That's why we always leave a staff member in the water."

Will inspected his fingernails. "I've climbed the ladder plenty of times in rough water and never fallen off before."

"There's a first time for everything, right?" Hope asked. "The important thing is we learn so this doesn't happen again."

"I'm sorry."

Alex leaned forward, giving Will a small smile. "Don't be sorry. Just be more deliberate. When you're in charge, you have to think worst-case scenario. It happens often enough." He turned to Jack. "You were great. Textbook rescue. If you hadn't been at the stern, the whole thing could have gone much differently."

Jack shook his head but was pleased with the praise. "You, Robert, or Tommy would have been right behind me. It's our job," he added with a shrug.

Hope stood. "I'm going to go back to the office so I'm there if Patti calls." She wrapped an arm around Tommy's and Robert's waists. "Why don't you gentlemen come with me? I need to fill out an incident report, and you can help fill in the details."

Jack couldn't help a smile. Hope was so smooth he didn't mind being maneuvered. But he wasn't quite so ready to let his brother off the hook.

After the trio left, Will turned to Jack. "You still pissed at me?"

Alex shook his head. "We're not angry, Will."

Will snorted. "Oh, Jack was pretty furious, Alex."

Jack tipped his head back and forth in a so-so gesture. "Yeah, I was pissed at you, Will. You should know better."

And I feel like an idiot for asking Alex to go out of his way to mentor you. Especially when you make a dumbass move like that.

Will's face was even longer than usual. "You've both been telling me I'm too green to lead dives and need to take this more seriously." He swallowed, his eyes becoming haunted. "That guy got hurt because of me. Because of a decision I made. Maybe I'm not cut out for this."

"You can't change jobs every time things get tough, Will," Jack said, starting to thaw. "Or dull. That's a part of every job. I've seen a huge difference in your diving since you moved here. You're doing fine. And I think you just got the attitude adjustment you needed."

Alex crossed the deck and sat on Will's other side. "I know a lot about making decisions that get people hurt. I've made decisions that got people *killed*. You can't take back what happened, but you can learn from it, and grow from it, and do everything possible to keep from repeating it. You got lucky today, Will. That guy is going to be fine."

"You don't know that," Will said. "He's on his way to the clinic right now."

Alex gave him a small smile. "I do know that. Hope would never let a potential head injury refuse a medical evaluation, and neither would I. But I sat with Rob the whole way back. I've got plenty of experience evaluating injuries in the field, Will. He's fine."

Will looked at Alex, the desire to believe clear in his eyes, then finally nodded. "I have a favor to ask. I know I'm working with Robert this afternoon and Jack's taking the other group. Do you have anything really important going on?"

Alex shook his head. "Just working up the plans for turning the dive shop into the new gear room."

Will cleared this throat. "Could you and I work in the bay here instead? Maybe go over more emergency procedures? I kind of glossed over those, and my rescue course was basically a joke."

Alex nodded, and the hard knot in Jack's stomach finally unfurled, pride filling his chest. *Good on you, little brother.*

"That sounds like a hell of a lot more fun than arranging

furniture," Alex said. "Let's eat lunch and get to it." He turned his gaze to Jack and grinned. "Don't want your brother getting a swelled head after this morning. I'm sure he and Robert can get the boat ready for the afternoon dive without our help."

Jack clapped Will on the back. "We'd be happy to."

Chapter Thirty-Three

A LONG ROLL of thunder sounded overhead as Sara stood at the entrance of Aqua, a giant pair of scissors in her hands. *I refuse to let the dreary weather dampen my enthusiasm.*

I've worked too hard for this!

The storm that had caused Will's ladder accident had swept out of the area, followed by two weeks of sunny, gorgeous weather. Until yesterday, when she'd awoken to thunder and rain. Now, just before 10 a.m., rain pounded down even more, though the air held a fresh, clean scent. The entryway to the spa was covered, and earlier Tommy and Jack had added a large pop-up tent next to it to keep people dry.

The current storm hung over the island, but at least it wasn't accompanied by wind, much to the dive staff's relief. Will had become a new man since his mishap, listening closely to both Alex and Jack. All three were on the boat now and would miss Aqua's grand opening. But a spa wasn't exactly their thing anyway.

A long turquoise ribbon ran across the smoked-glass entry doors and a small crowd huddled under the tent, including a photographer from the *St. Croix Chronicle*.

Hope stood next to Sara, dressed in a blue staff polo and black slacks. "Go on. Cut it!"

Sara was dressed more formally in a long silver and blue gown. Chest tightening, she stepped forward and cut the large ribbon. Both sides fell to the ground, and Hope picked them up with a delighted smile.

Feeling like her heart was about to burst, Sara turned around. "Ladies and gentlemen, welcome to Aqua!"

Heather, Patti, and Selena applauded enthusiastically, and Cindy had come too. In addition to the photographer, who was also writing a publicity article about the opening, a dozen curious patrons craned their heads, eager for a look inside.

With a flourish, Sara opened the door and waved everyone inside. "Please enter and we'll get started on the grand tour."

Hope waggled her eyebrows as she entered last.

After fighting for so long to make the spa a reality, Sara had been dreaming of people's first reaction to the facility, imagining the applause and exclamations. She entered the building after Hope, eager to finally show Aqua off.

The crowd was completely silent.

Oh my God! Don't they like it?

All the water features were turned on. Besides gently trickling water, the only other sound was the shutter of the photographer as he turned in a slow circle. Many of the staff had seen Aqua, so Sara concentrated on the potential patrons who had come for the opening. Her stomach twisted hard in a way that had nothing to do with her surging hormones.

Two women had been chattering non-stop as they waited under the tent for Sara to cut the ribbon. Now both stood side-by-side, their eyes open wide as they turned in a slow circle like the photographer. But still not uttering a word.

Sara's confidence fled like a cat escaping the rain, but she did her best to put on a smile as she asked them, "What do you think?"

The nearest woman startled, as if she had forgotten other people were present. Then she turned to Sara, still wearing a stunned expression. "This is the most amazing thing I've ever seen. Look at that wall!"

Sara turned, confirming the feature wall was indeed stunning. The waterfall shimmered as it trickled over the stacked stone. The light-colored wooden shelves contrasted beautifully, with their white ceramic pots and green plants.

The photographer laughed. "Yeah, when the editor sees my photos, you might get more than a casual mention. This is incredible."

Hope applauded, and soon a wave of cheering filled the room.

Tears filled Sara's eyes and she tried to blink them back, but several escaped. She wiped her eyes. "Thank you. If you follow me, we'll start in the massage wing. We have treatment rooms on both sides, so clients can choose a rainforest view—" She caught Hope's sly smile. "—or an ocean view. All rooms are air-conditioned, and we also have several outdoor pavilions for the full natural experience."

As Sara stepped forward, she caught sight of someone standing at the back of the room, near the beach entrance. Jack stepped toward the group, wearing gray slacks and a yellow button-down shirt, a giant smile lighting up his face. She stumbled slightly before smiling back, her heart filling even more.

He came!

But she had a job to do and carried on toward the massage wing. Her expression must have shown her shock, because Hope winked as Sara walked by.

· · ·

AN HOUR LATER, the group was back in the lobby, the tour complete. Sara had drawn names for giveaways while showing off both sides of Aqua, and one of the massage winners was present. Selena led her into a room, mentioning she had the honor of being Aqua's first client. Selena and Violet, the newly hired receptionist, both wore the official Aqua uniforms of a shimmering turquoise smock, embroidered with silver threads that rippled like water.

Sara swept an arm toward the glass café counter. "We have a sample of the foods Aqua will have on order, so please take a moment to enjoy yourselves. We also have an outdoor patio with a beautiful view of Half Moon Bay, but today might not be the best day to enjoy that."

Right on cue, thunder crashed, and laughter rippled around the room.

As the group dispersed, Sara quickly moved to Jack, who had attended the entire tour. She wrapped him in an embrace. "I can't believe you're here!"

"I wanted to surprise you, and I wouldn't miss your big day for the world."

She gave him a private smile. "There's been quite a few big days lately. And more to come. Who's filling in for you?"

"Alex and Will are leading the two groups. Alex and I both think Will's ready to lead a group on his own now."

"That must make you very happy."

"Happy and relieved." Jack leaned in and kissed her cheek. "Congratulations, darlin'. You worked hard and refused to give up, and now it's paying off. And you managed to stay out of jail too!"

Sara laughed. "Thanks, it was a near thing a couple of times."

Movement caught their eye as *Surface Interval* streaked by

offshore, headed back to the pier. "Guess that's my cue to get to work," Jack said.

"Aren't you a little overdressed?"

He laughed. "I've got a change of clothes down at the pier."

"I need to get to work too. My first official Aqua client is waiting."

They brushed hands softly, then Jack ambled out the back door, giving her one last smile before he left. Sara sighed, swallowing the thickness in her throat. Then she turned around, searching.

There had never been any doubt who her first client would be. She peered around the room, finally spotting her with Cindy. Sara approached where the two women stood. "Well, are you ready?"

A smile brightened Hope's face. "One hundred percent. Let's go!"

"I'm comin' in tomorrow," Cindy said. "This is definitely an upgrade compared to Yolanda's old place."

With help from Patti, Sara had hired an extensive staff, including three other stylists. The feather in her cap was hiring Yolanda, Cindy's stylist. Sara had always admired Cindy's hair, and Yolanda brought an extensive clientele with her. "I hope people enjoy the serenity here," Sara said. "But most of all, I want everyone to feel comfortable and welcome."

"I think you've accomplished that," Hope said, and nodded goodbye to Cindy. "See you tonight."

Hope looped her arm through Sara's as they crossed to the salon. Sara's station was at the far end. She wanted her staff to have the more central stations. Hope sat and Sara placed the cape around her neck. "You wanted several hours blocked. I take it you want more than a trim?"

"I do. Make me a redhead, Sara."

Sara ran her fingers over the thick strands of Hope's shoulder-length hair, evaluating. "Your hair already has a reddish tone, so we can darken it and make it brighter. Maybe add some blonde highlights. Do you have anything specific in mind?"

Hope shook her head. "Nope. Surprise me. I have complete confidence in you."

Sara nodded and removed her shears from the drawer, trimming the ends of Hope's hair.

"You're not going to let the rain cancel our Girls' Night Out, are you?" Hope asked.

"No, rain's never stopped us before. GNO must prevail! And I don't think any of you would let me off the hook tonight anyway, since it's a celebration. No matter how tired I am."

"Damn straight, sister."

And she was tired. The nausea came and went, but fatigue hit her like a train some days. And she couldn't help but feel a qualm as she chatted with Hope about the opening. More than anyone else, Sara wanted to tell her sister about the baby, but she'd been waiting for the right moment.

Now that the opening is out of the way, things will settle down. Soon...

SARA WAS the last to arrive at Marimba. The rain still fell steadily, creating puddles on top of the sand, but the group stayed dry under the thatch roof. After entering, Sara stopped by the bar to get a glass of ice water, then took a seat next to Hope. Bartender and owner Ted was putting two bowls of chips and salsa on the table when Selena pushed a filled champagne flute toward Sara.

"Here," Selena said. "We splurged and got the good stuff in your honor. Drink up, Sara—you've earned it!"

Sara stared at the clear liquid, rows of bubbles rising to the surface.

Ok, how do I get out of this?

She thought fast. "You know, after being on my feet all day, I'm just really thirsty. I'll probably drink this water in one shot." Sara smiled at their server. "Ted, could you bring a big pitcher of water?"

"You got it. Comin' right up."

"To Aqua!" Cindy said, holding up her flute. All the glasses met in the center of the table. As Sara clinked her large, out-of-place pint glass of ice water, Hope froze. Very slowly, she turned her head toward Sara, her eyes narrowing.

Ok, maybe I won't need to tell her.

Sara mouthed, "Later," and took a long sip. She hadn't been lying—she was parched. Smacking her lips, she searched for a subject change, pronto. "Hope had the honor of being my first client at Aqua. How does she look as a redhead?"

Ooohs and aahs sounded, and Sara had to admit she'd done a good job. Hope's hair was cut in a sharper A-line. The color was a reddish-brown that brightened considerably under direct light. It would be even brighter in the sun. Blonde highlights added an additional touch, and the whole style made her even more beautiful.

"Thank you, ladies," Hope drawled. "I'm very lucky to have the best stylist around, and she'll even clear the decks for me when I need it." She laughed, leaning forward in her seat. "I think Alex likes it too. I met him in the dive shop before coming down here, and he was speechless. That doesn't happen often. I'm looking forward to a lovely evening ahead," she said with another subtle stare at Sara, who just smiled blandly back, now enjoying keeping Hope guessing.

"I'm glad one of us is," Selena said, frowning as she put her phone back in her pocket. "I've got to head to my uncle's house after this. He can't remember where he put his wallet and wants my help. My mom is tryin' to get him to move in with her and my dad, but he's stubborn as a goat."

"It's hard to give up your independence," Sara said. "Jack has an elderly friend who was in a similar situation."

"I know. I love him to death. I just wish he wouldn't put *me* in the middle."

"Speaking of relatives," April said. "How's Will doing?"

"Much better," Sara replied. "In fact, he officially led his first group for Half Moon Bay today, and Jack said he did great." She turned to Hope. "Thank you for arranging that, by the way. I was shocked to see Jack there this morning."

Hope grinned. "You're welcome. Alex and I came up with it together. He was ready to turn Will loose, and today seemed like the perfect day."

Hope turned to April. "How are things with you? How was your weekend in St. John?"

April's lovely, happy face fell, and the table grew quiet. "Brian and I are officially no more. The weekend was a disaster. Well, for me, anyway. He was so in love with the island he decided to stay. Without me."

"Oh, I'm so sorry!" Cindy said. "He just up and left St. Croix?"

"He stayed an additional week in St. John to line up a job, then came back here to pack up. I haven't talked to him since I left him there. I haven't seen him at the restaurant, so I'm sure he's gone."

"You two couldn't work it out?" Cindy asked.

April sighed. "Brian wasn't interested in working it out. He wanted something new, which didn't include me."

"Screw him," Sara said, incensed. "You deserve better, anyway."

April laughed, but it was forced. "Thanks. I've been talking with my friend Maia more. She said the same thing. She wants me to move to Florida."

"Oh, don't do that!" Selena said, wrapping her arms around April's shoulders. They had been neighbors for several years. "We'd miss you!"

"We'll see." April darted a quick look at Hope before returning her gaze to the flute in front of her. "Sometimes I feel like everyone falls in love at Half Moon Bay but me. Maybe I need a new start too." Then she shook herself. "Enough of being a downer! We're celebrating. To Sara and Aqua!"

The storm intensified, and the party didn't last much longer. Rain pounded on the thatch roof above, falling to the ground in a solid sheet. Everyone rushed through the rain to their cars. Hope's Jeep Wrangler was parked next to Sara's SUV.

Holding her purse over her head, Hope grabbed Sara's arm, turning her around. "Ok, Sara. What's going on? I got a very weird vibe from you when you first sat down."

Sara scowled at Hope's hair. The rain was flattening all her hard work. "I don't want to stand in the damn rain talking about it. Why don't you follow me home and we can talk inside, like two civilized people?"

Hope nodded. "Excellent idea. I'll be right on your tail."

Chapter Thirty-Four

"OH, GODDAMMIT! ANOTHER ONE?" Jack ran to the kitchen and pulled yet another pan—their last—from under the oven and ran over to the newest leak. Returning to the living room, he slid the saucepan in just as another drop plinked into the metal container. He glared at the ceiling.

The hollow, sinking feeling in Jack's stomach had begun the previous day, when the rain had started in earnest. And sure enough, when he'd gotten home, the leak Sara had discovered while he was in St. Thomas had returned. He'd started with a frying pan under that one, but soon graduated to a large plastic bucket. Then he'd crossed his fingers against further water incursions.

A fruitless gesture.

When he'd come home from the third dive today, there had been several new puddles on the tile and wooden floors. Not much could be done about the problem until it stopped raining. But a new roof wasn't optional anymore.

Two car doors thumped outside, and muted women's voices drifted toward him. One of them was Sara, and the other sounded like Hope. He was peering at the ceiling, looking for more potential problem areas, when a loud, delighted scream came from outside.

Jack jumped, then headed toward the door, not one hundred percent positive the sound was due to happiness and not a giant centipede. As he neared it, the door exploded open and Hope rushed in. She saw him and repeated the shriek before encompassing him in an embrace that almost knocked the wind out of him.

"Oh my God! Jack, I'm so happy for you guys!"

He shot a bewildered glance at Sara, who crossed to join them.

"I take it you told her?" he asked.

"Actually, I didn't. She guessed."

Hope shot Sara a wry look. "After what you've been through getting Aqua ready, when you refused your celebratory champagne, I knew something was up." She grasped Sara's hand. "How are you feeling about this?"

"I started out in mortal terror. But I've gotten more used to the idea—now I'm only petrified."

Jack slid up to her and kissed her temple. "You'll be great."

Hope looked back and forth between them. "I take it this wasn't... planned?"

"No, it was most definitely a surprise," Sara said.

"But such a wonderful surprise. I'm going to be an aunt!"

"Don't tell anyone, ok?" Sara asked, a line between her brows. "We're not ready to say anything yet."

"Oh, of course! But what about Alex? Can I tell him?

Sara laughed. "As if you could keep it from him!"

Hope scowled. "I can keep a secret."

"From acquaintances, yes. But Alex would know within two seconds that something was up with you."

"Yeah, you're probably right." Hope looked at Jack. "You haven't said anything to him?"

"Not a peep. You're the first person who knows."

"Oh!" Hope broke into a dazzling smile, then it faded as she examined the room and its assortment of pots, pans, and containers on the floor. She lifted her gaze to the wood beam ceiling. "Having a bit of a leak?"

Sara stared at the ceiling, open-mouthed. "Oh no. This is much worse."

"Yeah," Jack said. "I've been playing catch-up since I got home today. Looks like a new roof is in our future." He scowled at the wooden ceiling. "Assuming I can get Calvin to pony up."

"He has to," Hope said. "You can't be expected to live under a roof this leaky."

"I plan to tell him that tomorrow," Jack said.

"Where's Will?" Hope asked.

"He went out for a beer with some guys he met. I haven't checked his room for leaks yet."

"Oh, good," Sara said. "He'll also have a nice surprise to come home to."

"He doesn't know about the baby?" Hope asked.

Jack shook his head. "The conversation will probably coincide with telling him his room is going to be turned into a nursery, so we're waiting until he's a bit more settled."

"According to Alex, he's a new man since he fell off the ladder. So hopefully you'll be able to tell him soon. Well, I'd better get going. I can't wait to tell Alex!" Hope screamed again and hugged them both before rushing out the door.

"Do you think Alex will be as excited as she is?" Sara asked.

Jack laughed. "I can just picture him looking up from a scuba magazine and saying 'Oh, cool,' before going back to his article."

"That sounds about right. But I don't want to talk about Hope or Alex. I haven't even said hello properly." She slid her arms around Jack's neck and pressed her lips to his, quickly opening her mouth to deepen the kiss.

Happiness thrummed in Jack's chest as he broke the kiss. "That's what I call a welcome. And how is Mama tonight?"

Sara leaned her head against his chest, and he wrapped her up tightly. "Tired—oh, that feels good. It was a wonderful, but very long, day."

Jack slid his hand up and down her back, and he let it slip around to cup her breast. "How tired are you, exactly?"

"Mmm, keep that up and I won't be tired at all."

"That's the idea."

"Then let's head to the bedroom and you can convince me some more."

JACK WOKE to a large drop of water splashing onto his face. He sputtered and bit back a curse just in time, not wanting to wake Sara. It was still dark out, and the clock informed him it was just before 5 a.m. He patted the covers, and his hand came away wet just as another droplet hit his arm.

The roof was mostly leaking on his side, and he was torn between making sure Sara stayed dry and letting her sleep. Tossing back the blankets, the cool air caressed his wet, bare chest, and he grimaced as he tried to wipe away the moisture.

Guess this leak has been going on for a few hours.

Jack grabbed his phone and went into the bathroom, shutting the door behind him as he opened his weather app. "Thank God," he muttered. "The rain should be stopping soon." He put some clothes on to check the damage in the rest of the house, his mood steadily blackening.

As he crept across the floor and opened the bedroom door, he was met with a loud, "What the hell? Oh my God—yuck!"

He couldn't see in the dark room, but had no issue deciphering Sara's problem. "Yeah, we've got a leak right over the bed."

"Great. Guess we're up now." She rose and shuffled grumpily toward the bathroom. Jack smiled as he watched her mutter blackly. She was adorable when pissed off. Then another patter hit him on the head and the smile disappeared.

He left the room and was surprised that Will's door was wide open. With a deep sigh, Jack padded into the living room. Water dripped into the various receptacles, and the room was alive with steady plinking. A couple of pans had overflowed, leaving puddles on the wooden floor. As Jack passed by the exterior kitchen door, he spotted Will curled up on the porch couch, sound asleep.

Jack snorted. "Figures. Outside is the driest place in the house. Calvin, you're gonna do something about this, whether you want to or not."

Or maybe it's time for us to find a new place to live.

He flicked on the lights, figuring Will might as well get up too, and made a pot of coffee. Sara emerged from the bedroom, dressed in a long tunic and leggings, and scowled at the original leak, which dripped steadily. Jack quickly swapped out an empty bucket and dumped the full one down the sink.

Will came in, yawning hugely as he stretched both arms over his head and went straight for the coffeepot. "Guys, I hate to tell you this, but your roof has a leak."

"Thanks for the news flash," Jack said with a glare that made Will grin.

"Are you going to call Calvin this morning?" Sara asked.

"Better than that," Jack said. "I'm going to make him come out here this afternoon and look at this. So don't clean anything up, including our bed."

"Your bed?" Will started laughing.

"Why else do you think we're up at this ungodly hour?"

Sara asked before yawning, both hands wrapped around her mug.

"This is ridiculous," Jack said, slamming his mug on the counter. A splash of coffee spilled over. "The place is falling down around us—one thing after another."

Sara padded over and brushed his arm. "Don't get too worked up. A new roof will solve all the leaks."

"And probably shake a bunch of new problems loose. Maybe we ought to look for a place further inland."

As soon as the words were out of his mouth, Jack regretted them. Sara stepped back, her eyes becoming round. "We can't leave!"

"You gotta admit," Will said. "Not too many properties have their own house reef."

"Great. Both of you are ganging up on me?"

Sara twitched a corner of her mouth. "When we're right, we're right. You can take your frustration out on Calvin."

"Too bad I won't be here to see the fireworks," Will said, washing his empty mug. "Alex and I are working on the coral nursery this afternoon. But I expect to hear all the juicy details."

CALVIN EMORY'S beat-up old truck rumbled into their driveway and Jack forcibly relaxed his shoulders, not wanting to intimidate the older man. Bright sunshine reflected off the windshield, and all traces of the storm were nearly gone. All morning, Jack had been glued to his weather app—the app Tommy used, not the one that came standard on his phone. Fortunately, sunny skies were forecast for the next week.

The driver's side door gave a rusty shriek as Calvin opened it, and another as he hinged the door shut. Jack had called him between dives, saying they needed to meet him at the house.

The landlord hadn't been altogether pleased at Jack's insistence they meet in person, but he had relented.

The wooden stairs creaked under Calvin's weight as he slowly climbed them. His ebony skin was covered with a long-sleeved shirt and jeans, and he wore a battered St. Croix base-ball cap. Jack moved to the edge of the porch to shake hands. Calvin didn't closely resemble Jack's elderly friend Dexter, who had moved to South Carolina the previous year. But there were enough similarities that Jack's irritation took a back seat as he greeted the man politely.

Calvin nodded. "Afternoon, Jack. Well, here I am. What couldn't we talk about on the phone?"

"This is a case where describing the problem doesn't quite do it justice. Come on in." He opened the door to the multiple pots, pans, and plastic containers still spread all over the floor.

Sara was painting in one corner. Calvin's gaze lingered on a framed wedding photo they'd hung on the wall. One evening, Robert and Heather had joined them, and Robert took sunset shots of the newlyweds. Hair and makeup immaculate, Sara was fully dressed up in a flowing white gown with a proper bouquet. Jack wore a gray suit—a much more wedding-appropriate couple for photos. But that didn't stop them from delighting in the ones Robert had taken during the ceremony and the video he had produced.

Calvin tipped his hat to her. "Good afternoon, Missus. Congratulations on your weddin'."

A smile graced Sara's face as she put down her brush and joined Jack's side. "Thank you, Calvin. We appreciate you stopping by."

The older man cast a long look over the floor. "I'm guessin' the roof didn't do so well with the hard rain."

"You got it," Jack said, making sure his voice stayed even.

"Calvin, we need this roof replaced immediately. Not repaired —replaced. You can see there are leaks everywhere."

The older man sighed. His shoulders slumped as he ran his eyes over the room, rubbing the back of his neck with one hand.

Jack stayed silent, ignoring the pang twisting his gut. *I've got a family to take care of now.*

"Yeah, I know," Calvin said. "This place has reached the point where it needs a lot of repairs."

"We love living here," Sara said. "We just want the maintenance better taken care of. And a solid roof would be nice too."

Calvin gave her a smile, his lined face brightening. "It would indeed."

Jack wasn't ready to be so conciliating. "This place hasn't exactly been what we were expecting. It might be time to look for something lower maintenance."

Sara stiffened next to him but didn't say anything.

Calvin didn't reply immediately. He walked around the great room, looking in all the receptacles lining the floor before studying the couches and wall décor. "You two have fixed this place up real nice."

Jack inhaled deeply, anger rising back up, but Sara placed a restraining hand on his back, and he slowly let the breath out. "Yes, we have. I've put in a lot of work here, Calvin, and I'm pretty much at the end of my rope. I have better things to do than be your handyman. And honestly, it just feels like we're doing the work and you're the one benefiting."

Calvin darted his eyes back to them. "There's some truth to that, and I don't deny it. I'm not as young as I used to be and have sold off most of my rentals. Too much trouble." He paused, bouncing his eyes between them. "What if you two were the ones benefitin' from your work?"

"What do you mean?" Jack asked.

Don't try to get out of this, Calvin!

"Would you two be interested in buyin' this property?"

Sara gasped and stepped forward. Now Jack was the one restraining her with a gentle hand on her upper arm. Calvin's question was the last thing he'd been expecting, not that it mattered much. "There's no way we could afford to buy this place!"

Sara deflated next to Jack, making him feel like a complete asshole. But this property was pretty much the definition of biting off more than you can chew.

Calvin smiled, then nodded his head toward the back door. "Let's head out back and talk a bit."

Jack opened his mouth to decline, but Sara's hopeful face changed his mind. The group descended the stairs and stood behind the firepit, currently full of water. The furniture around it had been relocated to the porch.

"This is the kind of property most people dream about," Sara said. "But Jack's right. I don't see how we could afford this."

"You might be surprised." Calvin smiled again, then pointed to both heavily wooded ends of their cove. "The parcels on each side of this one are county conservatories, all the way out to the edge of the bay. Protected by the government and can't ever be developed."

"I would think that would make this place even more valuable," Jack said, his patience thinning rapidly.

"Here's the thing," Calvin replied. "This property is less than a quarter of an acre. Just the little slip of land with the house and the beach." He swept his hand out, encompassing the entire cove. "Almost all of this is the conservation land. The actual parcel I own isn't nearly as large as you think by lookin' around here. And the dirt road is deeded access that can't be taken away."

"What exactly are you saying?" Sara asked.

"I need to figure out fair market value with my lawyer. But buyin' this might not be as much as you're expectin', simply because the property is so small. And I'd be willin' to credit you for the rent you've already paid. You want me to get you some details on a purchase price?"

"Oh yes!" Sara called out, her voice echoing off the water. "That would be fabulous."

Jack's heart sank as he put his hand on the small of her back. "Never hurts to look at the figures, but we'd need to think long and hard about this, Calvin. You said yourself the house needs a lot of work."

"It does. But I'd go so far as to say you might never get a better opportunity to own an oceanfront house. I'll get you a sale price by tomorrow. If you decide you want to buy the place, we'll go from there." The old man grinned and resettled the baseball hat on his head. "And if you do decide to buy, *you* can pay for the new roof."

Jack had to laugh. "That would only be fair." Sara's eyes were imploring as she stared at him. "All right, let us know what you want for the place—including the rent credit—and we'll think about it."

Chapter Thirty-Five

THE NEXT AFTERNOON, Sara sat in her office—her very own private office!—waiting for Calvin's email. Which still hadn't come. As far as offices went, hers wasn't fancy. Just a small room with white walls she had decorated with two of her watercolors to give it some color. A soothing zen fountain trickled on a table in one corner. Her office phone rang, and she picked it up, glad for the distraction. "Aqua. Sara speaking."

"Hello, Sara. So nice to talk to you again."

Sara's eagerness fled at the sound of Diane's drawling voice, but she wasn't about to let the awful woman know that.

"That's nice to hear, but I'm afraid I'm not sure who I'm speaking to."

"It's Diane."

"Diane who?" she asked in her most polite voice.

There was a pause and Sara let a smile rise, even as her heart took off at a gallop. She could practically hear Diane's teeth gnashing. "Diane Powell."

"Oh, *that* Diane. You kept Jack's last name? How old-fashioned. What can I do for you?"

"I've become quite the fan of your spa. I've been following its progress on the Facebook page. And the resort looks so lovely! I had no idea. I thought maybe a visit might be nice."

Sara sat back in her chair.

But instead of dread and insecurity flooding her, all she felt was a tired irritation. And an urge to wipe her hand on her pants.

If only I could wipe her off so easily...

Her eye was drawn to a framed copy of her and Jack on their wedding day. Robert had taken it after they'd changed into street clothes, standing at Amalie Grill with the beautiful blue waters of the bay behind them. "You're right. Half Moon Bay is a lovely resort, and the spa is exceeding my wildest expectations. Though it's mostly a couples resort. If you came here looking to hook up, I think you might be disappointed."

"Oh, I don't know about that. Seeing Jack again made me realize how much I've missed him. Maybe there's something still between us."

Sara sighed, tired of the woman and her inane mind games. "Drop it, Diane. Jack told you in no uncertain terms *months ago* he never wanted to hear from you again. Get a life. If you've been stalking our Facebook profiles, did you know we're married now?"

A strong protective urge came over Sara. She placed a hand on her stomach, not about to tell this vicious woman about their child.

Diane gasped through the phone, and Sara's grim smile rose again. "You didn't know that, huh? Oh, that's right! You couldn't, since Jack blocked your number. You have to call my office phone to cause trouble."

"I'm not! Trust me, Sara. If I wanted to cause trouble, you'd know it. I hear St. Croix is lovely this time of year."

Sara leaned forward, almost wanting to laugh now. Jack's pathetic ex-wife was no match for Hurricane Sara. "Know what? Come on down here, Diane. That way you can hang out in your bungalow. All alone. Because no one wants anything to do with you. Because the only joy you get out of life is trying to make other people miserable. You want me to check availability for you? We're usually fully booked, but maybe I can pull a few strings so you can get in here."

Diane breathed heavily, the sound echoing through the phone. "Go to hell. You're not worth my time." The *click* was deafening as she hung up.

Sara laughed gleefully as she dropped her phone on the blotter. "Oh, that made my day. Goodbye, Diane. I think we're finally done with you once and for all."

She was drawn back to the picture on her desk. Jack's happiness lit him from within as he stood behind her, resting his cheek against her head. Again, she traced her hand softly over her stomach.

Diane is nobody.

Sara's email dinged on her phone, and she picked it up absently, still concentrating on the picture. But her vision sharpened when she saw the email was from Calvin. Inhaling sharply, Sara opened the message. She bit her lip, scanning the contents, then sat back numbly.

Calvin wanted $600,000 for the Love Shack.

Hope and Alex had purchased a portion of land at the north end of Half Moon Bay recently for $1.7 million, so Calvin's price was much less than she'd expected. Though the property was also much smaller.

But I have no idea if we can afford it.

The day-to-day household financials were more Jack's area than hers. But she wanted to be fully informed before speaking with him. "I know who can help me figure it out." Sara texted Hope.

> Sara: Are you free right now? I need some help.

> Hope: Is something wrong? Do I need to call 911?

Sara snickered. "Jeez, overreacting much?"

> Sara: No, lol. Bump is doing just fine.

> Hope: Bump?

> Sara: Baby's name for now. Long story. I need some financial advice.

> Hope: I'm working from my home office. Come on down!

After leaving word with Violet where she was going, Sara hurried to the south end of the beach. She was soon patting Cruz on the head as she entered Hope and Alex's house through the back slider. The sisters moved to Hope's office and sat behind her desk. Sara briefly thought about bringing up Diane's phone call but didn't see the point. She was no longer threatened by the pathetic woman. Instead, she got right to their potential real estate purchase.

"That would be amazing!" Hope said, her voice breathy. "That cove is so private."

"I need to know what our monthly mortgage would be."

Hope nodded, and her fingers flew on her keyboard. "How much would you want to put down?"

"I have no idea."

Hope paused, her fingers drumming on the keyboard. "You still have the $100,000 that you had intended for Aqua, right?"

"Yes, but that's supposed to be for the spa."

Hope lifted a brow. "It was a gift, with no strings attached. What else do you have for a down payment?"

Sara's stomach flopped over. "Not much. We've saved some since moving in together, but nowhere near that much."

"Then you're probably going to need to use all of it."

Sara dropped her eyes, pursing her lips together.

Hope smiled and patted her hand. "You're still co-owner of Aqua, with or without the capital infusion. We were saving that money for an emergency reserve fund. From our initial projections, Aqua should turn a profit very quickly. I don't think we'll need your money. But mortgage companies hate big gifts as a part of the down payment. The fact that the money has sat in your bank for almost two years will help a lot. How much is in the account?"

"About $120,000."

Hope started typing again, then pointed to the screen. "There. With insurance and taxes, you'd probably be looking at $2600 or so per month. Maybe a little more."

Sara's mouth went dry. "We can afford that. It's about what we were paying before Jack got the rent reduced."

Hope nodded, a grin lighting her face. "With your salaries combined, you can swing this. Even adding Bump into the equation." Then she sobered. "Do you want to work full time after the baby is born?"

Sara blinked. "I haven't even thought about it. I'll have to take several months off, but I want to keep working. I need to keep my identity, Hope. I've worked so hard for this!"

"I know. There's plenty of time to figure this all out, so don't worry. But, as for your immediate quandary, I'd say you can afford that house if you want it."

"It needs a lot of work."

"Oceanfront properties usually do. It's a constant battle, believe me. Good thing your husband is a fixer."

Sara still experienced a thrill whenever she heard Jack referred to as her husband. "He wasn't too sold on the idea when Calvin brought it up. Jack is the more practical one."

"Sounds like you guys have another big decision to make."

JACK LED his group through a narrow channel with towering walls on either side. White rippled sand extended below him, and a prism of colorful soft corals lined the walls, earning the site its name Technicolor Alley. An adult yellow-tail damsel fish darted into a crevice, bringing a smile to his face. Since Sara was pregnant, diving was off the table for her, and he'd been diving their reef with Will and giving her updates on her fish family. The babies were now nearly adults, not quite to the stage as this one, with its royal blue body and bright yellow tail. His smile got bigger remembering that she referred to the fish as her babies.

Not anymore...

Thoughts of Sara and their cove made him wonder if Calvin's email had come in yet. It hadn't before he left on the afternoon dive, and he couldn't figure out if he was hoping or dreading to find out if they could afford the property.

Back on board, Jack scanned his email. His heart lurched when he saw Calvin's email was there.

Here goes nothing. Probably way over a million dollars.

He saw the sales price and swiped a hand over his beard.

Shit! That complicates things... Can't just reject the idea out of hand.

Jack worked double time to finish for the day, and less than an hour after returning, he and Will drove from Half Moon Bay in opposite directions. Will went to hang out with his new friends in Frederiksted while Jack headed home. His mind was swirling, and he had a strong gut feeling he and Sara could afford the house.

But he was also worried the property would be nothing but expense after expense.

Good thing Will's out of the house this evening. That will give us plenty of time to discuss the situation.

When he'd texted Sara to make sure she got Calvin's email, she'd just replied yes and that they'd talk more that night. But he knew how she felt about the place.

The house was empty when he entered, so he headed toward the back porch, where Sara sat on the couch, watching the ocean. After kissing her hello, he said, "I'm guessing you're not just enjoying the view."

"It's a lot to think about, isn't it? All of this could be ours."

Jack let his gaze roll over the serene cove. The water lapped onto the salt and pepper beach, and the area was silent except for nature. "Yeah. The price was lower than I was expecting. I'm sure Calvin is giving us a deal."

"I went over to Hope's this afternoon and got her help with the numbers. Our monthly mortgage wouldn't be that much more than we pay in rent, Jack. And that money would be going *toward* something. I could use my $100,000 for the down payment, and Hope said this is a great investment."

"I know. I also know great investments can easily turn into money pits."

Sara took his hand and squeezed. "What would make you feel better about buying this place?"

"A good—dry—night's sleep with you next to me. I just don't want to make a rush decision. Let me mull it over a bit."

She broke into light laughter. "Yeah, leaky roofs don't make for great sleep. I know you're worried about all the repairs, but we can make a building inspection a condition of purchasing."

"Oh yeah. That's non-negotiable." He sighed. "Sara, I'm responsible for you and a baby now. I don't want to get in over our heads here."

"I love you for that. But you're not by yourself in this. I should bring in good money from Aqua."

He looked into her eyes and saw his future. *I just want to make you happy.* "I'm making more too with the classes I'm teaching. Let me chew on it for a while."

"You got it." She darted her eyes away, looking back out at the ocean, her eyes clouding.

"What's that look about? The house?"

Sara blinked rapidly. "Oh, I didn't realize I was making a face. No, it's nothing to do with the house." She hesitated, then turned to him. "I'm not sure why it even popped into my head, but I should tell you. Diane called me today."

At first, Jack just stared at her, trying to make sense of her words. Then his blood pressure went through the roof.

His anger must have shown, because Sara smiled and pressed a hand to his face. "Don't be upset. It was nothing. She's nothing. She wanted to stir up some trouble, and I slapped her down."

Jack still wasn't happy she'd had to deal with Diane, but he was distracted by the notable change in Sara's reaction. When they'd left Texas, she'd been nearly shattered—insecure and despondent. The woman sitting next to him now was calm and completely confident. A smile cracked his face. "I'm sure you did."

"Diane is officially in the past. Let's leave her there."

"That's music to my ears." Draping an arm over Sara's shoulders, Jack pulled her close and kissed her forehead. She settled against his chest as they watched the waves tumble onto the beach. After several minutes, Jack asked, "What are you thinking about?"

"The house, and how I can't believe this could be ours soon."

"As long as it doesn't fall down around us. And on top of us."

She laughed softly. "What's the latest on the roof?"

"Calvin texted me this morning. He's got a roofer lined up to start in a few days. Who pays the bill depends on what we decide."

"If we pass on this place, we'll probably have to move."

"Why do you say that?"

Sara turned to face him fully. "Calvin said he's getting out of the rental-property business and wants to sell. If not to us, I'm sure he'd be happy to take someone else's money."

Jack sighed, resting his head against the wall. "I'm sure you're right."

"A good night's sleep cures all kinds of problems."

He leaned over and brushed his lips over hers. "Thanks for not rushing me."

"This needs to be a mutual decision. And you might need to do a fair number of repairs, so I don't want you thinking I steamrolled you into buying the place."

Jack laughed. "I won't think that. You might be able to steamroll others, but I'm on to your tricks. I love this place too—I just want to make sure it's the right move for our family."

"Speaking of family, where's Will?"

"He went into Frederiksted for a drink." Jack brushed a hand over her hair. "How do you feel about telling him about Bump?"

"It's time. He needs to find a new place to live."

"I know. I just feel bad kicking him out when he doesn't have a solid job lined up."

"Alex hasn't said anything?"

"No. The two of them are getting along much better, though. Alex is just being cautious. I'll wait until I'm alone with Will and tell him about the baby."

Sara raised a brow. "And that he has to move out."

"That too."

Chapter Thirty-Six

"JACK, I can't believe you're even hesitating," Will said as he rolled the rack of dripping BCDs into the new gear room. They had moved the essentials of the dive shop upstairs now that it was empty, and Alex had created an office in the old massage room. The old dive shop was now becoming their gear storage room. The scuba classroom remained just off it—being air-conditioned, there was no need to relocate it.

Jack hung the two regulators he carried on their wall pegs, a project he was currently in the middle of building. "This house is a hell of a big decision, Will. And it's not exactly cheap either."

Jack had told him earlier about Calvin's offer, though he had remained silent about the baby. He was curiously shy about telling Will, finally deciding to inform him over a beer after work. Both men would be free as soon as they finished cleaning up.

Will turned around, propping his hands on his hips. "How often do you get the opportunity to buy a beachfront house on a tropical island, for God's sake?"

"Don't swear. It's not becoming of a priest."

"Uh-uh. Not being distracted by that old ploy. I can't believe he only wants 600k for that place."

Jack shrugged. "I know. I almost wish the price was out of our reach, so this decision would be easy."

Will stood square, eyeing Jack evenly. "That's kind of weaselly."

Anger flaring, Jack opened his mouth for a retort, but he snapped it shut.

Will was right.

One of the main reasons he and Sara had had problems early in their relationship was because of Jack's fear of telling her how he felt. He'd been a chickenshit little weasel.

And now I'm doing it again. Maybe Will's smarter than he looks.

Will burst into laughter, leaning against the rolling rack. "What now? I can practically see the lightbulb over your head."

"I just realized you're right. I am acting like a coward. Sara wants this house like crazy, but I'm afraid it will be a huge mistake."

"Or maybe it will be perfect. Happy wife, happy life, and all that."

Jack laughed. "I'm considering it, ok?"

Just then, Alex walked in the door and shut it behind him. "Afternoon dive go ok?"

"Really well," Will said.

Alex looked at Jack, who nodded. "Will's a first-rate divemaster, boss. The guests love him."

The tall man gave him a smile and leaned back against the closed door. "That's why I'm here, actually." He turned his attention to Will. "I'd love to have you on my team full time. You interested in a permanent divemaster position?"

Will's face lit up, and Jack almost sagged with relief.

That's one huge problem solved.

"I'd love that!" Will said. "Thanks for the opportunity."

"You're welcome, but you earned this, Will. I wouldn't hire you if I didn't believe in you."

Jack grinned as Will's chest expanded, obviously soaking in the praise. Since his blunder on the boat ladder, Will's attitude toward Alex had completely changed. He listened closely and had paid his dues without complaint. Not to mention he'd developed a great respect for the former SEAL.

"Welcome aboard," Alex said, shaking Will's hand. "With Jack and I both teaching, we need more divemasters. In fact, I'm probably going to put Zach through a course soon. There's been a lot of changes around here, that's for sure." Alex slid his eyes to Jack and nodded. He'd congratulated Jack in private about becoming a father but had kept silent otherwise.

Jack nodded back, then turned his attention to Will. "We're just about done here. How about we head to Breakers and celebrate?"

"Absolutely. You want to come too?" Will asked Alex, but he shook his head.

"I'm knee deep in projects this afternoon. Another time. By the way, has Hope talked to you about that couple?"

Will broke into laughter again and nodded.

"What?" Jack asked, perplexed.

"There's a couple coming soon who want an underwater wedding," Will said, still smiling. "So I'll get another chance to break out all the gear."

"For which Tommy and I are both very grateful," Alex said and laughed.

"Robert and I are working together and created a website advertising underwater weddings. He shot such great video of Jack and Sara's wedding we wanted to use it for promotional purposes."

Jack smiled at Will. He still had the same goofy sense of

humor, but there was a new confidence about him. "Looks like things are working out for you, little brother. Let's head out and get you that beer."

Jack and Will sat at the bar at Breakers, a beachfront bar north of Frederiksted. Maurice, the gigantic bartender, came over and placed two coasters on the wooden surface in front of them. "Afternoon, guys. Two Leatherbacks?"

Will nodded, but Jack said, "Just a Coke for me, please."

Maurice went to retrieve their drinks while Will broke into laughter. "Coke? Since when did you become a teetotaler? I've noticed the beer in the fridge only decreases when I drink one."

"That's one of the reasons I wanted to sit down with you."

Maurice brought their drinks and Jack spun his Coke on the wooden bar, shy once again about broaching the subject.

"Well, are you going to spit it out, or am I going to have to break out the thumbscrews?"

Taking a breath, Jack turned to him. "I'm going to be a father."

Will paused, the beer halfway to his mouth. Then he slowly returned it to the coaster. "Seriously? For real?"

Jack nodded, a ridiculous smile he had no control over washing over his face.

Will clapped him on the shoulder. "Congratulations! When does the little bundle of joy arrive?"

"December," Jack said, and took a drink.

Will's eyes followed the movement, and he grinned. "So why are you going dry? You do realize Sara's the one actually having the kid, right?"

Jack frowned and pursed his lips together. "I want to support her. If she can't drink, neither can I."

"You are *so* made to be a husband." Will laughed and shook his head. "Does Mom know?"

"Not yet, but I'll tell her soon."

"You'd better! She was pissed at both of us over you and Sara eloping."

"Yeah, but I think this will make up for it."

Will clapped him on the back. "I'm really happy for you, Jack. I mean it."

"Thanks. I'm nervous as hell but can't wait—all at the same time." Then he took a deep breath, gearing up for the next subject. "With the baby coming, I also need to talk to you about something else."

Will affected a wide-eyed, innocent look. "What would that be?"

Jack stared at him narrowly. "You know exactly what I'm going to say, don't you?"

"Wait! I want to guess. Since you're buying your little oceanfront paradise, you want me to live there forever and start paying rent to help you with the cost."

Will's eyes were sparkling, and Jack couldn't help laughing. "Just the opposite, asshole. I'm kicking you out. We need to turn your room into a nursery."

Will grinned and took another drink. "Yeah, I know. I've been working on getting a place for the past few weeks."

"Really?"

"Living with newlyweds isn't my idea of a long-term situation, Jack."

"But now you can add a baby screaming at night to the list of positives."

"Incredibly tempting, but I'm going to pass. I know a guy who owns a house in Frederiksted and needs a roommate. Now that I've got a full-time job, I'll move in there. I can be out within a week."

Jack nodded. "Sounds like a good plan. Alex had good timing today."

"No joke! I'm pretty proud he wants me to work there."

"So am I. Half Moon Bay's got probably the best reputation on the island. A lot of divemasters would love to be in your shoes."

"Yeah, but how many of them are ordained ministers?"

Jack laughed and raised his can. "You've got me there. Let's get out of here and get home so we can tell Sara the big news."

"That I got the job?"

"No, stupid. That you're moving out."

The two brothers grinned at each other, then fell into a hug as the sun drifted closer to the western horizon.

SARA STOOD in the corner of the great room, adding a final swath of green to the hillside she was painting. The scene was their cove but viewed from the ocean toward the house. She'd captured the weathered brown structure and contrasted it vividly with emerald-green hills behind. Standing back, she smiled. "This one's going straight to Ember."

Voices accompanied clomping feet climbing the front porch stairs. The door opened, Jack and Will laughing as they entered. Will made straight for her, embracing her tightly. "Jack just told me about the baby. Congrats."

Jack gave her a thumbs up behind Will's back and she smiled at her brother-in-law. "Well, thank you. This baby was a surprise, but we're getting used to the idea."

"Will's got some news of his own." Jack rocked back and forth on his feet, grinning hugely. Sara raised her brows at Will.

He held both arms out from his sides. "You're looking at the newest divemaster for Half Moon Bay Resort!"

Relief washed in a long wave through Sara's body. "Oh, that's great news!"

Will laughed. "Yeah, yeah. Don't worry—Jack already told me my days here are numbered."

"I hope he didn't make you feel like you have to leave tomorrow."

"Not at all. He gave me until the weekend."

Jack punched him in the upper arm. "Did not, you jerk."

Will told her about his new living arrangement.

"That sounds perfect!" Sara said. "Two bachelors living it up."

Will's text tone went off and he read the message. "This is him now. I'm going to go over there, and we'll iron out the details. Don't wait up for me, kids."

After he left, Sara gave Jack a long, deep kiss. "You must be happy about how that went."

"Very happy. And grateful I got a chance to speak with him. He helped me sift through all the garbage I've had in my head about buying this house."

"Sift through, huh? And what was left over?"

"That buying this place is too good of an opportunity to pass up. This house has cemented our relationship from the beginning. When we moved in together, and when we got married. And now we're starting a family. We need to stay here. Let's buy a house, darlin'."

Tears filled Sara's eyes. She let them spill over, laughing and crying at the same time. Jack smiled as he wiped them away.

"Sorry," she said. "It's the hormones."

"Much more than that." He picked up her left hand and pressed their palms together. "This baby is another sign that we've always been meant to be together."

She stared at his hand, studying it. Rougher than hers, yet artistic and gentle too. Strong enough to be whatever she needed, and sensitive enough to make her body sing. She lifted it to her mouth, brushing her lips over the surface. As she slipped her tongue over his warm skin, she lifted her eyes to his.

Jack's look of tenderness was quickly being overcome by desire. Sara drew his index finger into her mouth, closing her lips around it, and Jack groaned. He stepped forward, and they pressed their bodies together.

"You are so incredibly sexy," he whispered in her ear.

He removed his finger to cup her face with both hands. He kissed her softly, tenderly, and his mouth tasted sweet. Sara opened her lips, probing his tongue with hers. Her core flared in throbbing surges. The only noise in the room was their deepening breaths.

Jack nuzzled her ear. "Good thing we got the bedroom put back together again."

"We wouldn't let that stop us anyway."

Sara led him by the hand to their room. The blinds were closed, creating a dim twilight as they kissed again. She wore a loose dress, and Jack unzipped it. It fell to a puddle at her feet, and he quickly unhooked her bra. Sliding both hands around to grasp her breasts, he broke the kiss to watch as he cupped them gently. "I think your breasts are bigger."

"Not as much as they will get. And they're much more sensitive. Right now, that is a very good thing." She closed her eyes and tipped her head back as he moved his head to one peak, rolling his tongue in circles. Waves of desire traveled up and down her body, and her skin was aflame. They removed the rest of their clothes, tossing them aside before sliding into their bed.

The skin on Jack's back was smooth under her hand, the muscles beneath hard. Sara rolled him onto his back and straddled him. She sat up, brushing her fingers over his chest, then his abdomen. "You are such a beautiful man. I love to watch you."

The corner of his mouth twitched. "That's right. You like to watch."

Smiling, she bent down to his face. "Only you, Jack."

"Only you, Sara."

She slowly moved down his torso. She kissed the center of his chest, then drew her tongue down the line of hair descending from his navel. As she enveloped him with her mouth, Jack moaned and drew both knees up, pressing them gently against her head.

His breath deepened, and when he made a long thrumming sound in his chest, she withdrew, knowing him well. She rose above him and slowly lowered herself. Jack's eyes were half lidded as he watched her slowly grind against him. Sara leaned forward and he rubbed both thumbs over the peaks of both breasts, making her groan.

Their eyes locked, watching each other.

Quickening her movements, Sara sat upright again, still holding eye contact. and his hands fell from her breasts. He slid his right hand to her center, rubbing in time with her movements. Faster, then faster again.

"Oh God, Jack."

Sara closed her eyes, moving hard against him now, and placed her hand over his, pressing harder.

She cried out, calling his name. The force of her orgasm tumbled her forward, and she collapsed against Jack's neck, only then noticing he was calling out too. Both of them twitched, and she contracted, making him gasp. Settling against him, she traced a slow circle on his damp chest.

"I love you, Jack."

"I love you more."

Sara twitched one side of her mouth. "You always have to one-up me, don't you?"

Laughing softly, Jack kissed her hair. "I'm always going to

try." Then he tightened his arms around her. "We're not hurting the baby?"

"No, the doctor said it's fine. Though we might have to get more creative toward the end."

"Mmm. I can't wait."

"Easy for you to say. You won't be the size of a house."

He lifted her chin, his large eyes staring straight into her soul. "You'll always be beautiful to me. Now more than ever. Do you believe that?"

A smile rose on her face at how easily she could answer that question. "Yes, I believe you."

Chapter Thirty-Seven

JUNE...

Lacy lavender clouds streaked across the sky as the sun neared the horizon. Once again, a group of champagne flutes clinked around the table at Marimba. But this time, all were filled with sparkling cider.

"I'm really happy for you, Sara," Cindy said. "But I hope you don't think I'm goin' to be like Jack and not drink for the rest of the year."

Sara's bubbly laughter burst forth, her heart full at the support around her. "I certainly don't expect that. Of you or Jack, but he insists on it."

Selena sighed blissfully. "I think it's romantic."

"So did my friend Marissa back in Charleston," Sara said. "With the baby, I might finally get her down here for a visit sometime. She can't resist babies." Sara had hung up the phone just prior to driving to GNO. Marissa was her most long-term friend, though their calls had slowed since Sara moved away.

Fortunately, they had the kind of friendship that could pick up where it left off even after long absences.

"You and Jack must enjoy having your house all to yourselves again," Heather said with a sly grin.

Sara shrugged, not denying it. "Will's a great guy, but three was becoming a crowd. Now we can start decorating Bump's room."

Hope laughed. "You really don't want to know the sex of the baby?"

Firmly shaking her head, Sara replied, "Nope. Jack and I talked it over, and we both want to be surprised."

"I don't think I could stand not knowing," Heather said. "How will you know what clothes to buy—blue or pink?"

"And why should Bump have to wear blue or pink?" Sara asked, waving an index finger. "There are plenty of other colors to choose from."

"I think it's beyond romantic that the baby was conceived on your wedding night," April said.

"It's a guess, but it had to be close to that," Sara said. "And that night was... very special. Certainly more special than having my ass scraped raw up against a brick wall, like Jack wanted the night before."

Selena choked on her cider, sputtering. "You had outside sex in *Charlotte Amalie*?"

"No, I put the brakes on, and Jack eventually came to his senses." Sara laughed at the memory. "I told him people don't actually do that, despite it being a staple in movies and books."

Cindy burst into laughter, holding a hand to her lips.

"What's so funny?" Sara asked.

Still laughing, Cindy couldn't answer, but removed her hand to point at Hope. Sara followed her finger, which revealed Hope sitting with a studiously blank face. A bright-red face.

Sara joined Cindy's laughter, snorting. "Oh, I sense some

good gossip. I know that face, Hope. Apparently, I've been misinformed."

"Well... maybe. Alex and I... it was only once."

"Where?" Selena asked gleefully, leaning forward.

The entire table was rapt now, everyone wearing giant grins. Hope's face turned even redder as she muttered, "In an alley in Frederiksted."

Howls erupted around the table. Eventually, they diminished enough for Heather to ask, "How is that even possible, anyway? Did you sit on a garbage can or something?"

Hope bore a close resemblance to a tomato. "No... Alex is a very strong man, you know. He, uh, lifted me and held me against a brick wall."

"Oh my God—I'm dying!" Sara said, wiping her eyes. "So did you get a scraped-up ass?"

Hope drew herself up, staring regally at Sara. "I didn't notice. I was too busy concentrating on other things."

More laughter resulted from this, and Hope held her hand out. "Subject change! You're not getting any more details out of me."

"All right," Sara said. "I think we've picked on you enough."

"I sold another painting of yours today," Heather said with a wink.

"Good. We're going to need the money!" Sara sipped her cider while a round of laughter went around the table, then asked Heather, "Is Robert still providing prints to Ember?"

"Yes, and they're selling even faster."

"Did he agree to double the price?" Hope asked.

Heather laughed and swept her long, red hair over her shoulder. "Yes! He thought you'd finally gone too far, but you were right." She sighed. "It's a good thing Alex hired Will. I'm not sure Robert will be doing anything but photography from now on. Since the St. Croix tourism promo took off, he's booked solid."

"He deserves it," Sara said. "His photos are spectacular." Then she couldn't resist a little fishing. "Any wedding bells ringing for you two?"

She was rewarded when Heather blushed as much as Hope had earlier. "No, but we've discussed it some. In general terms." She narrowed her eyes at Sara, who just smiled sweetly back.

April raised her glass. "To finding true love. Maybe the rest of us will get there some day."

After the party broke up, Hope and Sara walked back to their cars. "Alex and I were thinking about going to the grotto later this week. Why don't you and Jack join us? We'll take all the keys so it will be private."

Sara smirked. "We don't want to crash your party. I'm sure there are some tree trunks you still need to try out."

Hope briefly squeezed her eyes shut. "I should have just kept my mouth shut."

"We would have gotten the details out of you anyway. Your face gives away everything, and the redder you get, the better the story is."

"It's so embarrassing—I hate blushing. But back to the grotto. We just wanted to get away from the resort for a while. You wouldn't be intruding."

"Sounds fun. Count us in."

Hope drew Sara into a tight embrace. "I'm so happy for you. About everything. Good luck tomorrow."

"You're ok covering Aqua while I take the afternoon off?"

"Oh yes. Take as much time as you need. This is an important appointment."

THE NEXT AFTERNOON, Sara stood with Jack inside Will's old room. Half a dozen paint chips were taped to the white wall, and they studied them. She slid an arm around Jack's waist and pressed a kiss against his neck, his beard prickling her lips. "Which one do you like best?"

He returned the embrace, pulling her tighter. "The one that's in my arms right now."

"Be serious! All right, we'll start with the easy choice. Yellow or green?"

"What if I want purple?"

Sara cocked her head, glancing around the room. "That's not a bad idea. Lavender would be a great color in here."

Jack sighed. "I was kidding. I have no idea about any of this. You decorate, I'll repair. How's that?"

"Play to our strengths, huh?"

"Exactly."

Sara took stock of the bare room. Its white walls were contrasted by the original wooden floor, which was clean but showing its age. They had moved the furniture into the smaller third bedroom, which had served as storage, but would now be the guest room. "It sure is empty in here now."

"Not for long," Jack said. "And Will's enjoying his new bachelor pad."

"I owe him a lot."

"What do you mean?"

"If Will hadn't moved here—" She snorted laughter. "—to the wrong island! We wouldn't be married right now, and we might not be buying this house, either."

"Yeah, he's not too terrible, as brothers go." Her ire must have shown, because Jack laughed. "He made a big difference in helping me realize I wanted to buy this place after all. I'm glad he's here. On the correct island."

Jack was still laughing when his phone rang. He pulled it out and glanced at Sara. "It's Mama. Can I tell her?"

"Absolutely, Jacky."

He shot Sara a dirty look as she giggled, excited for Trish's reaction.

Jack answered the call. "Oh, not much right now," he said. "We're just standing in Will's old room. Hey—we need your opinion. Do you think yellow or green walls would be better for a nursery?"

There was a long pause on the phone before a loud scream emanated from it. Jack held the phone out from his ear, wincing even as his smile grew. "Yep, you're going to be a grandma again. In December."

He met Sara's eyes as a soft warmth enveloped her like a warm blanket. "I'll tell her. You're absolutely right—she will be a great mother." Jack glanced at his watch. "Mama, we need to run. I'll fill you in on all the details later, ok?"

Jack still smiled after ending the call. "She's pretty excited." He held out his elbow to Sara. "Let's hit the road. We don't want to be late for this."

Thirty minutes later, they pulled to a stop in front of an older green and white plantation-style building. The shingle out front read Alistair X. Montgomery, Esquire. Jack held the door open, and Sara entered a warm, wood-paneled lobby with a squeaky wooden floor. The scent of lemon furniture polish tickled her nose.

A plump receptionist led them down a narrow hall with black and white pictures of St. Croix hanging on the walls. Sara studied them closely. "These photos look really old."

The woman glanced backward, her dark face breaking into a smile. "They were taken of the island in the early twentieth century. A lot has changed, but some of those buildings still remain." She stopped before a closed door at the end of the hall, opened it, and ushered them in before closing it behind her.

Sara was looking forward to this meeting. Jack had met Alistair Montgomery once, when he'd accompanied Dexter Ridgeway during Hope and Alex's purchase of the older man's property. The attorney had made an impression on Jack.

Sara understood why when the thin man with chocolate skin and closely cropped black hair rose from a massive mahogany desk, gliding toward them. Montgomery's fingers were long and shapely as he buttoned the coat of his pale orange suit, accented by a lime-green tie. He moved elegantly, smiling at them warmly as he shook hands. "Pleased to meet you, Mrs. Powell." Then he shook hands with Jack. "Nice to see you as well, Mr. Powell. Please have a seat."

He indicated a pair of gigantic black leather wingback chairs in front of his desk. The leather was impossibly soft as Sara sat. The wood paneled room was dominated by a wall of floor-to-ceiling bookcases filled with legal tomes.

"Please call us Jack and Sara," Jack said. "No need for formal address."

The attorney inclined his head before speaking with a very faint Caribbean accent. "As you wish. And please call me Alistair, or Al, if you'd like." He brushed a smooth, manicured hand over a thick file on his blotter. "I have all your documentation prepared, so this proceeding should be concluded rapidly." He smiled at Sara. "My interactions with your mortgage company went smoothly, other than the issue with your down payment."

Sara laughed. "I'm not sure I'd call it smooth."

Alistair lifted one shoulder. "Closing on properties is rarely a completely frictionless procedure. Once Hope signed a document stating your gift was given with no expectation of repayment, they were satisfied."

That had been a stressful day, and Sara had been afraid the

entire deal was about to fall through. But, as usual, Hope took charge and got the entire thing taken care of by simply calling the bank and filling out an affidavit.

"We're here now, and that's what counts," Sara said to Alistair.

The attorney smiled as he handed them two fountain pens and opened the thick file folder. Inside, a stack of documents was separated by flags, marking places for signatures. "Shall we begin?"

Less than thirty minutes later, Sara's hand was about to cramp, but they were finished. She massaged her sore appendage as Alistair carefully restacked the documents within the file folder. "Normally, this is where I would hand you the keys. But as you are already in possession of them..." He smiled.

"That's it?" Sara asked, curiously disappointed at how anti-climactic it was.

"The paperwork must travel through official channels, but essentially, yes." Alistair smiled at both of them as he folded his hands on the blotter. "Congratulations. You just purchased what I believe is the single best buy on the entire island. The property has appreciated tremendously over the years, and there is no reason it won't continue to do so."

"Thank you," Jack said. "We've got some plans for the place, and it's nice to know we can do whatever we feel like now." He turned to Sara and held out his hand. "You ready to head home?"

He placed a slight emphasis on the last word, and she grinned back. "I am. Let's get started."

Chapter Thirty-Eight

DAPPLED SUNBEAMS SPARKLED on the cobalt-blue surface
of Half Moon Grotto. Sara had been there a few times, and the
quiet grove always instilled a sense of serenity. She breathed out
a big sigh and inhaled the fresh air.

Hope and Alex had already stripped down to swimsuits.
Alex cannonballed into the cool water, but Hope took her time
entering, cautiously wading in with her lips clenched.

Until Alex rose from the depths and swept her underwater
in his arms. Her screech echoed through the deserted glen as
Sara and Jack both laughed. She raised a brow at him. "Do that
to me and you'll be sleeping in the guest room, mister."

Jack gave her a peck on the end of the nose. "Nah. I won't
deny it looks tempting, but scaring you is a dangerous idea. And
not just because of the pregnancy."

She grinned at him. "Glad you realize that."

He stripped off his shirt and tossed it on a nearby boulder.
Jack's trim form was perfect to her. She pulled her loose cover-
up over her head, revealing a black one-piece swimsuit, and
waded into the water. Jack dropped his eyes to her stomach and

smiled. Warmth spread through her at his expression. Sara reached out a hand, and they entered the water together.

Hope had finished splashing Alex back, though he was completely unrepentant. Now she turned to Sara, and her eyes became round. "Bump has earned his name!"

"Or her name," Sara said mildly. "But yes. I'm definitely showing now."

Alex and Hope swam into the middle of the pool, and a dark, yawning mouth loomed behind them. Hope turned back. "You want to check out the cave?"

Jack began swimming toward them, but Sara held back. "I'll pass. I've seen bats come out of there. I don't think breathing the air would be good for the baby. You go on ahead."

Jack stopped cold and started back with leisurely strokes.

"Oh, good point," Hope said. "Guess you have to think about all kinds of things now that you never worried about before."

"You can go with them," Sara said to Jack as she watched Hope and Alex disappear into the cavern.

"I've seen it. And the view here is much better."

She laughed as he swam over, but it faded to a soft mew as he pressed his lips to hers.

Regretfully, she broke the kiss. "Come on. Let's unpack the picnic while they're exploring."

Jack spread a blanket over a grassy area next to the beach. Sara reached into a large backpack Alex had carried and removed an insulated container containing blackened fish sandwiches. Steam escaped when she unzipped the container to check the temperature. "These are plenty hot."

Hope and Alex were on their way back. Alex jackknifed his body and dove on the far side of the pool while Hope swam with strong strokes toward the beach. She climbed out and toweled off. Just behind, Alex exited the water, pulling Hope back against his chest.

"You've got everything ready!" Hope said. "Who says you're not a domestic goddess?"

Sara smirked. "Gerold did the cooking. I didn't want to interrupt you two while you were exploring. Let's eat."

They settled on the blanket. Sara and Jack drank from their stainless-steel Half Moon Bay Resort water containers while Hope and Alex shared a bottle of white wine.

Sara smiled at their wineglasses. "Thank you for not tiptoeing around me."

"Jack might be a martyr, but that doesn't mean we have to be." Alex grinned as he said the words, but respect glinted in his eyes as he held his glass up to Jack.

"I'm glad someone realizes that!" Sara said. She leaned back on one arm, enjoying the soft breeze.

The blanket began trembling under her hand. At first, she thought she had to be imagining it. Then the leaves on the trees shivered and several dropped to the ground around them.

The shaking ended as quickly as it began.

All four people sat up, looking around. "Was that an earthquake?" Sara asked, flabbergasted.

"More like a small trembler," Alex said. "The Caribbean is pretty active, though I've never felt one here before."

Sara scowled at Hope. "Great. Now you tell me."

Hope broke into laughter. "That was a first for me! I had no idea."

Birds had stopped singing, but now started up again as Jack looked around the grotto. "Seems over, anyway. Never been in an earthquake before. That was kind of cool."

"As long as it isn't repeated," Hope said, her brows drawn.

They continued their lunch, but the shaking wasn't repeated.

Hope turned to Sara. "So, how's the nursery coming?"

"We settled on a soft yellow color and are going to decorate with a seashell theme."

"Very gender neutral," Hope said.

"And the new roof is completely done," Jack added.

"That'll help in the next rain. You can have your pots and pans back," Alex said.

Jack grabbed some more potato chips. "Just in time. I read there's a weather system coming in."

Hope stared at the sky, absently rubbing her left upper arm. "Yes, rain is coming."

Sara watched her for a moment. "Does your arm still bother you?"

Hope looked down and started, as if surprised to see herself rubbing her arm. "Not really, but it acts as a barometer sometimes."

Sara nodded. Alex's face was glued to Hope's arm. He swallowed hard and put his sandwich down.

Jack's brows lowered. "Why is that?"

Hope darted her eyes to Sara, who shook her head. "I've never said any of the specifics of what happened."

"Sara told you I was in an abusive relationship when I was much younger?"

"She mentioned something about it."

"He put me in the hospital. My arm was broken in several places, and I still get twinges now and again."

Jack stared at her. "That's terrible."

"It was," Sara said. "But Hope's finally put it behind her. With Alex's help."

Alex breathed out forcefully, his face tense, and Hope stroked his forearm. "Yes, with his help." They held eye contact for a long moment before Alex relaxed his shoulders, rolling his neck around on them.

Sara cocked her head. "Do you ever hear from his parole officer?"

"Now and again. Last I heard, Caleb was in prison, convicted of a bunch of different crimes."

Alex snorted. "Good. He better stay there."

Something about the way Alex said that made Sara look closely at the former SEAL. He was still tense, and obviously didn't enjoy hearing the details of what Hope had been through. Which only made Sara like him more, and she didn't want to see him uncomfortable. "Are you enjoying having your dive shop upstairs at long last?"

Alex darted his eyes to her and smiled, acknowledging her change of subject. "It's getting there, but we're operational, and that's what counts."

"I'm adding a resort gift shop in there too," Hope said.

Alex turned to Jack. "I've got several people next week who want classes. Let's get together tomorrow and divide them up."

Jack nodded. "I saw we have three groups on the morning trip."

"Good thing we've got Will now, but it's not enough," Alex said. "I'm planning on putting Zach through a divemaster course soon."

Sara smiled. "He'll be happy about that! He's been dying to lead dives since he started."

"He's earned it," Hope said. "Zach was a great hire."

"What we really need..." Alex said, looking at Hope. "Is a fill-in divemaster. Someone who can cover for sick calls and last-minute additions."

"No argument there," she replied. "But that sounds like a tough position to fill."

"It is," he said, a small smile playing at the corner of his mouth. "The job calls for someone who's already at the resort and can jump right in when needed."

A line formed between Hope's brows. "We don't have any divemasters like that."

"No, but we could. I know the perfect candidate."

Jack and Sara both broke into grins at Hope's blank face.

"Tommy?" she asked. "He's never expressed interest to me in wanting to be a divemaster."

Alex rolled his eyes. "You, Boss Lady!"

Hope sat up straight. "Me? I can't lead dives!"

"Why not?" Sara asked. "You're a great diver."

"Because, because..." Hope opened and closed her mouth a few times while Alex raised both brows at her. "It's never even occurred to me."

"Well, I've thought about it a lot," he said softly. "You'd be great at it, baby."

"I'm not sure."

Sara burst into laughter. "Hope, when have you ever failed at something you put your mind to?"

A tiny smile rose on Hope's face. "I'll give it some thought."

"Do that," Alex said, and leaned over to kiss her forehead.

Conversation turned to other subjects, with a thorough discussion of how well Aqua was doing. Alex's eyes kept sliding to the far edge of the pool.

"I've hired two more massage therapists and one more person to do mani-pedis," Sara said as Alex narrowed his eyes, gazing at the blue water. "I saw you free dive in the pool, Alex. Is there something wrong down there?"

He snapped his head back to her, then grinned. "No. I dove down to check the gate over the pool passage."

"Have you guys ever gone back in the cave tunnel?" Jack asked.

"No, we explored that thoroughly," Alex said, then his eyes slowly drifted back. "I've been looking for a new challenge, and that passage off the pool has been calling to me."

Jack shuddered. "Better you than me."

Hope laughed. "Not interested in joining the expedition?"

"Not in the slightest. I don't mind swim throughs, but underwater caves are a different story."

"Even if I could dive, you'd never get me in one of those things," Sara said.

Alex stroked a long finger down Hope's thigh. "What about you?"

She leaned forward and grinned at him. "A divemaster course *and* cave exploration? Mr. Monroe, are we about to have another adventure?"

A slow smile rose on his face as he stared straight back. "Absolutely, Mrs. Monroe."

LATER SARA STOOD at the waterline of their cove, the salt and pepper sand racing from underneath her feet as a wave swept out. She stepped forward, enjoying the warm water bathing her skin. As she and Jack had driven home, there had been a newsflash about the earthquake, but it had been an isolated incident, measuring less than 4.0 on the Richter Scale.

Jack came up behind her and wrapped both hands around her waist.

"It's hard to believe how much our lives have changed, isn't it?" he asked.

She smiled and leaned her head against his chest. "I know. Not even two years ago, I was afraid to even think about settling down. Now I'm married and going to be a mother."

Jack laughed softly. "You didn't even sound terrified when you said that."

Sara turned around in his arms, staring into those beautiful brown eyes. "Because I'm not." She took his hands and placed them on her stomach, then covered them with her own. "Hope and Alex aren't the only ones looking forward to an adventure, are they? The future holds something even more incredible for us."

She closed her eyes and pressed her forehead to his. The only sound in the cove was the gentle Caribbean Sea moving in its timeless rhythm over their feet. Jack's wedding ring was slightly cooler than his hand as she ran her thumb over it.

Two people were becoming three. Yet somehow, all were one.

***

THANK you for reading *Half Moon Aqua*! This book was an absolute blast to write, especially the two chapters featuring poor Mr. Janssen.

But the Half Moon Bay series has one entry left. After reading that final chapter, hopefully you're eager for the next installment.

Yes, Hope and Alex are BACK!

The eighth, and likely final, book is titled *Crowning Hope*.

CROWNING HOPE: HALF MOON BAY BOOK 8

What happens when the couple who refuse to be kept apart … is?

Hope Monroe has watched her sleepy resort in St. Croix transform into a sold-out sensation. Keen to take on the new responsibility of being a divemaster, she soon finds out how much she has yet to learn. A final reckoning with her abusive past forces her to face painful wounds again.

Alex Monroe faces a crisis of confidence. Mishaps in his dive operation have him questioning his influence. An old friend's visit makes him realize how far he's come, and ignites a yearning for a challenge. A new cave diving adventure seems like a perfect way to bring his team together.

When disaster strikes, the couple is torn apart. Separated.

Can Hope become the leader Alex has always seen in her, and bring them together again? Or will this be Alex's final adventure?

Crowning Hope is the eighth novel in the Half Moon Bay series. This thrilling adventure romance features the two devoted soulmates at the heart of Half Moon Bay, nail-biting excitement, and hot, steamy romance.

Order Crowning Hope today!

HAVE you read my bonus scene for Sara and Jack yet? It's a free bonus available to all subscribers of my Beach Read Update (www.erinbrockus.com/sara). The scene takes place shortly after they move into their new beach cottage. It's both touching and funny!

My Beach Read Update subscribers hear about all my free content, plus exclusive offers and sales. I'd love to have you along!

Sign up to download this exclusive bonus today
(www.erinbrockus.com/sara).

IF YOU'RE ALREADY on my list, I've got you covered! At the bottom of each newsletter is a link to all my free content for subscribers. Just find your last email from me to read this bonus, as well as any others you might have missed. Or you can simply sign up again—you'll have your bonus in a flash.

KEEP READING for my Author's Note, and the first chapter of *Crowning Hope*...

Author's Note

Well, Sara has been on quite a journey of growth, hasn't she? I thoroughly enjoyed transforming this character from a sassy yet immature and flighty woman to a committed wife and mother-to-be. She even got to realize her great wish of a spa like Aqua in the process.

The design for Aqua was loosely based on a spa at one of my favorite resorts in Bali. My husband and I have stayed there several times. I immediately fell in love with the tranquil stream running through it. The Bali spa also had wooden bridges to cross to get to the treatment rooms, but the stacked stone feature wall is all Aqua.

Fans of the series from the beginning hopefully enjoyed the chapters featuring Mr. Janssen. I had an absolute blast writing them. I wanted one more obstacle to throw at Sara, and knew it was going to be the final permit process. Throwing poor Mr. Janssen into the mix was the perfect solution. He really was no match for Hope and Sara combined!

I also enjoyed letting Jack be the hero while Alex stood on deck, unable to help. The incident described is a combination of real-life experiences I've had while diving. In the Bahamas, a furious squall blew up while my husband and I were diving. When we surfaced, the boat ladder was rising completely out of the water, only to come crashing down as the entire stern submerged. I was terrified to go near it. I made a mad dash for the ladder, and the boat captain picked me up *bodily* by my tank valve and tossed me on board! I've also fallen off a ladder backwards. Fortunately, only my husband (a scuba instructor) was behind me, and knew to keep well away. Getting back on boats is dangerous, folks! It's shocking how quickly situations can change when diving.

The other big surprise while writing this book was Will. He was designed to be a minor side character who would show up in St. Thomas to marry Sara and Jack, but he just kept talking and elbowing his way into the story. And now he's employed at our resort, so I guess he got the last laugh!

Thank you for being a part of the Half Moon Bay family, and keep reading for an excerpt of the next, and likely last, book in the series, *Crowning Hope.* For the final book in the series, I had to return to Hope and Alex, where it all began.

Get ready for some nail-biting adventure romance...

Erin Brockus
March, 2023

Crowning Hope Excerpt

The afternoon St. Croix sun warmed the wooden railing beneath Hope Monroe's hands. She stood on an elevated deck overlooking the aquamarine Caribbean Sea. The deck was attached to the second story of a long building halfway down a wooden pier, a large palapa at the end. A lock of reddish hair blew in front of her face, and Hope tucked it behind her ear. Her fingers paused on her neck, and a smile rose as a memory flashed into her mind.

A vivid, life-changing memory.

She had stood in this same position nearly four years ago, though the railing had been replaced since. This was where she and dive operations manager of Half Moon Bay Resort, Alex Monroe, had shared their first kiss. And just the previous month, they had celebrated their two-year wedding anniversary.

Her gaze drifted to the right, taking in the long crescent of white sand beach which gave the resort and bay its name. Hope shook her head. What she saw now hardly resembled the humble resort of her arrival. Since taking over—and especially since she and Alex had married—they had nearly doubled the number of guest bungalows, as well as building an art gallery and spa toward the northern half of the beach. She inspected a bare stretch of land at the far northern end, her next big project.

But not quite yet.

Hope's smile lingered as she turned around and opened the glass door at the other end of the covered deck, entering a wonderfully cool open room, now in its third incarnation. Originally, the area had been Alex's apartment. But after a hurricane, he had moved in with her and she had turned the space into a modest spa they had quickly outgrown. Once Aqua, their new destination spa on the beach had opened the previous spring, Alex had been quick to reclaim his territory, moving the dive shop to take advantage of the newly freed area. She'd had a few ideas for the space herself.

Now Hope looked around the finished product, very pleased with the result. The long check-in counter was the only thing left from Hibiscus Spa. Two thirds of the wide-open room was taken up by the dive shop, filled with wetsuits, regulators, buoyancy compensation devices, and other diving necessities. The other third was the resort gift shop, an idea she'd wanted to implement for years.

As usual, the first thing that caught Hope's eye was the group dive staff photo on the wall. Specifically, the picture of Alex, smiling at the camera. His crystal blue eyes, sandy hair, and tall, muscular body only increased her desire for the real thing.

Alex, along with their dive boat *Surface Interval*, was out on the afternoon dive trip, so the shop was deserted except for two people working in it. An average-height young man with closely cropped black hair turned from arranging dive masks on a wall display. His dark face breaking into a smile, Zach Turner spoke with a lilting Caribbean accent. "Hey, Hope. What brings you by?"

Twenty years old, he'd worked at the resort for over two years and was addicted to diving. Alex was slowly bringing him along and had plans to make Zach a divemaster for the resort. Often, the young man worked on the boat, assisting the staff, but he was covering the dive shop that day.

And helping orient their new employee.

Hope smiled as a nineteen-year-old young woman approached from the gift-shop side of the room. Jasmine Olson lifted her lips in response, an irresistible expression of brilliant white teeth against her caramel-colored skin. She had a tiny, upturned nose that gave her pretty face a youthful cast.

"I just came by to see if Jasmine had any questions," Hope answered Zach, then turned to the young woman. "Is he treating you ok?" She'd hired Jasmine to work in the gift section, but Zach and Hope would cross-train her to work the dive shop as well.

"Oh, yes!" Jasmine said. Like Hope, she was dressed in the usual uniform of a staff polo and capris. Her shoulder-length straightened hair was pulled into a low ponytail. "I'm learnin' the ropes, and Zach's showin' me where everythin' is."

"Sorry you couldn't go out on the boat, Zach," Hope said. "But after Alex starts our divemaster class, you might be longing for an easy afternoon in air-conditioned comfort."

Zach widened his eyes, his expression aghast. "No way! I can't wait to start. Do you know how long I've wanted to be a divemaster?"

Hope laughed. "Pretty much as long as I've known you. Unlike me." She shook her head. "I'm still a little surprised Alex wants me to take the class too."

The young man shrugged. "Don't know why. You've been divin' a lot longer than me."

Hope had never thought of herself as an expert diver. She'd come a long way since her near-drowning shortly after becoming certified, but she still viewed diving more as recreation than profession.

Better change that line of thought.

"We'll figure it out together, just like we've been doing." Hope smiled at him. She and Zach had been partners in their last two classes. The previous summer, Alex had brought them through the rescue diver course, the prerequisite for divemaster, which had been a challenging and fulfilling class. Hope was proud to be one of the only non-dive staff members who could assist in water emergencies.

"Leadin' people on dives is a lot of responsibility," Jasmine said, giving Zach an admiring smile.

He visibly puffed up. "It's just a matter of gainin' confidence. Maybe I'll show you sometime." The two couldn't tear their eyes apart, their mutual interest obvious. Hope refrained from groaning.

Oh, boy. I should have foreseen this!

Though she couldn't exactly cast stones in this area, now could she? At thirty-nine, Hope was a long way from young, blushing love, and her experience with first love had been a disaster. An abusive relationship had wounded her spirit deeply, and it wasn't until she met Alex that she was able to trust completely. Old demons still rose to the surface now and again, for both her and former Navy SEAL Alex. But neither Zach nor Jasmine had experienced their traumas. Hope wished them every happiness, but she wasn't paying them to make moon eyes at each other.

Behind Jasmine stood a half-full display of resort-themed coffee mugs. An open carboard box sat on the floor. "Did the mugs arrive undamaged?" Hope asked.

As desired, her question brought Jasmine back from

admiring Zach. She whipped her head toward Hope. "Oh—yeah. I'll just get back to unpacking them."

"Excellent," Hope said. "I need to head over to Aqua and check on things there. See you two later."

After stepping back into the afternoon heat, she headed down the staircase to the wooden planks of the pier, passing through a tunnel created from the gear room on one side and compressor room on the opposite. The dive shop spanned overhead.

Hope continued, stepping down onto the white sand beach. An emergency station sat next to the stairs, a life ring and flotation device ready to assist rescues. An identical station was placed near the spa. Heading north along the beach, she passed a rectangular infinity pool with a restaurant behind and pool bar to one side. The resort faced due west, giving it a full view of the sun as it made its daily progress toward the western horizon.

Hope approached a seventy-year-old woman laying her towel on a chaise lounge. "Getting a little sun this afternoon, Peg?" Hope asked. The woman was vacationing alone, so Hope had made a point to talk to her and make sure she felt welcome.

"I'm lathered in sunscreen, but I just love the heat," Peg said, ruffling a hand through her short, wavy gray hair. "I'll head into the ocean if it gets too much."

"It's a beautiful afternoon, so enjoy."

Hope continued toward the white building in the distance. The left third of it was encased in smoked glass, streaks of red and orange running through it. The art gallery Ember had been a success from the very start, benefitting its exhibiting artists as well as the charities Hope donated profits to each month. A local pet shelter, veterans support center, and domestic abuse shelter were her primary beneficiaries.

Aqua took up the other two thirds of the building. The same smoked glass graced a large wall with a patio facing the ocean.

Tables were placed on the brick pavers, and several guests were enjoying an afternoon drink. The ocean-facing row of massage rooms also incorporated the one-way glass, allowing the guest to enjoy the scenery and stay cool.

Hope entered Aqua's lobby and was met with soothing spa music. A meandering four-feet-wide river ran through the lobby, leading off to the salon on one side and the massage wing on the other. She crossed a bamboo bridge, enjoying the trickling water as it flowed through the river-rock-lined channel below. On the far side of the room, a long aquamarine-colored glass counter stretched before a gigantic stacked-stone wall. A sheet of water flowed over it.

Aqua's receptionist, Violet, stood behind the counter. In her mid-forties, she was tall and willowy with a natural elegance Hope admired. Her black hair was arranged in a neat bun at the base of her neck. She smiled at Hope's approach. "Afternoon! You here for a little pamperin'?"

"No, I'm here to talk to Sara. Is she in the salon?"

Violet's smile faltered slightly. "Yes. They're just finishin' up. Sara doesn't seem to be feelin' real great today."

Hope kept a straight face as she clucked sympathetically. Her empathy was as much for the Aqua staff as her sister Sara. Due to give birth in a few weeks, Sara's crankiness increased with the size of the baby she carried.

As Hope crossed over a bamboo bridge and entered the salon, Sara stood in the far corner, sweeping her station. Hope strolled over two more bridges as the river ambled across the salon. "How's my favorite sister today?"

Sara looked up and drew her brows together. Dressed in a voluminous lavender maternity dress, her dark-brown hair was styled in ringlets falling down her back. "Glad the day is over. My back hurts, and just look at my ankles!" She thrust a leg out, tapping one sandal-covered heel on the white tile floor. "Correction—cankles!"

They were rather swollen, and Hope winced in sympathy, genuine this time. Sara had never been known for a meek personality, and she became ever fiercer as her pregnancy progressed, causing the staff to treat her with wary respect. Even Sara's husband Jack, one of the most easy-going people on earth, treaded carefully around her now.

"Well, why don't we get some smoothies and sit on the patio? You can put your feet up."

Sara's irritated frown softened, and a smile peeked out as she set her broom aside. "Thanks, but I just want to go home."

"I don't blame you. I came in here to let you know I talked to Patti, and she agreed the two of us can manage Aqua just fine while you're on maternity leave." Patti Thomas was the general manager of the resort. She dealt more with the housekeeping and guest-relations side of the resort, but was a quick learner and wouldn't have any issues adapting to being a temporary spa manager.

Sara grunted, placing both hands on the small of her back. "At first, I was so scared of this baby coming. Now I can't wait for the birth so this damn pregnancy can be over."

Hope shifted from one foot to the other. With no children herself, she was at a bit of a loss around Sara these days. "Can I help with anything?"

Sara shoulders fell, then she gave Hope a hug. "No, you're a sweetheart for putting up with my bitching. Not as much as Jack is, but then again, he's responsible for this. So I refuse to completely give him a free pass."

"I think it takes two."

Sara made another derisive noise, then lifted her eyes to the windows facing the ocean. "Go on and get out of here, sis. The dive boat's coming back, so both our husbands will be off soon.

And Alex doesn't have to tiptoe around you." She sighed and gave Hope a crooked smile. "I'm married to a saint."

Hope couldn't help but breathe a sigh of relief as she left the salon, but the soft breeze restored her good mood. The life ring from the spa emergency station hung askew. She was heading over to straighten it when she was distracted by a much more appealing sight, *Surface Interval* snugging up to the dock. Quickening her steps, she was eager to see Alex and discuss the other adventure they were planning, involving a submerged tunnel exploration.

Peg's empty lounger lay just past Aqua, and Hope shielded her hand as she walked, looking for the older woman in the water. Peg was further out than Hope expected, and she waved to her. The woman waved back and Hope smiled, continuing on her way. A few moments later, she looked again.

Peg was nowhere to be seen.

The ocean's surface rippled somewhat, but the waves weren't large enough to hide a person in the troughs. Hope raised both hands to her brow as she stopped at the water line. Peg surfaced and feebly raised one hand over her head, making no noise.

Instantly, Hope kicked off her shoes and sprinted into the water, heart racing. She swam toward the woman with fast, powerful strokes, grateful that swimming was a regular part of her fitness routine. In their rescue class, Alex had explained that drowning people rarely splashed and screamed.

They simply slipped beneath the waves, exhausted.

As Hope neared Peg, the woman surfaced again, gasping for air. Then she disappeared beneath the waves.

Hope dove after her.

Grab your copy of Crowning Hope now

About the Author

Dive into steamy small-town romance, where passion meets paradise!

Erin Brockus writes steamy small town romances that transport readers to exotic, tropical destinations, and provide a perfect beachy getaway from everyday life. Her mature, relatable characters are impossible not to root for, and she weaves breezy romantic adventure into her stories, emphasizing scuba diving and the ocean.

Drawing on her twin passions for diving and travel, Erin infuses her characters and narratives with a sense of excitement and passion. Her idea of the perfect day involves sipping a cocktail on the beach after exploring the ocean depths.

Erin lives in Washington wine country with her husband, who is also a scuba instructor. She is currently hard at work on her next island adventure. When she's not writing, you might find her out for a run or cycling through the countryside on the next quest for adventure.